Mimicry of Banshees

An Alexis Parker novel

G.K. Parks

This is a work of fiction. Names, characters, places, events, and other concepts are the product of the author's imagination or are used fictitiously. Any resemblance to actual persons, living or dead, places, establishments, events, and locations is entirely coincidental.

No part of this book may be reproduced in any form or by any electronic or mechanical means including information storage and retrieval systems, without express written permission from the author.

Copyright © 2014 G.K. Parks

A Modus Operandi imprint

All rights reserved.

ISBN: 098919583X
ISBN-13: 978-0-9891958-3-6

Thank you for the continued support and encouragement

BOOKS IN THE ALEXIS PARKER SERIES:

Outcomes and Perspective
Likely Suspects
The Warhol Incident
Mimicry of Banshees
Suspicion of Murder
Racing Through Darkness
Camels and Corpses
Lack of Jurisdiction
Dying for a Fix
Intended Target
Muffled Echoes
Crisis of Conscience
Misplaced Trust
Whitewashed Lies
On Tilt

BOOKS IN THE JULIAN MERCER SERIES:

Condemned
Betrayal
Subversion
Reparation

ONE

"I'm heading out," I told Mark Jablonsky as I placed a twenty on the bar. "And just so we're clear, I'm not consulting for the OIO again. I'm done, and in case there's any doubt in your mind, my letter of resignation is sitting on top of your desk."

Picking up my purse, I maneuvered around the barstools. The mirror behind the bar caught my image, white dress shirt, black blazer, and long brown hair pulled into a severe bun. There was a time in my life that was all I wanted, but I had run from the pain associated with the job. Even after coming back for a month long gig, I couldn't do it. The reflection in the glass wasn't me. Not anymore.

"Director Kendall isn't going to be happy about this," he responded. "To be honest, Alexis, I thought you were going to stay this time." I shook my head. "If it makes any difference, you were instrumental in helping crack the museum robbery wide open."

"Thanks, but it doesn't matter." I headed for the door, ready to be free from my consulting contract with the Office of International Operations.

Agent Mark Jablonsky had originally been my supervisor and mentor when I started work as a federal agent almost five years ago, but after resigning to follow my own pursuits in the private sector, he and Director Kendall had convinced me to give the OIO one more chance. My own pigheaded stubbornness led to a final stint to reinforce my true reason for leaving; I didn't want to be tied down by bureaucracy and all the other red-tape legalities law enforcement agencies have to endure.

Stepping into the cold night air, I exhaled slowly and watched my breath float away. Alex Parker, you're free, my internal voice happily cheered. I had been working the private sector for almost a year, taking a few consulting jobs here and there. Going back to my former agency was the most recent venture in my sporadic work schedule. But it required one too many sacrifices, and I was glad to leave it behind.

My personal life had been put on hold while I waited for the gig at the OIO to conclude. What was initially supposed to last a couple of weeks had taken almost a month to resolve. During that timeframe, I had neglected both my retainer contract as security consultant for Martin Technologies and my somewhat erratic and brief attempt at a romantic relationship with James Martin, the company's CEO.

Arriving home, I checked the time. I promised Martin, once I was liberated from the government bureaucracy and both of our lives settled down, we would give our relationship another try. The only time we attempted to date, Murphy's Law had reigned supreme. First, a sadistic crime boss had gotten in the way, and then Martin was busy vetting his company's new VP and undergoing surgery to remove scar tissue from an injury sustained during my first private sector job, working as his bodyguard. I counted the weeks in my mind, trying to determine if his rehab would be completed by now. By my best estimate, he still had another week or two to go.

Even though it was after one a.m., I dialed his number. It had been a month since I heard his voice, and I missed him. The phone rang five times before his voicemail picked up. After leaving a message for him to call whenever he had a chance, I went to bed. There was no reason to rush things since I was a free agent once more.

*   *   *

It felt as if I had only closed my eyes when the phone began ringing incessantly. My bedroom was bathed in a warm glow, and I knew it must be morning; although, people should know better than to call this early on a Saturday. Grabbing the receiver, I answered, "Parker," out of habit.

"Miss Parker?" a voice I didn't recognize responded. "Alexis Parker?"

"Yes," I grumbled. I had a feeling this was a telemarketer. "I'm not interested." And I hung up. It was too early in the morning to deal with someone selling subscriptions to cable television. Rolling over, I buried myself under the covers. The phone rang again, and I sighed loudly and picked it up. "What?" I snarled.

"Miss Parker, this is Alan Ackerman," the voice identified himself. "Are you still under contract with Martin Technologies?"

"Uh-huh." Calls this early never bode well, and I knew something was wrong.

"Miss Parker," he continued, "I'm James Martin's attorney. Have you been watching the news?"

"What's happened?" A feeling of fear and dread settled in the pit of my stomach. "Is he okay?"

"It'd be best to discuss this matter in person." He rattled off an address. "Please do not speak to the press or anyone from the media until we have a chance to meet."

As soon as our conversation was concluded, I turned on the television. Flipping to the local news channel and turning the volume up, I dressed and prepared to depart for Ackerman's law office. Mr. Ackerman hadn't provided any hint as to what was brewing, and given Martin's recent history, I hoped he wasn't hurt or worse. How many times could a person be threatened in the span of one year? Thankfully, before my musings could become more morbid, I went into the living room and caught the story toward the end.

"The police are still investigating the suspicious death of Caterina Skolnick, a model rising to fame at the Tate Agency. Skolnick was discovered on a yacht belonging to CEO James Martin. As more information becomes available, we will continue to update you," the news anchor informed the viewer before the story changed to a scene of a fire at a preschool.

Taking a deep breath, I left my apartment for the law office. I was irritated. The reason I had stayed away from Martin for the last month was to keep him out of trouble and protect him from the dangers associated with my line of work. Apparently he was talented enough to get into hot water with or without my presence.

Arriving at the office building that housed Ackerman's law firm, Ackerman, Baze, and Clancy, I waited impatiently for more information. The assistant indicated a few empty chairs in the lobby and promised Ackerman would be available momentarily. While I sat in an uncomfortable chair near the reception desk, my phone rang. I hated being this popular.

"Parker," Detective Nick O'Connell's voice instantly calmed my nerves, "have you heard what's going on?"

Nick was a good friend. We had a general understanding of quid pro quo. He had come to my rescue when I was Martin's bodyguard, and he had risked his neck to watch my back when dealing with the sadist from one of my recent cases. My work had helped him earn a commendation, and typically, I tended to make his job much easier. Although, we weren't always in agreement on that last part.

"Only tidbits," I responded. I would have loved to ask some questions, but now wasn't a particularly pertinent time.

"I can't say anything, but I wanted to let you know Martin's in holding." I swallowed and shut my eyes. Great, he was arrested for murder. Could today get any better? "I'll keep an eye on him and make sure he's okay," Nick promised.

"Thanks." I didn't know what else to say. A man emerged from an office and gestured for me to join him. "I'll be by as soon as I can."

"Miss Parker," Ackerman greeted, extending his hand, and we shook.

"Alex, please." He ushered me into an office and shut the door. "What's going on?"

He picked up a file and flipped through some pages. "You're on retainer as security consultant for Martin Technologies. It's also been indicated that you originally worked private security for James Martin, prior to your position at his company." I nodded. "Former federal agent, meritorious service award, excellent percentage of closed cases, and you have a private investigator's license and your own consulting firm." I didn't need this jerk to read my file to me. I wanted to know what was going on with Martin. "It appears Mr. Martin is in need of an investigator at the moment, and he holds your skills in high regard."

"Fill me in."

Ackerman flipped over a confidentiality agreement to sign, along with who knows what other types of forms. I didn't bother to read; I just put my John Hancock seamlessly on each of the Xs and waited.

"Last night, the Coast Guard received a distress call from Mr. Martin's yacht. When they boarded, they found Caterina Skolnick's body on the main deck. Only the preliminary ME's report has come back, but she was stabbed repeatedly and suffocated. The only other person on the yacht was James Martin." Rubbing my face, I leaned back in the chair. "Mr. Martin placed the distress call, but given his proximity to the body, he's been arrested on suspicion of murder."

"His call wouldn't have done anything to alleviate such suspicion," I replied, automatically running through basic police procedures. "Has it been turned over to the locals?"

"Yes. Until other suspects are identified, it is in the best interest of our client to hire a team of investigators to look into the murder as well."

"Martin and I have," I paused, "had, might have had, a personal relationship." There was no easy way to categorize our past history, but I needed to divulge this information. Even though I was positive he hadn't committed murder, he couldn't afford any part of his defense to be tainted with impropriety. Ackerman acknowledged this without any surprise. After all, personal relationships with employees were an all too common occurrence in Martin's past.

"Okay," he pressed his lips together in thought,

"don't investigate on your own, but if your law enforcement friends offer any relevant information, please pass it along. Or if you can convince them to drop the charges altogether, I wouldn't mind that either." Excusing myself, I left the office and went to the precinct.

Pulling into a parking space near the out-of-service patrol cars, I noticed some news vans lingering near the front of the building. Apparently they couldn't wait for a few tantalizing snippets on this high profile murder. I headed to O'Connell's desk in the major crimes unit and found him flipping through some casework.

"Hey, Nick," I greeted, sitting down in his partner's chair. He looked up, smiling slightly.

"Funny, I thought you would have been here twenty minutes ago. Now I owe Thompson ten bucks. What took you so long?"

"I'm glad you're taking things so seriously," I growled. I bit my lip and shut my eyes, trying to force myself to be more pleasant. "What can you tell me? Can I see him?"

"I can't tell you anything. It's an ongoing investigation, so don't look in this file." He pointed to the folder on his desk. "I'm going to grab a cup of coffee. Do you want one?"

"Yes." I eyed the folder, glad that he had dropped the by-the-book attitude he had when we first met. "Cream, sugar, and shaved chocolate on top would be nice. Maybe you need to run to the store to get some."

He snorted. "I'll be back in five minutes."

As soon as he was gone, I glanced around the room. No one was paying any attention, so I picked up the folder and began reading the report. Caterina Skolnick was stabbed three times to the left side of her torso; however, the cause of death was asphyxiation. I skimmed through the crime scene photos and located the possible murder weapon. There was a standard bed pillow next to the body. From the coroner's report, there were obvious signs of sexual activity prior to her time of death, but there was no tearing or injury to indicate it was anything other than consensual. No semen or DNA was present, but spermicide was found. Whoever she had been intimate with wore a condom. I swallowed and continued to the next page.

From Martin's statement, it was clear he had no recollection of what happened once they arrived on his yacht. He claimed to have passed out, and when he came to, he found Caterina, attempted to perform CPR, and radioed for help. There was a note indicating a toxicology screening was ordered for both Martin and the deceased. Hopefully, this would help to exonerate him.

Closing the folder, I placed it back on O'Connell's desk and tried to process everything I just read. If Martin slept with her, it would add to his suspicion. I didn't want to think about that possibility either, but it was in the report so personal feelings needed to be pushed aside for the moment. Although, if there was spermicide, then where was the condom?

I grabbed the folder again and carefully scanned through the crime scene photos, cross-referencing the scene markers with the list of evidence. There was no condom present. Maybe she had sex before getting on the boat. This could point to a plethora of possible sexual partners and would help cast some dispersion on Martin's guilt since there was the possibility of an unknown third party being involved. Spotting O'Connell returning with the coffees, I put the folder down.

"I brought you a regular, black coffee. This is a

police station, so I couldn't find your fancy chocolate shavings," he teased, setting the cup in front of me. He lowered his voice and leaned down. "I don't think he did it."

"Me neither. Why don't you cut him loose?"

"It's out of my hands." He took the folder to a filing cabinet and stuffed it inside. "It's not my case. I've got too much past history with the accused."

"A lot of that going around. When can I see him?"

"I'll find out. The last I heard, his lawyers were working on getting him released. I'm sure he'll be out of here in a few hours. He's only been here since four this morning, anyway." I waited for O'Connell to return. I hadn't seen Martin in a month, and this was not the way I intended our reunion to go.

TWO

I was in the basement, standing outside the bars of one of the holding cells in lockup. O'Connell had done all he could, and he made sure Martin was given his own cell as secluded from everyone else as possible. Given that it was a Saturday morning, the only other detainees were passed out in the drunk tank down the hall, and the hardened criminals were either upstairs in the interrogation rooms or moved to another facility, awaiting transfer. At least he wouldn't get shanked while in lockup.

"Hey, stranger. Long time, no see." I tried to sound upbeat.

Martin was lying on the bunk of his cell, staring at the ceiling. I had been standing there for a few minutes, but he didn't notice my presence. At the sound of my voice, he sat up. His dark brown hair, which was usually so carefully styled, was mussed, and his impeccable clothing looked almost as haggard as his facial features. His green eyes seemed dull, and his toned, athletic build looked somehow diminished against the backdrop of the metal bars and the dingy beige walls. The smallest sign of relief crossed his features before being replaced with resentment.

"If I had known the only way I was going to see you again was by getting arrested, then maybe I should have had this happen sooner," he responded. "But quite frankly, I'm not sure it was worth it." Someone was in a bitch of a mood, and I did my best to let his hateful comments go.

"Do you want to tell me what happened?"

He stiffly got off the bunk, holding his right arm firmly against his body as if it was still in a sling. Obviously, the cops confiscated it before putting him into a holding cell for fear he might try to strangle himself. I made a mental assessment of the stab wounds on the victim. They were all focused on the left side of her body. I didn't think, given Martin's currently immobilized arm, he would have been capable of such actions. Hopefully, his attorneys reached the same conclusion and weren't complete morons.

"Why? Do you think I did it, too?" he asked bitterly.

"Cut the crap," I snapped. "I know you damn well didn't do this, and I'll do whatever I can to get you out of here." I tried not to let him continue to push my buttons. "Ackerman called this morning, read me in, but I can't investigate."

"Really?" He sounded cynical. "You gave me up for the job, and now you're giving the job up, too? Why the hell are you here? What good is any of this doing?"

"Goddamn you." I didn't need this. He could stay here and rot. It's not like it should matter to me. Dropping my tone to a barely audible whisper because I didn't want to risk my anger causing this asshole to get into even more trouble, I retorted, "Whenever you do manage to get out of here, just ignore the call I made to you last night. After all, you were probably busy screwing the dead girl at the time." Turning, I stomped down the corridor.

"Alex," his tone shifted to something more civil, "I wasn't. We didn't."

Fine, I cursed inwardly. Martin always had what I considered extreme mood swings; apparently some things never change. I pressed my lips together and counted to ten before turning around.

"Then what happened?" I asked, exasperated. He wrapped his hand around one of the metal bars, and I stood in front of him.

"I don't know." He looked lost. "Everything's jumbled."

"Okay." I noted how bloodshot his eyes were. "Start at the beginning. What'd you have for dinner?" It was a tactic I used when trying to jog a witness's memory. Often, it helped to have them start with something simplistic and unrelated.

He began his recollection with insignificant details relating to the gala. He always was philanthropic and got invited to a charity function at the marina, the same marina where his yacht was docked. Numerous influential guests flocked to this particular event, and he spoke to quite a few people from business associates to minor celebrities to models. As the evening progressed, someone introduced him to Caterina Skolnick, a twenty-six year old model. I attempted not to begrudge the recently deceased as he continued his story.

There was an open bar, and he drank continuously for a good part of the evening. "Things start to get blurry," he said, attempting to recall how he ended up on the yacht.

"When the police brought you in, they took a blood sample, right?" I was double-checking what was in the report.

"Yeah, they wanted to run a full tox screening." He looked perplexed.

"To see what your blood-alcohol level was," I clarified. It was painfully obvious he was extremely hungover.

"Great, they'll probably think I'm a drug addict, too."

"Why?" I didn't like where this conversation was going. "What the hell were you doing?"

He looked at his arm before glancing back at me. "Doctor prescribed pain medication, but I took them as directed," he quickly interjected, hoping I wouldn't go off on a tirade.

"Are you trying to kill yourself? Can you not read the warning label saying something along the lines of no alcohol or limit alcohol intake? It's no wonder you can't remember anything. It's a fucking miracle your heart didn't stop." His attempt to avert my wrath failed miserably, and I rubbed my eyes, trying to think my way through his unhelpful commentary. We stood there silently for a few moments. "What's the next thing you remember?"

"I was at the party, and then we were walking down the pier to the yacht. We got on board."

"Was anyone else with you besides Caterina? Were you followed?"

He frowned and slammed his open palm against the bars, causing me to jump. "I don't know what happened after that. It's all blank." He sat on the cot, leaning his good elbow on his knee and resting his head in his hand. The briefest desire to wrap my arms around him crossed my mind, but I pushed that out of my head. I wasn't even sure if, aside from his current predicament, we would be on speaking terms.

"Did you call the police?" Since I knew he placed

the distress call, maybe jumping ahead in the story would help jog his memory.

"Eventually. I must have blacked out because when I came to, I was on the floor. We were still on the main deck." The blood drained from his face, and he looked like he might be sick. "I reached for the bench seats, and I felt her arm. It was cold."

"Cold?" I parroted the word.

How long had she been lying there dead? Body temp takes awhile to drop. How cold was it last night? Did the coroner's report list an estimated time of death? I didn't remember seeing it, but since he had been in lockup since four a.m., TOD had to be sometime before three o'clock at the earliest. If she was cold, she could have been killed several hours before that, maybe even around the time they first boarded the yacht.

"Yes." He looked nauseous. "Unnaturally cold. The first thing I noticed was her eyes. They were open and filmy, but she wasn't seeing." He had never encountered a dead body before last night. That alone could be traumatizing enough without the added stress of being arrested for the crime. "I felt for a pulse, tried to revive her, and then I called for help." I nodded for him to continue. "The Coast Guard towed us to shore. The cops were called, and then I was brought here. They photographed, fingerprinted, and took my blood, and that's pretty much it. Hell of a day." He had been processed and booked.

"How far from shore were you? Were you questioned? Did you have counsel present?" Improper procedure was as good an excuse as any to be exonerated.

"I have no idea, but I could still see the harbor lights. So it wasn't far. It couldn't have been." He sighed, screwing his eyes shut and trying to gain insight. "I was questioned, and my attorney was present. He instructed me not to say a word, but," he met my eyes, "maybe you've rubbed off on me. I told the authorities everything I remembered because I don't want the person responsible to get away with this."

Smiling sadly, I remarked, "What a dumb idea." He graced me with the briefest smirk I've ever seen. If everything he said was true, and there was no reason not to believe him, then whoever murdered Caterina had been inches away from him. The realization was chilling. If Ms. Skolnick was the intended target, then without any solid proof, Martin could theoretically provide the real culprit's defense attorney with the ability to cast plenty of reasonable doubt on any trial proceedings.

"Alex," he pulled me from my reverie, "why did you call last night?"

"Did you have your phone with you?" I ignored his question as a thought worked its way through my brain.

"Of course." He was standing close to the bars again. "But I must have been out of it by then. What time did you call?"

"It was around one. I had just left Mark at the bar." Maybe my call could help establish a timeline. The cops needed to pull the surveillance from the charity event and get some witness statements in order to determine what time Martin left. If he truly was passed out when I called, and if it could be corroborated by either the marina security cameras or his toxicology screening, maybe he could get out of here sooner rather than later.

"You're still working for Mark?"

"No," I replied harshly. "Look, one thing at a time. I need to run some things by O'Connell or Ackerman or whoever the hell will listen. I said I'd try to get you out of here, so sit tight. I'll be back." Turning on my heel, I headed for the stairs.

"Alex," he murmured my name and something about missing me, but maybe I was hallucinating. After all, given the way our encounter started, I wasn't sure he would want me around once the current crisis was resolved.

THREE

I was sitting in my car, speaking to Ackerman over the phone. He already heard Martin's recitation of the evening's events, but perhaps my background could shed some light on the inner workings of police procedure.

"They are still collecting evidence, but it all seems suspect and highly circumstantial," I concluded my diatribe.

Through the speaker, Ackerman could be heard pecking away at a keyboard. "I've been trying to put a rush on the arraignment in order to get Mr. Martin released on bail." Despite his attorney-client privilege, I signed my life and soul away to the ABC law offices, so I was allowed to be in the know on such things. At least this deal with the devil didn't require a signature in blood. "He's a high profile client and an upstanding citizen with no previous criminal record. If everything goes as planned, he should be home by late this afternoon."

"All right." My mind was a million miles away. "I'll stay at the precinct until he's moved to the courthouse. If I can do anything else, give me a call."

Disconnecting, I went inside to see if I had any pull at the police station. Since the major crimes unit achieved worldwide notoriety after I acted as bait to lure out the French national hell-bent on killing me and I provided them all the pertinent evidence on a local murder-for-hire conspiracy, maybe it was time to call in some favors.

"Back so soon?" O'Connell asked, and I shrugged, trying to figure out the best way to be tactful.

"Who caught the case?"

He jerked his head to the corner of the room. "Heathcliff's working the case, but his balls are in a vise because of it." He picked up his pencil and tapped it on the desk. "Martin isn't our typical suspect. Wealthy, connected, personal friend of the mayor, goes golfing with half of city council." He was embellishing since I didn't know Martin to golf, ever. "Every move Heathcliff makes is being sent up the ladder."

Politics be damned. The brass was so concerned with making sure everything was done perfectly that it was going to take even longer than usual. Meanwhile, any actual leads were growing colder by the minute. It would be best to go over Detective Heathcliff's head and straight to the major crimes lieutenant, a man I had only briefly encountered in the past, Dominic Moretti.

"Where's Moretti's office?" Someone needed to get the ball rolling and not just Heathcliff's.

O'Connell swiveled in his chair and pointed to the door with the metal nameplate. "Try not to go in with guns blazing. The LT doesn't respond well to dramatics." I acknowledged his advice and marched to Moretti's office, knocking somewhat timidly.

"Enter," Moretti bellowed from inside.

"Lieutenant Moretti? I'm Alex Parker. I don't know if you remember me."

"Parker." He nodded slightly to himself. "The Parisian shooting, right?"

"Yes, sir." I sat on the edge of the chair. "I was hoping to speak with you about the Skolnick case."

"In what capacity? Are you still working for James Martin? Or are you back with my old pal, Mark Jablonsky, at the OIO?" He was eerily aware of everything pertaining to me, and I wondered if O'Connell tipped him off earlier.

"I'm guessing overly observant and concerned citizen isn't an option?" I tended to be sarcastic and make bad jokes at the worst possible times. He didn't waver, waiting for me to be serious. "I finished consulting for the OIO yesterday. Today, I'm just a Martin Tech security consultant."

His eyes crinkled at the corners as he laced his fingers together and rested his hands against the desk. "Why don't I begin with what you're going to say, and if I get it wrong, you can correct me. Fair enough?"

He looked like a bulldog with drooping jowls and unyielding eyes. He was the definition of a hardened, no-nonsense cop. I agreed to his terms, and he began his spiel. Or maybe it was mine. I could no longer be sure.

"Martin's at a party, gets a little drunk, things don't mix well, so he goes outside to get some fresh air. The vic, Caterina Skolnick, goes with him. Maybe she's interested in a good looking man, or maybe she thinks his Rolex has its own attractive qualities. Somehow, they end up on his yacht. Maybe they have sex." He shrugs, lifting his hands in a 'who knows' gesture. "Martin's unconscious on the boat. Someone else finds Caterina, finishes her off, unties the yacht, and then when Martin comes to, he calls it in. And we end up here."

"So why are you holding him?" Moretti's theory sounded even better than mine.

"Gotta hold someone. There's a dead model on a yacht and no one else around. My department's already given a bad enough rap for being incompetent when we do our jobs. How would it look to let some rich SOB walk away from a crime scene?" He raised a challenging eyebrow, making me wonder if the question was rhetorical or if he actually expected an answer.

"Dammit," I muttered. This was bureaucracy at its worst.

"Eh," he assessed my reaction, "cheer up. It gave us a chance to have this pleasant moment together. Plus, the toxicology just came back a couple of minutes ago. They were both drugged. Rohypnol was found in both of their systems. We're pursuing other avenues, especially since the DA won't touch Martin with a ten foot pole now that he might also be considered a victim. All the charges are being dropped."

"You could have started with that tidbit of information." I was trying to keep the resentment out of my voice and failing miserably.

"I guess, but it's more fun to watch people squirm. Side effect of working this job too long." He grinned, amused. "I'm not pretending to be psychic," he continued, "but I'm guessing if you're still working private sector for him, our paths might cross again on this case. Do you think he'll hire his own team of investigators to assist in figuring out who drugged him and why his yacht was used for the staging of a homicide?"

I hadn't considered any of these possibilities. My singular concern was to get Martin released, but Moretti had a point. "I don't know. If so, are you open to having some assistance?" He evaluated the situation, weighing his options.

"O'Connell's vouched for you a couple of times, and Jablonsky swears by your skill set. If it comes down to it, we'll work with you, but just make sure he doesn't hire some imbecilic private dick that's going to bumble around and botch the entire investigation."

"All right. Thanks, Lieutenant." I was in the process of shutting his office door behind me when he asked if I would give Martin the good news, and I nodded. Things were beginning to look up.

As I went past O'Connell's desk, I gave him a big smile and a thumbs-up. Nick must have assumed I lost my mind, but he knew me. He probably figured there wasn't much left to lose anyway.

I headed for the stairwell, hoping not to be stopped en route to the holding cells. I was on the landing when my phone rang. Ackerman was calling with the good news and to request, if I could manage it, that I somehow get Martin out of the building and away from the media circus. Lovely, the media, I thought frustrated. One thing at a time.

Nodding to the cop working the desk, I continued my trek to Martin's cell. "The charges are being dropped," I told him. He was sitting on the bunk, looking miserable, but at my words, he produced the first genuine smile I'd seen in far too long.

"How?" He was relieved but confused. "You must be a miracle worker."

A small part of me wanted to take credit because I didn't want to risk dealing with his resentment, but the truth would come out soon enough. "It wasn't me. They didn't have any hard evidence. You were in the wrong place at the wrong time, and you were drugged." He approached the bars, wanting to ensure he heard all of the good news. "Both of you were. The tox report came back. I don't know much else, but the DA's dropping all charges."

"You're still saving me," he said quietly, grasping the metal bar that separated us.

"I'm going to catch up with O'Connell while we wait for someone to release you. But fair warning, the media circus is going to be a bitch. When I got here, they were already outside, circling like sharks. But we might be able to slip out the back, and I can take you home. My pathetic subcompact is less obvious than your chauffeured town car."

"Okay." He was at a loss for words. That was a first for him, or maybe it was only a side effect of the roofie and the hangover.

*   *   *

A couple of hours later, Martin was a free man. Whether or not he was free from suspicion was still questionable, but the district attorney and police commissioner came to the precinct to personally apologize for the inconvenience. Martin took their apologies graciously, more graciously than I would have, and signed off on receiving his personal property as he exited lockup. He was attempting to fasten the clasp on his watch when I met him in the corridor.

"O'Connell and I have planned the perfect escape," I said, handing him a pair of sunglasses, a baseball cap, and a windbreaker. "We thought you should disguise yourself since you are public enemy number one and all. My car's around back with the patrol cars, so your departure shouldn't be plagued with paparazzi claiming to be journalists for the local news stations."

"Aren't they journalists?" he asked, somewhat bewildered. His lack of sleep had impacted his ability to comprehend my witty banter.

"Yes, but never mind." There was no point in explaining my failed attempt at a joking remark. We made it uneventfully out of the police station and to my car.

"You're actually taking me home?"

"Yes." I wondered what prompted this strange question.

"Because I just assumed you were still hung up about going back to my place. You haven't been there since the shooting a year ago." His tone was accusatory; however, given everything he had been through, he earned the right to be bitchy. But since I was nice enough to rescue his sorry ass, he needed to hold his snide comments in check.

"If you're that concerned, I'll let you out here, and you can walk." He remained silent as we continued the drive to his house. Finally, a thought crossed my mind, and I knew once I asked, we'd be fighting again. Screw it. "Where the hell was your bodyguard last night?"

"Bruiser?" His bodyguard's name was Jones, but I always insisted on calling him Bruiser. I was surprised Martin referred to him this way too.

"Yes." I glanced at him before returning my gaze to the road. "Why didn't he make sure no one drugged you or murdered your escort? I'm pretty sure that's bodyguarding 101."

He snorted derisively. "It was a charity function. I didn't think I needed a babysitter at a party." I cast a sideways glance at him. "Fine, I was wrong," he admitted. "And just so you know, she wasn't my escort."

"Doesn't matter to me." His remarks and behavior from earlier annoyed me, and I realized I was trying to pick a fight. The problem was I couldn't help myself. A month ago, we agreed to try again. That didn't entail going to parties and scoping out models. "I'm just curious," my tone was flippant, "since you can't remember too much about last night, how do you know you didn't screw her? The police assumed you did, which was also why they figured you were good for the murder."

"I didn't kill her," he snarled. "And I didn't sleep with her."

"I know you didn't kill her," I responded matter-of-factly. "But if you were with her, would you even tell me? It's okay if you were. It's not like we're together."

"Unbelievable. You make it sound like this is my fault when you're the one who decided we were taking two weeks apart, so you could go back to the OIO for some moronic reason, even though you didn't want to be there in the first place. You said I needed time to recover in peace from my surgery, which was just another pathetic excuse to avoid me. Then I don't hear from you for a whole fucking month. If I hadn't gotten arrested last night, you'd probably come up with some other reason why this wouldn't work. You show up out of the blue today for god knows what reason, and you get me out of trouble. I appreciate it, but right now, I'm not sure if I can stand to be around you."

"The feeling's mutual." The rest of the drive to his house was in total silence.

FOUR

I pulled to a stop in front of Martin's compound, located on the outskirts of the city, and parked in front of the southern garage entrance. Martin got out of the car and entered the security code, so the door would open. He glanced inside and then turned back to me, unsure of exactly what to do now that we were at his house.

"Is Bruiser here?" I asked through my rolled down window, prepared to make a quick getaway.

"No. Neither is Marcal." Marcal was his driver and valet.

Leaving him alone didn't seem like a good idea after everything that happened in the last twelve hours. Even though his estate was situated at the end of a long driveway that connected to a private road which linked the residence to the main highway, someone from the press would eventually track him down, and god knows who else might be looking for him.

I blew out a breath. "If you want me gone, I'm gone,

but I'd feel more comfortable if you weren't here by yourself. There's a good chance the hounds will be barking at your door soon enough." Or maybe the murderer might want revenge since you made a pretty pathetic patsy. However, he would deem this comment too dramatic and impractical, so I let it float around the paranoid recesses of my mind instead of saying it aloud.

"Fine." He was less than pleased by being stuck with me, but he got back into my car and indicated that I should pull into the garage.

I hadn't been to his house since my days working as his bodyguard. A team of mercenaries was sent to eliminate him, and part of his residence had been decimated in the resulting firefight. The house had been restructured, but I still found it unsettling. Too many bad memories.

Parking my car, I turned off the engine. Martin was already out the door and halfway up the stairs to the main level. I steeled my nerves and followed, noticing that the first floor not only contained the garage, with all of his expensive sports cars on display, but a new gym area complete with boxing ring, heavy bag, and the like. Maybe he was taking up a new hobby or planned to once his shoulder rehab was completed.

I emerged onto the main level to find everything looked as it had before. Martin was in the kitchen, pouring a glass of water. Pulling out a chair, I watched as he picked up his prescription bottle from the counter.

"I wouldn't," I stated, and he turned. Maybe he was surprised I was still here. "I know you must feel like shit." I was trying to be sympathetic, not that the bastard necessarily deserved it, but maybe his remarks hadn't been a hundred percent unwarranted. "But you should let the Rohypnol and the remaining alcohol work their way out of your system first. You don't need to mix any more drugs with what's already inside of you."

"I was roofied?" He seemed genuinely amused by this fact. "Guess that's what I get for ordering two of the same drink and trying to be a gentleman. Clearly, no man should ever order a cosmopolitan. They're too girly and apparently come with the added bonus of containing date rape drugs. The FDA really should take a firm stand against that." He shook his head. "I knew I should have stuck with the scotch, but it was some cheap ass scotch, though." He was talking to himself.

"Get some sleep. You need to get your priorities in order. I'll wait until Bruiser shows up, and then I'll go, like you asked."

Without another word, he went upstairs. I put my head in my hands and shut my eyes. The kitchen was neutral territory; nothing traumatic had occurred here. I willed myself to sit quietly and wait for Bruiser. Unfortunately, I wasn't particularly patient. Also, I was easily distracted.

About fifteen minutes later, I was rummaging through my purse, looking for a pen. Once the pen had been located, I began searching for paper. Finally, I located a small notepad in one of the kitchen drawers. Martin's kitchen was still familiar as was being this close to him. We had been friends for a year, ever since he hired me, but our one month hiatus had made everything awkward. Or maybe that came from our attempt to cross the line into something more than friendship. Now we were back to square one. He was insufferable, and I was employed by his lawyers to get him out of a jam.

Focusing on work, I jotted a few notes concerning Skolnick's murder. Lists were an integral part of my process, and I wrote down all the necessary information needed to conduct a proper investigation: surveillance footage from the charity event and from the cameras posted at the marina, witness statements, an interview with the bartender, Skolnick's phone records, the Coast Guard's report regarding the location of the yacht and their initial scene impressions, background on Skolnick, a list of her friends and enemies, a list of everyone at the party, the ME's report, the tox screenings, and the official case file.

When I couldn't come up with anything else, I paced the kitchen. Why wasn't Bruiser there last night? All of this might have been prevented if Martin's bodyguard had intervened. Maybe the girl would still be alive. Why didn't Bruiser insist on going? And where the hell is he now?

I thought about calling O'Connell, Mark, or pretty much anyone since I was spinning in circles with no place else to go outside of this fourteen by eighteen foot room. I freed Martin from his holding cell to simply put myself into a prison of my own design. Sliding to the floor, I pulled my knees to my chest, staring at nothing.

Martin was angry with me. He was feeling the leftover effects of the Rohypnol and the alcohol. That combination mixed with his painkillers probably created a god-awful headache which was compounded by being processed and booked at the precinct, interrogated, and locked up for a few hours. His odious demeanor likely had more to do with his current physical discomfort than with my failure to see him for the last four weeks, but he had a point. What good did any of this do? I left him in an attempt to protect him, and yet, that plan completely backfired. Now I was stuck in a purgatory I created.

Damn ethics. Some lines should never be crossed, and we never should have tried to become more than we were.

A few hours later, Bruiser arrived. His sudden appearance jerked me out of my self-inflicted mental torment, and I automatically pulled my nine millimeter from its holster and pointed it at the sound of the disturbance.

"Parker," Bruiser acknowledged as I lowered my weapon, "I didn't mean to scare you." He was a large, burly man with vast amounts of tactical training. He was hired as Martin's bodyguard after I insisted someone competent and well-trained be my permanent replacement.

"Yeah, well," I sighed, "where the hell have you been?" I tried not to sound angry.

"The boss gave me a couple of days off." I stood up stiffly from my place on the floor and leaned against the counter, waiting for the feeling to return to my legs. "In fact, I'm actually twenty minutes early."

"Martin failed to mention that. It seems he's failed to mention a lot of things. I'll get out of here and leave everything in your capable hands." I picked up my purse, moments away from escape. "Did you hear the news?"

"What news?" he responded uninterestedly.

"Your boss was drugged last night and arrested on suspicion of murder. You did a real bang-up job as his bodyguard." Martin's resentment had leaked into my own tone. Obviously, that was another hazard of the two of us being in close proximity to one another.

"Hmm." He looked smug, and I halted my retreat. "You realize what the problem is, right?"

"Enlighten me." I stormed back into the kitchen, feeling the overwhelming need to yell at someone.

"James doesn't listen to anyone. He does what he

wants, when he wants. When he tells me to take the night off and leave him alone, I take the night off." He furrowed his brow thoughtfully. "We aren't all like you, Parker."

"What's that supposed to mean?"

He tried to ineffectually hide the slight grin on his face. "You're just like him, too damn stubborn to listen." I narrowed my eyes, trying to make him take his remark back, but he wasn't intimidated. At least that was one point in his favor. "By the way, good luck getting out of here." He jerked his chin in the direction of the front yard. "There are five news vans parked near the entrance to the private road."

"Lovely." I sighed. "So how'd you get here?"

"I drove around, parked about two miles away, and came on foot through the back. If I didn't have to go through all that extra trouble, I might have been a couple hours early instead of twenty minutes." He chortled. Apparently he didn't listen to orders very well either, regardless of what he wanted me to believe. "Now it makes sense why the news people were outside. I thought they were lost or looking for aliens."

"Aliens?" Martin commented, entering the kitchen. "Resident or unidentified?" He looked a bit better. He changed his clothes and smelled of soap and expensive cologne. A few hours of sleep had hopefully improved his attitude too. He looked at me. "I thought you were leaving," he said, awaiting my reaction.

"I was." I reached for my list, but he grabbed it before I could, reading it quickly and placing it back on the table.

"And I thought you couldn't work this case," he challenged. Bruiser sensed the tension in the room and quietly excused himself.

"Just an exercise in killing time." I snatched the

paper off the table and shoved it into my pocket. "If you'll excuse me," I said bitterly, brushing past him. He stepped out of my way, and I headed for the garage.

"Unfortunately, Miss Parker, I believe you missed your window of opportunity." Story of my life. "Since I don't need any more speculation or news coverage regarding my presence at a crime scene, you'll have to stay here and wait it out." I assessed his expression, knowing he was a world-class manipulator. He also tended to believe his unilateral decisions were all that mattered. "Plus," his tone shifted to something slightly more pleasant, "a brilliant security consultant I know might have mentioned that one person cannot be a twenty-four hour protection detail. It looks like Bruiser might need some help." He tried to fight the grin off his face, but the corners of his lips curled upward.

"You son of a bitch." My tone was somewhere between playful and incredulous. "You promised that there would be no more bodyguard work ever."

"Things change," he surmised, pulling an icepack from the freezer and tucking it under the strap of his sling so the cold could ease the pain in his shoulder. "By the way, how long do you think it'll be before I get some actual relief from this infernal headache and painful throbbing?" He was making an incredibly dirty joke in his mind, but given his vile comments today, he decided to keep it to himself. Classic Martin, full of inappropriate jokes only a teenage boy would find amusing.

"Apparently, someone's already feeling better," I retorted, tossing my purse on the counter in defeat.

FIVE

Later that afternoon, Martin's team of lawyers arrived at the compound which unfortunately encouraged the news vans to idle even closer to the house. I snuck a peek out the window and figured if any of them were foolish enough to actually encroach on private property, they could be arrested for trespassing.

"Miss Parker." Ackerman's voice interrupted my thoughts, and I turned to face him. Along with Ackerman, there were two junior partners from the firm seated at the kitchen table. "Would you care to join us?"

I regarded Martin. This wasn't my business. As far as I was concerned, none of this was my problem. Maybe he wasn't attempting to bully or persuade me to get out of his house, but there was still an unpalatable tension between us. The slight reprieve didn't last.

"Take a seat." He reached over and pushed a chair out. I didn't like being told what to do, but at the moment, I was stuck.

"The district attorney's office has issued a formal apology," one of the junior partners mentioned. I missed the introduction, so I was simply referring to them as Frick and Frack. Frick was perusing a copy of the apology. "The story will be made public, per your request. There should be minimal fallout since the turnaround was less than twelve hours."

"I'll have the PR department handle the related business issues," Martin replied. He picked up his phone and sent a quick e-mail to the vice president of his company, Luc Guillot, so things at the office could be set in motion between now and Monday.

"At least there are no criminal charges to consider," Ackerman sounded pleased and winked at me, but I pretended not to notice since I really hadn't done anything. "However, we don't want to risk any of this getting away from us. There is a strong possibility Skolnick's estate will file civil charges. Assuming you want to get ahead of this, we're prepared to hire our own investigative team in order to be proactive." I was beginning to understand why I was asked to sit at the table with all the legal eagles.

"Alex?" Martin said my name cautiously, hoping I would offer my services. I knew what he was asking, and I wanted to behave and not fight with him in front of his lawyers. In the event I slapped him, there didn't need to be witnesses who were also officers of the court.

"What about ethical issues?" I asked Ackerman, ignoring Martin for the moment. Ackerman looked from Martin to me and back again.

Martin shook his head and interjected, "I think we're in the clear." I stared at him, ready to protest. "Oh, come on," he rolled his eyes, "you never gave us a chance to get off the ground. What's the worst that can happen? In the unlikely event any of this ever goes to trial, what are they going to do? It's not like our business relationship is tainted with scandal. They'll throw you on the stand and ask if we had an intimate relationship. Obviously, the answer is no."

"Yeah, and if they ask for details, what do I say? I'm sorry, your Honor, but he just couldn't get it up."

"Ha!" We were in the middle of a very ugly argument at the worst possible time. "How 'bout I couldn't even touch you without you wincing or freaking out over my damn bullet wound."

"Says the guy who couldn't tear his eyes from the electrical burns on my chest, who stood in the doorway of my apartment hypnotized by the bloodstain left by someone he never even met."

"We'll give you two a minute," Ackerman muttered, and he and the other lawyers quickly extricated themselves from the kitchen.

"You never gave me a chance to process everything that happened before you blindsided me. I'm sorry I had difficulty accepting the fact that you forced me to stay away, even though you almost died." Martin was still arguing, even though we both needed to calm down and act more civil. "The only thing I asked was that you not shut me out again, and you said you couldn't do it. You had to protect me. Is this how you protect me?" He gestured obliquely to the room, the lawyers, and the entire situation.

"I told you I would try. We would try, once we both had a second to breathe. You had so much going on at work, and I had..." I stopped. Why were we fighting about this now?

"You had what?" He pushed for an answer.

"We can discuss our personal life later. Right now, we scared off your lawyers."

"You had what, Alexis?" He wouldn't let it go.

"I had to figure out if I could walk away from the OIO and not go back. I had to choose. It or you." My voice was a low growl, and my breathing was harsh. If I were a dragon, smoke would be coming out of my nostrils.

"What'd you decide?" His green eyes bore holes through me.

"At the moment, neither." My voice was deadly.

"Fine." There was a self-satisfied expression on his face. "Then there's no reason why you can't be lead investigator." My jaw dropped at his insanity, and I made the conscious effort to close my mouth. "Ackerman," he called into the living room, "I think we've settled things."

The trio re-entered the room, having enough sense to pretend our screaming match didn't just happen and they couldn't hear every single hideous word we uttered to one another. Immediately getting back to business, Ackerman produced copies of my previously signed documents, which he double-checked.

"Miss Parker," Frack spoke, "you're a seasoned investigator. We shall defer to you for the hiring of third parties and the allocation of any resources you deem imperative for the proper execution of an investigation. You will coordinate all discoveries through me." He held out his business card, and I took it and read his name. Jack Fletcher. Fletcher, Frack, close enough, I reasoned.

"With any luck, none of this will come to fruition," Ackerman replied, standing and shaking hands with Martin, "but it's pertinent to compile the information while it's still new and fresh. I know how you are, James." He patted Martin's good shoulder. "You like to be ahead of the curve on everything."

"Since I have the resources at my disposal, it would be ill-advised not to use them." Hopefully, he was talking about his deep pockets and not my skills since I was not a resource nor available for his disposal. Okay, so maybe I was angry, bitter, offended, and a few dozen other adjectives. There were some flaws in my personality which needed work, but I was only human, after all.

"We'll see ourselves out," Ackerman concluded.

I handed my business card to Frack/Fletcher, and he put it in his pocket and followed his boss to the door. "I'll walk you gentlemen out," I offered as a means to distance myself from Martin. Once the door was securely shut behind us, I pulled Ackerman aside. "Why'd you call me this morning? I did absolutely nothing to get him out of lockup. I gave the guy a ride home. That was it. So why did I sign a dozen different forms and risk all your attorney-client privilege shit just to sit around the police station, drinking coffee?"

"I can only act in regards to my client's wishes," he responded with a brief, knowing smile that made me uneasy. "If you want answers, you're going to have to ask Mr. Martin."

I felt myself blush, embarrassed that these complete strangers had witnessed my unraveling. "Yeah, that would be easier if we were on speaking terms." He chuckled and got in his car, and I went back inside the house, hoping a tactical assault team might be waiting to put an end to this misery. No such luck.

"I've discovered something." Martin was speaking from the couch in the living room, and Bruiser was nowhere to be seen. Going into the living room, I sat across from him. We needed to clear the air before things got further out of control. "You and I are really great at fighting, world-class level of yelling and arguing. My god, we should have our own reality show."

I snorted. "People would think it was scripted."

"I'm sorry." He appeared genuinely repentant. "I've had a shitastic day, and you were only trying to help."

"I probably should have been a bit more considerate." My words didn't sound sincere, but I wasn't feeling particularly sincere. "We need to get over ourselves before we scare off even more of your hired help." I looked around the room. "Bruiser's gone AWOL, after all."

Martin smirked. "He's downstairs."

"Oh." We sat in the awkwardness for a while, recovering from our screaming match.

"We're going to table the current situation for the next ten minutes." He looked at his watch. "Think of this like you would any other day. Nothing's happened. Pretend I answered my phone when you called last night." I stared at him as if he were insane. "Humor me," he insisted. "You said we need to get over ourselves, so let's just fast forward through all the yelling, screaming, and whatever other types of emotional torture we were going to inflict upon one another."

His idea was absolutely ludicrous, but there was no way I'd be able to stay here and investigate if I wanted to kill him myself. I tried to organize my thoughts, and he waited patiently for me to begin.

"I finished the case with Mark last night." My tone was low. There was an underlying feeling of defeat I just couldn't shake. "I told him I was done, and there was no way I was going back again."

"How did that go?" His tone was equally subdued.

"About as well as could be expected. They weren't happy with my leaving, but I wasn't happy with the prospect of staying." He wanted to say something but stopped himself. "I just thought I should tell you." It felt stupid saying any of this now, but he nodded thoughtfully. I was staring at my nails, considering getting a manicure, when he finally spoke.

"The two weeks, your plan that we'd see each other again in two weeks," he swallowed, "the job ran longer than you expected?" At least now I understood the reason for his anger. If we could learn to speak the same language, life would be so much easier.

"The paperwork was completed yesterday. It was more complicated than I imagined it'd be. Frankly, two weeks was just my best estimate, but I guess I never made that clear."

"When I didn't hear from you, I thought you went back for good," he admitted.

Shaking my head, I stared out the window. "Why didn't you call? Or you could have asked Mark." Mark and Martin were friends from way back, and Mark had introduced the two of us and encouraged Martin to hire me when I emerged onto the private sector security scene.

"I guess I didn't want to know."

"Understandable, I suppose." I was already tired of this conversation. "Let's just chalk it up to bad timing and another missed opportunity." I stared unyieldingly until he agreed.

"Okay," he mumbled, pressing his lips together. "Back to business then?"

"Back to business, as long as you stop being a complete asshole."

He smirked. "I'll work on it."

"Why'd Ackerman call this morning?" If we were back to business, then I might as well dive in head first.

"You weren't rushing to the precinct to spring me on your own volition?"

"I thought you were working on not being an asshole." He gave me a pointed look. Apparently, I needed to work on holding my tongue. "I was asleep and hadn't heard the news yet." I could see the question in his eyes. Sighing loudly, I relented. "If I didn't get the call, I still would have been there as soon as I found out."

"See, that's why you got the call." He was making no sense. Having no interaction with him for the last month had impaired my ability to comprehend his irrationality and insanity mingled in with his extreme mood swings and unilateral decision-making skills. I opened my eyes wide and made a face, trying to get him to connect the dots, but he cocked an eyebrow up, confused.

"I don't understand," I retorted, annoyed.

"If something happens to me," his tone shifted to serious, "I want to make sure you have access to all the information. I saw you work your friend's murder, if you don't remember. You couldn't let it go until you found the person responsible for his death."

"But he wasn't dead." I rubbed my forehead; Martin was giving me a headache.

"That's not the point." He was insistent. "I know you," he said simply. "You would do anything to find the truth and get justice. I just want to leave you with the best starting place possible." He smiled sadly.

"That is possibly the nicest thing you've ever said and quite frankly the most morbid. Are we talking your untimely demise or something along the lines of you being found in the back room of a stash house with stripper Barbie?" I tended to use sarcasm and bad jokes to avoid the more serious emotional moments.

"More the former, but obviously, you'd still be read in on the latter. Once again, I wasn't with Caterina." He was ready to argue this point. "Hang on." He wasn't going to let it go until he satisfactorily proved his fidelity or at least his fidelity when it came to not screwing the recently deceased. He rummaged through his jacket pocket, looking for the receipt showing his reclaimed belongings. "Read this."

I resisted the urge to roll my eyes and skimmed through the list: watch, class ring, cell phone, wallet containing three hundred and twenty-two dollars, three credit cards, license, one condom. I stopped reading.

"I believe you," I told him, and I did. My internal voice was already running through other arguments the DA could make if they were still pressing charges, but I silenced it. There was no need to fight anymore.

"Now that that's settled, is there anything else we need to discuss in order to avoid any more mimicry of banshees?"

"Well," I folded my hands together and tapped my knuckles against my lips, conveying an air of seriousness, "if I have any say in the matter whatsoever, I'd prefer upon your demise to get one of those nice sports cars you have on display instead of information regarding your untimely death."

"Any vehicle in particular?" he asked, playing along.

"The one with the doors that lift up." I tried to sound sincere.

"Which one? Almost all of them do that." He smirked.

"I guess you better manage to remain breathing until I figure that part out."

SIX

After being accused of murder and drugged, Martin wanted assurances that nothing like this was going to happen again. He would never admit it, but the whole situation had rattled him. So Bruiser and I devised a schedule, so the two of us could comprise a full-time protection detail to monitor his movements, at least for the next couple of weeks. During the week, I would meet Martin at the Martin Technologies building and guard him at work. This made the most sense since I was still a MT employee. It also gave Bruiser a good eight to ten hours of downtime before Martin would leave work, and Bruiser would then resume his normal bodyguard duties.

The only problem was determining weekends. It was a Saturday, and with the news vans out front, I wasn't going home tonight. Relenting, I had no choice but to stay at Martin's compound for the rest of the weekend. Then next weekend, Bruiser and I could split the days into twelve hour shifts, but we'd both stay on the property that way there was someone to rely on for back-up in case anything occurred. The seriousness of the situation was being completely blown out of proportion, but it was Martin's dime. After everything he had been through this year, I understood his reticence.

"Are you sure you're okay staying here?" Bruiser asked as I settled into the guestroom on the second floor. He was convinced our bodyguard schedule was going to fall to the wayside.

"It's not a weekend at the Poconos," I retorted, "but as long as I can avoid the third and fourth floors, I can manage a couple of days." He understood my need to avoid the parts of the compound where I had gunned down two mercenaries.

"You can take days, and I'll keep an eye out at night. Since you're running the investigation for the lawyers, a daytime shift would be better."

"Thanks. I'm sorry I gave you a hard time earlier."

"That's part of your job as my predecessor." He turned and walked out of the room.

I shut the door and put my gun holster on the nightstand. Then I took off my pants and shirt and hung them in the closet. I didn't have anything packed for the weekend because I didn't know I wasn't going home tonight. Obviously, I should know better, especially after four years at the OIO, but thankfully, Martin always kept his guestrooms well-stocked with basic toiletries, and I commandeered a bathrobe. Tying it around my waist, I set to work, developing an attack strategy.

I wasn't used to being back inside Martin's house, and even though the room I was currently occupying was completely foreign to me, I could still feel a knowing unease settle throughout my body. I pushed the thought away and worked on expanding the list I started earlier. Until I got a chance to review the official police reports, I didn't have much to go on. Picking up the phone, I dialed Fletcher.

"Jack Fletcher speaking," he answered.

"Hey," I greeted. "It's Alex Parker. Can you smooth things over with the local PD? It'd be easier to shadow their progress than to remain two steps behind the investigation."

"Ms. Parker," he sounded friendly, "normally, that's not how these things work. I don't believe we've ever been granted a tagalong status with the police department. Our firm deals mostly with corporate or civil cases, but on the few criminal cases we've worked, we're the defense."

"You're not the defense this time. Actually, you aren't anything this time."

He chuckled. "I'm glad you hold my job in such high regard," he commented, but his tone was teasing.

"You know what I mean. From the current legal standpoint, it's not a case for you, yet."

"That is true."

"Will it cause any anxiety attacks at your office if I convince the cops to let me work with them instead of running something completely separate?"

"It shouldn't be a problem but let me double-check with the partners, and I'll get back to you by Monday morning."

"Good night, Mr. Fletcher." I was trying to put on a good face after everything he had seen and heard this afternoon.

After concluding the call, I went into Martin's second floor home office. I turned on his computer and began compiling as much information as I could find on Caterina Skolnick. My laptop had access to all the proper criminal databases, but it was at home. The same place I should be. For now, general internet searches would have to suffice. I printed a tome of

Skolnick's personal information, information on her modeling agency, her biggest gigs, estimated worth, and a few dozen pictures of her with various men taken at numerous events. Now I had a starting place.

"I thought you were taking days," Bruiser commented. He was sitting on the couch in the living room as the outside surveillance feed filled the big screen television. Although, there was a book opened on his lap, so I wasn't sure how well he was monitoring the perimeter.

"I am taking days," I insisted. "But it doesn't mean I'm not working nights too."

"Get some sleep, Parker."

Agreeing with his suggestion, I went into my room and shut the door. It was almost two a.m. when I turned off the light and got into bed. "Bad idea," I muttered, getting up and turning the light back on. The dark was eerie and suffocating. Why wasn't there a television in the guestroom?

I climbed back into bed and shut my eyes, re-evaluating everything I knew. Unfortunately, I didn't know much. At some point, I fell asleep, but I awoke just before dawn, gasping for air and trembling. The nightmares of fending off mercenaries and Martin getting shot had returned.

There was a knock at the door, and I unsteadily opened it. "You okay?" Bruiser asked, his gaze shifting from me to the rest of the room.

"Of course." I swallowed and tried to play it cool. "Why wouldn't I be?"

He narrowed his eyes. "I thought I heard you scream."

"I just wanted to make sure you were paying attention." He continued to scrutinize my expression. "Nightmares," I admitted, and he nodded and went back to the living room without another word.

Obviously, I wasn't the only one plagued by bad dreams.

A few hours later, I emerged, relieving Bruiser who promptly vanished into thin air. I was sitting on the couch. All of the information I printed last night was sprawled from one end of the coffee table to the other. I had a notepad in my hand and was attempting to create a proper timeline concerning Ms. Skolnick's career and life history. On a whim, I dialed Lt. Moretti for an update on the case. I was on hold, listening to some god-awful music when Martin bounded down the steps.

"Good morning," he greeted, a very obvious grin on his face.

"If you say so."

I sifted through the papers, looking for the most recent photo of the victim. Caterina was pretty, thin, blonde, and exactly what you'd expect from a model. There were dozens of photos of her from magazine spreads, modeling gigs, and parties with numerous suitors. As far as I could tell, she never went out with the same man twice which would make solid leads more difficult to pinpoint. She seemed lively and vivacious, not at all like the photo in the preliminary police report.

Martin leaned over the back of the couch to see what I was doing. "What do you want for breakfast?" His lips brushed against my earlobe.

"I'm not hungry." I really didn't understand his mood swings. Maybe after sleeping on things, he had a more positive outlook on life. Who knows?

"Fine." He kissed my cheek before standing up. "I'll just have to surprise you."

I turned and gave him my patented 'what the hell' look, but he had already moved into the kitchen. I shook my head and continued to be tormented by the agonizing music. Eventually, a woman's voice cut in, saying Moretti wasn't taking any calls at this time and I would have to try back tomorrow.

Sighing, I hung up and went into the kitchen. Martin was in front of the stove, cooking eggs and bacon. I poured myself a cup of coffee, before sitting down at the table. Once breakfast was ready, he put a couple of plates, some silverware, and the food on the table, humming as he did so.

"Did you bust into the painkiller bottle when I wasn't looking?" I joked.

"Not that I remember, but then again, if I did, would I remember?" He was being extremely playful this morning. "Oh, hang on." He disappeared from the room, and I picked at the eggs while I waited. Returning to the kitchen, he slid a personal check facedown across the table.

"What's this?" I asked, not bothering to flip it over.

"It occurred to me while I was getting dressed that I hired you yesterday, and we never had a proper negotiation. No champagne toasts. Nothing." He tried to appear ashamed, but his good mood was ruining the effect. "Needless to say, I calculated what you were paid last time, divided it by the weeks, and if it's not enough, we can negotiate."

"I'm sure it's more than adequate." I pushed the check away and reached for a piece of toast. "So much for you not being my boss and me not being your bodyguard."

"You can quit," he offered, knowing I couldn't let this go.

"Yeah, right." I ignored him, and we ate in silence for a few minutes. "I hate to ruin this mood you're in, but I need to ask you some questions."

"Oh goody, an interrogation." He was beginning to freak me out with his happy-go-lucky attitude.

"Okay, seriously, you need to stop. Yesterday, you were ready to bite my head off, and you pretty much forced me to stay here and work this case. And now you come down here happier than a kid on Christmas morning who just spotted a freaking pony in the backyard. What the hell is going on with you? You're confusing the crap out of me."

"Sorry," he toned down his attitude, "I'm sure I'm being completely inappropriate, given the circumstances." He swallowed, recalling the moment he found the body on his yacht. "But out of all the possible outcomes, I woke up this morning." He smiled. "And you're here." I got it. He was happy to be alive, but in a couple of hours, he'd probably be dealing with survivor's guilt or something equally negative.

"They need to put you on a mood stabilizer."

He chuckled and cleared the table while I went into the living room to retrieve the relevant information, but before I could return to the kitchen, he met me in the doorway. "It's more comfortable in here," he explained, taking a seat on the couch, "unless you wanted to handcuff me to something." He raised his eyebrows seductively, and I resisted the urge to smile. "My safety word is," he paused, trying to come up with something, "grenadine." I snorted. "See, I knew I could get you to smile."

"Shut up." I was great at the comebacks this morning. "Mr. Martin," I began, trying to derail his attempts at flirtation. Things were beginning to return to normal between the two of us, but I wasn't sure we were ready for that. Yesterday, we both said too much, and right now, he had bigger problems to contend with.

"Alex?" he responded.

"Martin."

"Alex."

"Well, now that we've both been properly introduced," I was getting annoyed with his antics, "when did you first meet Caterina Skolnick?"

"Friday night at the event hall." At least he was finally being serious. Thank goodness.

"So you and Miss Skolnick never crossed paths before?" I flipped through the photographs, but he wasn't in any of the pictures.

"Not that I know of." He thought back. "I would have remembered her." I let the comment go and began rattling off a list of parties and events she had attended. He furrowed his brow, considering each one before shaking his head.

"All right." I got up to pace. "How did you meet?"

"Her agent, Richard Sanderson, introduced us." His eyes followed my path, back and forth.

"How do you know him?" I picked up the notepad and scribbled the name on the paper.

"We've met a few times in passing." He was being cagey, so I stopped midstride and faced him, crossing my arms. "I don't really know the guy."

"What exactly do you mean by 'in passing'?" He stared at the floor, preparing what I imagined would be a completely diplomatic and positively vague response. "Don't make me get out my handcuffs and a phonebook."

"I might have dated a few of his former clients," he admitted. "There was Cynthia, Chelsea, and Beka," he paused before adding, "Shanna, Svetlana, Stana, something like that." Ladies and gentlemen, I give you playboy extraordinaire, James Martin.

"You dated six models?" And I thought the reason we weren't going to work out was because people were trying to kill one or both of us. Obviously, that was just the tip of the iceberg.

"No. Four." He made sure by counting properly on his fingers. "I can't remember the last one's name. It sounded foreign and started with an S." Rubbing my eyes, I tried not to gape at him.

"Sanderson was the agent for all of them?" This Sanderson guy sounded like a pimp.

"Yes, but I never made that connection before now." Probably because you were busy making other types of connections, but I kept the comment to myself. "It's been a couple of years since I've seen him."

"Why? Did you suddenly stop dating models?"

A thought dawned on him, and he nodded. "Things got busy at work when the company expanded, so I wasn't going out and about as often. Maybe I matured and outgrew them. Women need more substance."

"You probably just got too old to catch their eye." I was being catty. Martin was only in his mid-thirties. If Hugh Hefner could still find twenty-somethings to bang, then I was sure he could as well. You're only twenty-nine, my internal voice commented, pissing me off. Maybe I was the one with multiple personalities. "None of that matters anyway." Skimming over my notes, it might help if he rehashed the entire evening now that he had some time to let it ruminate. "Paint a picture of everything that occurred Friday from when you got up in the morning until you were arrested."

He recalled every minute detail of his day until he ordered the two drinks at the bar; then things began to get hazy. One of the cosmopolitans was intended for Caterina, and the other was for himself.

SEVEN

Martin ran through all the details, but there wasn't much I didn't already know. The only exception was the mental ping concerning Sanderson. I gave him the stack of photos and names to flip through in case anyone else rang a bell, but everything came up empty. I needed to review the official police reports while I waited to get back to the real world and do my own investigating.

"Tell me more about Sanderson," I instructed, slumping further on the couch. Right now, this was the closest thing I had to a lead.

"Why? Did you want to get into the modeling business too?" He was being exasperating as always. "Hell, you have the body for it."

"I'm too old, too short, and otherwise damaged goods." My mind wandered to my numerous scars, causing me to become even more annoyed. "How do you know Sanderson? Did he arrange for your dates?"

"They weren't prostitutes," he began as I

scrutinized him, unimpressed. "And to answer your question, he didn't arrange anything. I was dating," he tried to recall which model was his first, "Beka, no, it was Chelsea that introduced me to her agent. It was at the Black and White Ball. That was the first time I met Rick."

"It's such a relief to know you treat women as unique, separate individuals and not just tissues you can use once or twice and throw away." My glib response escaped my lips before I managed to restrain myself. Dammit, I cursed inwardly, hoping he would let it go.

"Is that what you think? I never treated you that way. I *would* never treat you that way."

"Sorry, I have Tourette's. So Chelsea introduced you to Sanderson at a party, and then you were randomly reintroduced to him at subsequent other parties when you were dating the others?" In my line of work, coincidences didn't happen like this. Not four times, anyway.

"Yeah. Small circles." He dismissed this happenstance easily.

"I'll try to keep the commentary to myself, but be honest, Ms. Skolnick wasn't your date?" I watched him, trying to determine the veracity of his answer.

"No. We met for the first time at the party." How did he end up being the unlucky bastard in all of this? "Can I ask you a question?"

"You just did," I replied automatically but waited for him to continue.

"Who's asking? Alex Parker, investigator? Or Alex Parker, my failed attempt at a relationship?"

"Does it change your answer? Because if it does, then you need to hire someone else, and whoever you employ to get to the bottom of this is going to need the truth."

"My answer is no, and it will always be no. That's the truth. We weren't dating. We weren't set up to date. I was standing at the bar, ordering a drink, when Rick approached me. We exchanged pleasantries, and then Caterina appeared. He introduced us, and we started chatting. But some woman pulled him away. After he disappeared, Caterina and I got to talking, and a couple of drinks later, I decided to give the girly cosmopolitans she was drinking a try and ordered two. The next thing I know, it was unbearably hot and stuffy in that room, so I excused myself to get some air. She joined me, and we strolled down the pier and ended up on my yacht." He really was just unlucky. "But you didn't answer my question," he pointed out, drawing me from my contemplation.

"Maybe both." I sighed, giving him a small, sad smile. "The funny thing is, before I woke up yesterday morning, I thought we still had a shot."

"We can, Alexis."

"Right now, you're my boss, and I'm already having a hard enough time separating my feelings and insecurities from this case. So no, we can't. Not now."

He pressed his lips together and contemplated my words. "After?"

I shrugged. "Do I look like a damn fortune teller to you?"

* * *

Monday morning, I drove past the news vans, hoping to avoid any muss, fuss, or fanfare. I went home, changed, and left for another day of pseudo-bodyguard work. I arrived at the MT building a little after ten and headed straight to the top floor. Martin should be in his office, so I wouldn't have to worry about tracking him through the seventeen floors in the building.

"Parker," Bruiser acknowledged, buzzing me into Martin's office, "I thought you might have gotten lost."

"One could only hope. Where's the boss?"

"Downstairs, giving a press conference." He was as vexed about this as I was about the entire situation. "He said to stay here."

"Take off," I jerked my chin at the door, "and get a lift with Marcal this afternoon when he picks Martin up from work." Not needing to be told twice, Bruiser left the office. That guy needed to stop following orders to such extremes. I took a seat on one of the leather couches and called Jack Fletcher.

"Ackerman, Baze, and Clancy," the assistant answered on the first ring.

I requested to speak to Mr. Fletcher, but he was with a client and would have to call me back. I was batting a thousand today. Guess I'd just have to do what I always do and wing it. Picking up the phone again, I dialed Detective O'Connell's personal line.

"O'Connell," he responded promptly.

"How's my favorite detective this morning?" I was laying it on thick.

"Parker." Sometimes, the way he said my name reminded me of the way people would mutter curse words. Strange coincidence.

"Is Moretti busy?"

"He's always busy, but if you want me to pass along a message, I guess I could do that."

"Well, you are there to protect and serve," I teased. "Typically, I call you for the protect part, so it's about time I get some use out of the serve factor."

"Anyone ever tell you you're a pain in the ass?"

"All the time. It looks like the ABC's have hired me to investigate Ms. Skolnick's murder and the events leading up to it. Ideally, I'd love to tag along with whoever's investigating, but if that's going to be tricky, can I get copies of the reports and interviews?"

O'Connell sighed dramatically. "Maybe I'll just have the LT give you a call. But shouldn't you be bothering Heathcliff with this request?"

"I've never met the man. Did you want to introduce us?"

"Keep your phone handy. Someone will get back to you."

I did a quick sweep of Martin's office. With the exception of his press conference, it was just a typical workday for him. Having nothing better to do, I went across the hallway and checked in at my small Martin Technologies provided office space while I awaited his return. Since Martin didn't want Bruiser attending the press conference, he didn't need me there either. Honestly, he didn't need anyone to babysit him while he was at work, but Skolnick's corpse had worried him more than he would ever admit.

I just got settled, with my door wide open, when the MT vice president, Luc Guillot, appeared in my doorway. "Mademoiselle Parker, lovely to see you again."

"Monsieur Guillot." I smiled. "Please." I gestured for him to enter. "What can I do for you, sir?" Guillot had recently been promoted and relocated from the Paris branch of MT. While he seemed pleasant enough, he had encouraged Martin to consider allowing my consulting contract to expire due to the job hazards related to other cases I may be working. I tried not to take it personally. After all, I didn't want to be romantically involved with the guy who signs my paychecks; although, that had turned into a complete bust.

"This is all such a mess." He sat across from my

desk. "I know I'm new here, but do things like this happen often?"

"It's beginning to seem that way." I didn't have an answer for him. "Mr. Martin's just run into a string of bad luck recently." Guillot frowned. "In case you have any doubts, please be assured, all charges have been dropped. He was not responsible for anything that occurred Friday night. In fact, he was lucky the assailant didn't target him too."

"No," Guillot attempted to clarify, "please don't misunderstand. I never believed James was guilty. I just don't understand how things like this happen."

"Me neither. It's the human condition, I suppose. Everything's just a mess of perceived haves versus have-nots. Money, power, sex, it eventually results in one animal making a bloody mess out of someone else for no good reason."

"And you try to stop it." Enlightenment dawned on his face. "That's why James hired you and then kept you on at MT."

"I can't stop it. I just try to clean up the mess afterward."

He nodded, as if to himself, and stood up. "Alexis, it is good to see you again." I offered a small smile, the only condolence I could give in this cruel world. "I hope you will consider the new job offer."

"What?" Maybe his English wasn't as good as it should be, but he left without elaborating, leaving me in complete wonderment.

"You're here." Martin popped into view, placing his thumb against the biometric scanner and unlocking his office door. "I need you for a meeting." Standing in the hallway were Fletcher and Ackerman.

"Gentlemen." I nodded to them. The three of us followed Martin into his office. Apparently, I solved the mystery concerning which client Fletcher was meeting with this morning. If only all investigations were this simple.

"Between the press conference and the PR department, the media has gotten its fair share of the story and will no longer find me interesting enough to stalk," Martin declared, multitasking as he spoke. I glanced at the attorneys, and they both agreed.

"The requested coroner's report was sent to our office this morning," Ackerman stated as Fletcher dug through his briefcase until he found the file. "As of yet, there has been no word from Skolnick's estate, but we wouldn't expect to hear from them this soon. There is still a possibility the actual guilty party will be apprehended." I stared at Ackerman, somewhat bewildered. How could he worry about the possibility of a civil suit being filed months from now when a woman's body was cooling in the morgue?

"We have discussed things at great length this morning," Martin spoke up. "It's been strongly recommended that I file a complaint against the police department for wrongful arrest and resulting damages."

"But the cops didn't do anything wrong, and you're going to screw them over for doing their jobs?" I growled. "After everything?"

"Doing their jobs would have resulted in a proper arrest of the actual murderer," Fletcher chimed in, and I turned, preparing an acidic retort.

Luckily, Martin intervened, rescuing the man. "However, as you've pointed out, that would not be very appreciative of the past assistance they have provided us." I rubbed my forehead. No one was making any sense at the moment.

"Ms. Parker," Ackerman took over the horse and pony show, "given the confidentiality agreement you've signed, I am able to divulge that Ms. Skolnick's insurance company has reached out to our firm. They need to verify the details surrounding her death, and since you are already investigating for Mr. Martin, we were wondering if you could run this investigation simultaneously. The threat of a potential lawsuit might just be the incentive the police department needs to grant you access to all the pertinent information."

My head was spinning. In the last seventy-two hours, I had gone from once again quitting my position at the OIO to returning to my old job as Martin's personal bodyguard, and now, I was supposed to be investigating a murder in order to solidify Martin's innocence and to appease the corporate requirements of an insurance company. I sat in the client chair across from his desk and sighed.

"You get me into more goddamn trouble than you're worth," I muttered.

His green eyes danced playfully. "Admit it, you love this."

EIGHT

I was particularly annoyed with Martin's representation and their attempt to manipulate the police department. I had to think about things before agreeing to work for them in any real capacity, especially now that he was officially cleared, and as of yet, there was no real threat of any lawsuits, civil or criminal, regarding his arrest or the murder of Ms. Skolnick. Screwing with the boys in blue wasn't something I was willing to do, and appeasing an insurance company wasn't on my list of priorities. These were all hazards of signing your life away to a law firm, I suppose.

Sitting in my MT office, I stared across the hallway at Martin, who was behind his desk, typing a report. "What are you doing, Parker?" I asked myself. It dawned on me that acting as his bodyguard was fatally flawed. Some time away from his manipulative tactics had made me realize this, and his check was folded in the corner of my wallet.

Before he left work today, I was returning it and providing my incredibly sound reason why I couldn't be his bodyguard. The last time we tried this, he pushed me out of the way of a bullet. Bruiser would just have to work some overtime, or he could hire someone else.

My phone rang, and I picked it up. "Parker." I rolled my eyes and made a mental note to consciously answer with 'hello' next time.

"I hear you want to play with the big boys." Moretti's voice echoed in my ear.

"I'm not sure I'd go that far." It was time to backpedal. "If I investigate for James Martin, I'd like to know I have your blessing, but currently, I'm having second thoughts."

"What do you think I am? Some mafia don?" he teased. "I just spoke to Agent Jablonsky. He says you were consulting at the OIO for the past month and really helped them out on a case, but you didn't want to stay because of all the legal mumbo-jumbo."

"You've basically summed up my entire career."

"Well, if you decide not to work for the ABCs, the commissioner's approved you for a consulting gig at the precinct."

"What?" My voice came out a high-pitched squeal, even Martin heard it through the glass and glanced at me. I shook my head and turned away, completely flummoxed and slightly embarrassed.

"You think I'm going to sit here and tell you how great you are?" Moretti sounded annoyed. "Honestly." He groaned loudly. "Ex-federal agent, international notoriety, James Martin's personal security consultant. Think about it. You do realize how beneficial it would be to the city if you work this case."

The police department feared Martin would file suit against them, and by hiring me, it would insulate them from any potential legal ramifications. Furthermore, I had a sneaky suspicion Mark called in some favors, just to make my life miserable for quitting on him again.

"Damn politics," I grumbled, and he chuckled.

"Oh, and lastly, O'Connell and Thompson tossed in their votes for you too. They figure, in the event there is the need for any undercover work, you'd be a more convincing model than most of the women in uniform." And people wonder why cops are referred to as pigs.

"I'll get back to you."

I liked it better when I spent weeks on end with no job prospects on the horizon. As I tried to figure out what to do, I realized I needed to talk to someone, and right now, there was only one person equipped to provide a proper perspective and answers to my questions. The only problem was he was sitting across the hallway, busy at work.

I spent the rest of the day playing solitaire on my office computer and practicing my three-point shot by tossing discarded pro/con lists into the trashcan. At four thirty, Monsieur Guillot wished me good night on his way to the elevator. After he was gone, I locked my office door and went across the hall.

"Perfect timing." Martin smiled briefly, buzzing me into his office. "I was just going to file this and tell you to go home for the day."

"Can I pick your brain for a minute?"

"Is this about the mouse in your office?" He shuffled through his folders, looking for the proper placement for his document. "Or was it a spider? I can never remember which one you're afraid of."

"Spiders, ugh." I cringed. "But no, there was no spider in my office. And I'm not afraid of them. I just don't like them. All those legs, ew." He had attempted to derail my line of questioning, but I was determined. "So, can we talk or not?"

"Those are the worst five words anyone can ever

utter."

"I don't know what I'm supposed to do." I decided to ignore him and just launch into my monologue, and if he deemed my speech worthy of a response, then that would be a plus. "Am I supposed to work the Skolnick case? Things have changed from the way they were Saturday morning. You're not a suspect, and the news nightmare has been handled. You were stuck in the middle, but now, you're on the outside looking in. Do you give a damn what happened, or would you prefer to leave it be? You have no reason to be concerned. You didn't know her. You're fine, and it all seems to have worked itself out, at least as far as your involvement in the matter."

He scratched his head and leaned back in his chair. "You don't want to work for Ackerman."

"I'd rather accidentally shoot myself." I slumped into his client chair, and we stared at each other as I tried to gauge what his feelings were toward tracking Skolnick's killer. "Her death, it's not your fault, and it's not your problem."

"It was my yacht." He pressed his lips together, and something flashed across his face. I understood the uneasiness of being that close to death and that close to a murderer. "I gave her that drink from the bar. I didn't know there was anything in it, but still," he looked away, "it's not fair I got lucky."

"You've never been lucky," I commented, "at least not as long as I've known you." He snorted but didn't remark. "The local PD offered me a consulting position to help them check into her case. I'll take it, if you want me to. But there is a catch. You won't be able to sue them."

"Don't do this because of me."

"Why else would I do it? Speaking of," I dug through my purse, locating the check, "I can't be your bodyguard. You should know better than to ask, and if you pull the same shit again in the future, then you're going to need to hire a few bodyguards to protect you from my wrath."

"Alex," he stared at the check, sitting on the desk between us, "I know you're good at what you do."

"Yeah, and last time, you got yourself shot, shoving me out of the way. I can't protect someone who's trying to protect me."

"So you quit?" His tone was mostly neutral, perhaps even bordering on amused.

"Do you want to get the bastard who drugged you and used your yacht to stage a murder?" I asked again.

"Yes."

"Okay." I dialed Moretti, and I was once again put on hold. Martin sat silently behind his desk, watching with utter fascination. When Moretti came on the line, I agreed to go to the precinct and sign all the necessary paperwork as soon as I was completely free from the ABC law offices. My soul had been signed over to those devils early Saturday morning, so it would be nice to get it back sooner rather than later, while some of it was still intact. "Looks like I'm in, after all. Tell O'Connell if I'm going undercover, he's going to be my gay stylist." I ended the call, and Martin attempted to hand back the check.

"Here. It looks like you're still working for me."

"I get my monthly stipend from MT, and the police department will pay my consulting fee. I don't work for you." He raised his eyebrows. "I just work for your company and, therefore, you. But you aren't giving me any more personal checks. I'm not a fucking call girl, so you don't need to leave the money on the dresser before business can commence."

He snickered. "I feel I should welcome you to the

dark side since I've made this argument at least a dozen times over the last year, and you never seemed to catch on." I flashed him my annoyed glare.

"I'm outta here. Do me a favor and stay out of trouble."

"I'll do you one better. I'll give Ackerman a call and make sure you're released from all the contracts and paperwork. Go ahead and get started at the precinct."

"Thanks."

"Anytime."

He started to reach for me but decided better of it. We were stuck in an awkward place. We had argued too much and too recently to be friends, but at the moment, we weren't more either. We were just in an uneasy limbo.

*   *   *

After I signed all the official paperwork to be considered a temporary consultant for the police department, Moretti led the way to Detective Heathcliff's desk and introduced us. Heathcliff seemed the strong, silent type, barely saying two words before handing over all of the reports and files pertaining to Caterina Skolnick.

"Those are copies," Heathcliff said. "You can take them home to read them. Bring 'em back tomorrow, and you can share any insights you might have at that time."

"Oh-kay," I said slowly. Obviously, he wasn't the warm, fuzzy type. I did as he said and nodded to Thompson on my way out. I was still slightly miffed by the commentary concerning my physical appearance, but maybe I should take it as a compliment.

Placing the files in the trunk of my car, I went to my office at the strip mall. I hadn't stopped by in the past month, and even though there weren't a million people lined up for my investigative and consulting services, the junk mail still needed to be cleaned out of my mailbox.

As I flipped through the stack of flyers, I listened to the answering machine messages. I was surprised to find any messages at all, but as the machine played, I realized the bulk of the six messages were telemarketers. I was about to press delete all when a woman's hysterical voice stopped me in my tracks.

"Is this Alexis Parker? I don't know if I should have called, but I didn't know who else to call. I might need help. Please call back." She left a phone number before hanging up.

I tossed the stack of mail into the trashcan and checked the date and time to see when the message was left. It was only three days old. Could I really have my first new client? A mix of emotions quickly ran their course as I dialed the number.

"Hello?" a woman answered.

"Hi, this is Alex Parker." Before I could say anything else, the woman interrupted.

"Thank god," she sounded relieved, "I didn't know who to contact. The police laughed me out of the station, but a friend suggested I call you."

"Ma'am, what's wrong? Who gave you my name?"

"It's my son." She inhaled sharply. "He's classmates with Thomas Guillot, Luc and Vivi's kid." Things were starting to make a tad bit more sense. "You must be very busy, Ms. Parker."

"It's okay. Tell me what's wrong, and I'll see what I can do."

NINE

"Mrs. Smidel," I was still speaking to the frantic woman on the phone, "what did you tell the police?"

"Just that something is wrong with my son, Roger." I had been listening to her for the last twenty minutes, and all I had determined was that Roger wasn't missing, arrested, or physically hurt. He sounded like a typical teenage boy who attended a private, upscale high school. "They thought I was being overly protective and suggested I buy some of those at-home drug screening kits if I had any more concerns." I had the feeling I was dealing with a hypochondriac.

"What did Roger's father say?"

"I'm a single parent, Ms. Parker. His father died a year and a half ago."

"I'm sorry. What exactly has Roger been doing that is out of the ordinary?"

"He's non-communicative, surly." She paused, thinking of other differences. "Sometimes, there are strange marks on his arms and neck, but by the next morning, they're gone. It's happened a couple of times."

My brow furrowed as I tried to come up with a reasonable explanation. "Does he play sports?" I inquired. "Maybe it's related to physical activity or the sporting equipment used." Unless it was somehow drug-related, which was not uncommon for a teenage boy in an affluent environment.

"He used to play lacrosse but gave it up after his father passed."

"Ma'am," I began slowly. There didn't seem to be a case here, and I wasn't sure exactly what this woman wanted me to do. "Perhaps your son just needs someone to confide in." A therapist might be helpful, at least for one of the Smidels.

"Ms. Parker," she sounded desperate, "I just want my son back."

"Okay, let me do some research. Can you come by my office tomorrow?" I gave her the address. "We can discuss things more fully then, and I will let you know if I'm able to help."

"Thank you." She seemed relieved. Deciding I'd done my good deed for the day, I locked up my office and went home before I could get into any more trouble.

*   *   *

My night was spent reviewing every scrap of information related to Skolnick's murder. There weren't any transcripts or videos in the file since, as of yet, no interviews had been conducted due to the limited number of persons of interest in the case. I rubbed my eyes and got another cup of coffee.

I stared at the scattered paperwork and crime scene photos, wondering how the police could have considered Martin a suspect. Skolnick had been drugged but so had he. My guess was the bartender was responsible for the dosing since no one else had access to her or her drink as far as I knew. Furthermore, the spermicide and lack of condom were clear indicators she met someone else at the party prior to Martin. Maybe her quickie got jealous. After all, jealousy and revenge were great motivators for murder.

Flipping through the materials, I found a few photos of Skolnick in affectionate embraces with an unknown man. He was a dirty blond, probably around 5'10, and in decent shape. His face was obscured, so tracking him down might be difficult. There was no guest list provided, nor a list of those working the event. Frankly, not much progress had been made on the investigation. The folder only contained the coroner's report, toxicology screening, and a thorough list and description of the items on the yacht and how the body was found.

I reread the notes I had scribbled on Saturday afternoon in Martin's kitchen. The police still had a lot of work to do, and as a consultant, maybe I could help steer them in a more productive direction. Leaning back in my chair, I rotated my neck slowly. Having me consult for the police department was an utterly ridiculous notion. The cops ought to know what to do and how to do it. Homicides were not my area of expertise, so it was no wonder why Det. Heathcliff wasn't too keen on having an outsider hovering around his case. As it stood, his hands were already tied by the police brass since this was such a high profile case which would explain the lack of relevant material. Anyone he questioned would be hounded by the media, and the entire event would turn into a circus. Everything would need to be done quickly, quietly, and only after finding irrefutable proof.

The finalized autopsy report provided a lot more relevant information than the preliminary report I had 'accidentally' read on Saturday. Caterina Skolnick was 5'10, 118 pounds, natural blonde, with numerous remodeled foot injuries. Most likely, she had been a ballet dancer in her formative years. I looked at the picture of the lifeless, empty husk. What a shame. I understood how she caught Martin's eye and probably her killer's too.

She was suffocated to death, and there were traces of down and cotton fibers in her throat and lungs from where the pillow had been held against her face. The lack of blood loss indicated her heart had already stopped beating before she was stabbed three times to the left side of her torso. There was a picture of a mold taken from the wound track. I was no expert, but it looked like the blade from a common steak knife. Maybe it had been taken from the charity event which would indicate this wasn't premeditated, but the Rohypnol would say otherwise, unless the drugs and the murder were unrelated.

No, I shook my head. Whether the drugs were part of the plan to kill her or not, they still provided the perfect opportunity to commit the crime. Maybe this was premeditated murder. Sighing, I knew I was running myself in circles. There wasn't enough evidence to speculate either way. The only thing I was positive of was the assailant obviously wanted to ensure she was dead. Why else stab her multiple times after suffocating her? The hair stood up on the back of my neck.

Martin really had gotten lucky. Maybe if he hadn't drunk to such excess or taken his painkillers, he would have been conscious and faced off against the killer. I dazed off into nothingness as my mind ran rampant into dark places. Putting all the documents back into the proper case folders, I called it a night before I could give myself any more nightmares.

*   *   *

The next morning, I met with Heathcliff and hoped some of the more pertinent clues could be dissected out of this mess. "Parker." He glanced in my direction. Good morning to you too, I thought cynically. "I have interviews scheduled with the bartender, the event coordinator, and the victim's agent."

"Did you get a list of guests and the hired help? What about surveillance from the party and the marina?" Hopefully, he wouldn't mind my input.

Smugly, he lifted a file box and dropped it unceremoniously on his desk. "Since you seem so eager, you can sort through all of this while I question some witnesses." I smiled warmly, hoping to get myself out of the doghouse and waited for him to vacate the area before I began to separate the contents into various subcategories.

"Yo," I called to O'Connell, who had just entered the room, "where do you guys set up your in-progress cases?"

He looked completely confused. "What the hell are you talking about, Alex?" he inquired, peeking into the box.

"We had a board, like a corkboard, at the OIO. We would just tack up relevant photos or evidence." He continued to stare as if I were speaking a foreign language.

"Hey, Thompson, you ever hear about any board to put the information from our cases on?" he asked his partner. Thompson made a face and shrugged, but the mischievous glint in his eyes gave it away.

"Hazing the new consultant," I muttered bitterly.

"And don't you dare think for a second your comment on my should be model status is going by unnoticed." He laughed and rolled out a corkboard from the roll-call room and handed me a box of tacks. "Thanks."

"Now, you better be careful because these are sharp," he pointed into the box, "and I don't want to hear you pricked your finger."

I glared at him. "Since you're so smart, read my mind." I narrowed my eyes, and he grinned before returning to his desk. I was being made painfully aware of my outsider status in the precinct, even though O'Connell and Thompson were simply busting my nonexistent balls because that's just what they do. Maybe I would make myself scarce after today to avoid stepping on any more toes.

The entire hour was spent sorting through everything in the box and turning the blank corkboard into a workable theory, or at least something close to a workable theory. The victim and all the relevant evidence found on or near her body was in the center of the board. On the left side were her known associates, a history of her past, career, and familial and friendly ties. On the right was a detailed list of the charity event and the final few hours of her life. When I was done, I rested my hips against the edge of Heathcliff's desk, chewing on the cap of my pen and trying to see if there were any connections I didn't notice before.

Her agent – Richard Sanderson, the bartender, and Skolnick's romantic encounter were the three individuals with the strongest motives. Sanderson, maybe not so much, but there was something off about him. When Martin mentioned Rick, it triggered an uneasy feeling in my gut, and I still felt there was more there than meets the eye. I wrote his name on a sheet of paper and stuck it to the right side of the board. "Who did this to you?" I asked the picture of Skolnick.

"Are you clairvoyant too?" Heathcliff inquired, coming around and taking a seat at his desk. "Talking to the dead. Isn't that clairvoyance?" I ignored him as he added some paperwork to the file folder and then spun in his chair to assess my handiwork. "Looks good." He caught my eye and winked, signifying I just earned his approval. "Did you catch up on some light reading last night, Parker?"

"I was hoping it'd be a novel and not a short story," I remarked. "Do you know if Skolnick had a boyfriend? Seems to me the ah...organ donor...might be a suspect."

"You just made a joke." He chuckled almost silently. "Never thought the feds had a sense of humor." I shrugged. Former fed, my mind filled in the blank. Maybe working with him wouldn't be as painstakingly horrible as I imagined. "We don't have a name yet, but the guy in the pictures," he pointed to the photo of Caterina embracing a man, "seems the most reasonable assumption. Eventually, someone will recognize him, and we'll see where it leads. In the meantime, I have to interview the bartender. Want to watch from the observation room?"

"That might just make my day," I replied, following him down the hallway. I took a seat and watched Heathcliff conduct his interrogation of the bartender, Raymond Alvarez.

"Mr. Alvarez," Heathcliff said, leaning back in the chair, "do you enjoy being a bartender?" At this rate, we were going to be here all day. Patience, Parker.

"What can I say, it pays the bills." Alvarez was calm and collected.

"Probably helps with the ladies, am I right?" Heathcliff continued. This was definitely a boy's club kind of thing.

"Can't complain." He was a decent looking man with dark hair, an olive complexion, and light brown eyes. Throw in a couple of free drinks and he'd probably had his fair share of one night stands. "Looking to change professions, Detective?"

"Not particularly," Heathcliff intoned, flipping through a file folder. "Have there ever been any complaints against you?"

"You tell me." Alvarez wasn't going to add fuel to the fire. "I'm sure whatever you're looking at has all the answers."

Heathcliff shrugged. "A couple DUIs and an order of protection against you taken out by a Ms. Linda Reynolds," Heathcliff read the jacket aloud. "Do you want to give me your side of the story?"

"Crazy bitch accused me of stalking her." I glared at Alvarez through the mirror. Most crazy bitches really weren't the crazy ones.

"Right, you were innocent," Heathcliff commented with a level of sarcasm I could only wish to one day achieve. "What can you tell me about the charity event last Friday evening at the marina? Any crazy bitches there?"

"No," Alvarez decided to tighten his responses, "just some fancy assholes showing off."

"Do you remember seeing her?" Heathcliff placed a photo of Caterina on the table.

"No. But trust me, I would have remembered her." Something about Alvarez's facial expression was unsettling. "I definitely would have remembered her. A hot little number like that," he made a whistling sound, "damn."

"She's dead." Heathcliff's tone was hard as steel. "You're sure you don't remember her? We have the surveillance tapes from the event. We know she was drinking, and you were bartending."

"A lot of people ordered drinks, but like I said, I'd remember her." Alvarez wasn't changing his story. "Are you arresting me?"

"Should I?"

"I know how this works, and if you are, then I'm not saying another goddamn word."

Heathcliff slowly circled the room before walking to the door and opening it. "Don't leave town," he threatened before gesturing for Alvarez to take off.

Alvarez stood, looking very self-satisfied and sauntered out of the interrogation. I would have loved to knock him around a bit. There was something innately slimy and repulsive about this man.

"Batting a thousand," Heathcliff mumbled, opening the door to the observation room. "The first interview with the event coordinator was a bust."

"Sleazy prick." He glanced up, making sure I wasn't referring to him. "Look, I have a meeting with a client," I said, checking the time. "I'll stop by later, and if you could provide the transcripts for the other two interviews, I'd appreciate the opportunity to review them."

"Fine." He seemed annoyed, but then again, I figured he was annoyed at pretty much everything at this point.

TEN

Hoping for inspiration on the Smidel case and the mysterious marks, I drove to Highland Preparatory Academy, the private school Roger Smidel attended, and parked in the designated visitor parking space and remained in my car, hopefully not looking like a sexual predator. From my parking spot, I could see the cars in the student lot. Bentleys, BMWs, Audis, Corvettes, and other similarly expensive vehicles lined the rows of spaces. I didn't see anything that cost less than fifty grand, and that was a low-ball estimate. These were the children of doctors, lawyers, politicians, and businessmen. The crème-de-la-crème.

The school grounds were vast and intimidating with gothic-style architecture complete with gargoyles. The grounds included numerous buildings, tennis courts, an expansive track, what appeared to be stables, and who knew what else. As I surveyed the area, a security guard approached my car. Rolling down my window, I flashed my most disarming smile.

"Good day, miss," he said in a tone that didn't sound as friendly as the words he was using. "Do you realize you are on private school grounds?"

"Yes." I tried to charm him once more. Maybe he hadn't seen the full effect of my previous smile. Unfortunately, he stood his ground, so I pulled out my private investigator's license and held it up for his inspection. "I was just looking around on behalf of a client." Being intentionally vague was another of my talents.

"If you plan to investigate the school or its students, you will need to speak directly with the headmaster. If not, please vacate the premises immediately."

"I'll be back," I winked, "so try not to miss me in the meantime." I rolled up my window and pulled out of the parking space, returning to the main highway. My P.I. license didn't pack the same punch my OIO badge did. Admittedly, being able to shout 'federal agent' was much more meaningful than 'private investigator, please ignore me while I snoop.'

Unsure of what to do, I drove to my office and turned on the computer to perform a search on Highland Preparatory Academy. Unfortunately, no scandals popped up in any of the internet databases. I tried entering it as the location of a crime in the criminal databases, hoping for a hit, but still no luck. Whoever worked PR at the school must be an absolute genius because there was no way those rich kids were all innocent little angels. Kids were kids, regardless of family affluence. The only difference was mommy and daddy's money could buy them out of a lot of trouble if need be.

As I sat at my desk, I tried to determine what could put temporary marks on a teenage boy's arms and neck, but I had no clue. Mrs. Smidel had been less than helpful in providing any real description of the markings or information suggesting what might have caused them. Even a heads up on Roger's daily routine might have shed some light on the situation. The kid was angsty and non-communicative, but he was a teenager. Angsty and non-communicative were the two things they did best, at least from what I remembered.

The situation was perplexing, but I remained confident there was no case here whatsoever. It seemed best to extensively question her, so she'd feel something was being done, and then tell her the conclusion I already reached and remind her that Roger was a teenage boy.

My mind wandered back to the Skolnick murder as I waited for Mrs. Smidel to arrive. I was typing Raymond Alvarez into the database, so I could review his jacket, when a small, impish woman entered my office. She stood in the doorway, frowning at my office furniture and cheap décor.

"Ms. Parker?" she asked uncertainly.

"Yes. May I help you?"

"I'm Lynette Smidel." She walked briskly to my desk and shook my hand. I indicated the empty chair, and she sat, turning to critique the rest of my office. My sparse furnishings were clearly a personal affront to her existence, but she remained silent. "I only have twenty minutes, but I still wanted to discuss Roger in person."

"Can you tell me anything more descriptive and concrete about what is going on?"

"He just isn't himself. He hasn't been for the last month or two. He doesn't talk to me." I waited for her to continue, but she just sat there. Maybe non-communicative was a genetic disorder.

"Have there been any physical changes to Roger besides the mood swings. A gain or loss in weight? A great increase in muscle mass?" Maybe the kid was on steroids or something.

"No, just the occasional marks."

"Tell me about them. What do they look like?" She closed her eyes, trying to recollect.

"They look like scratches but very shallow and superficial. He won't say where he got them or what caused them."

I was trying my best to give her the benefit of the doubt, even though she was a bit of a quack. "Do you have any pets? Or does Roger have any known allergies? What does he do on a daily basis? When you've noticed the scratches, was his daily routine substantially different?" I didn't know what to ask.

"No pets or allergies. And I don't invade his privacy, so I don't know what he does on a daily basis. I'd imagine he goes to school, hangs out with his friends, and comes home before curfew. He's a good kid. That's why I'm concerned. Everything he's been doing is completely out of character." She was annoyed by my nonchalance. "Frankly, Ms. Parker," she practically hissed, "I don't think you're going to be any more helpful than the police department."

"Probably not." I was a bit flippant. Obviously, my professionalism wasn't up to par either, just like my décor. "Everything you've said seems characteristic of a typical teenage boy. Teenagers are hormonal, moody, and they don't talk to their parents about their business. I'd be more than willing to help if there is a problem, but I don't see one."

"Miss, I don't particularly care for your attitude," she berated. "The Guillots are good friends and recommended you to assist in this matter. Clearly, they seem misinformed about your qualifications."

"Ma'am, most people don't care for my attitude, so I'm sure you're in good company on that particular assessment. But I am good at what I do. I just don't see any reason for you to waste your money on an investigation into why your son is acting like a teenager."

"It's my money to waste. Can I see a list of your so-called qualifications or a résumé?" I had to give her credit; she wasn't easily dissuaded. After providing the briefest rundown of my former federal agent background, I waited patiently as she mulled over this new information. "What's your going rate?" She pulled out her checkbook.

"Ma'am," I tried again, "this is your son we are talking about. How do you think he'll react if he finds out you hired someone to tail him?"

"Then you better make sure he doesn't find out." She wrote out the check and laid it on my desk. "One week. That is all the time I am willing to waste on you, Ms. Parker, before I find someone else who actually wants to do this job." The way she said the words sounded like a threat, but I wasn't frightened. Perhaps I was supposed to be. I mean, my goodness, she could probably squash me with that insanely well-endowed checkbook of hers.

After she left, I ran a quick background check on her and Roger, hoping something would turn up. No dice. I checked the time; it was almost four. Having a few minutes to spare, I decided to go to the MT building to see if I could have a moment of Luc Guillot's time before returning to the precinct. Maybe Heathcliff's day improved since mine certainly didn't.

The ride to the MT building was uneventful, and my brain was so scrambled from working two very unaccommodating investigations that I simply sang along with the radio at the top of my lungs. After exiting the elevator on the seventeenth floor, I noticed Martin's empty office on my way down the corridor. I knocked on Guillot's door, and he waved me inside.

"Mademoiselle Parker, what a surprise. Can I help you with something?"

"Do you have a minute? This isn't business related, but do you know a Lynette Smidel?"

"Ah," a knowing look erupted on his face, "Vivi gave Lynette your name. I hope that's okay. She has concerns about her son, Roger."

"Yes, I met with Mrs. Smidel earlier today. I tried to tell her I didn't believe her suspicions were warranted, but she refused to listen. I was wondering if you might have any insight to share." His brow furrowed as he considered my request.

"Perhaps Thomas, my son, would be more helpful to you," he suggested. "Why don't you come for dinner on Thursday? My wife will be pleased to see you again, and maybe she or Thomas will be able to help."

"That's very kind," I began, but he interjected.

"Please, we are new here. My wife has few friends. You're a trusted confidante of Mr. Martin. It would be our honor to have you for dinner."

"It would be my pleasure, sir." I tried to appear pleased even though this was the last thing I wanted to do with my Thursday evening. I edged toward the door. "I have another appointment this afternoon, but I will see you Thursday. Ciao."

"Bonsoir." He smiled as I left.

When the doors to the elevator opened, Martin rushed out, almost colliding with me. "Hey," he said, surprised. "What's going on?"

"Not much." I got into the elevator and pressed the button for the lobby. "I came to see Luc. It's nothing to worry about. I'm just working for a friend of his or something closely related to that." He looked confused and put his hand against the frame of the elevator to keep the doors from closing.

"Are you consulting for the police now?"

"On my way there, if the elevator doors ever close," I quipped. He smirked and removed his hand. "I'll give you an update when something concrete surfaces on the Skolnick murder."

"Thanks, Alex."

*   *   *

I was sitting at Heathcliff's desk, reading through his interview notes from the event coordinator and Caterina's agent, Richard Sanderson. The event coordinator had provided detailed lists of the guests, the work crews, and those involved in the catering and decorating. Heathcliff was in the process of running through the names, checking for criminal records. The surveillance footage from the event had been provided, and Caterina's mystery man was identified as Jake Spencer, one of the photographers often used by her modeling agency.

Unfortunately, the interview file from Richard 'Rick' Sanderson left a lot to be desired. He hadn't hashed out his whereabouts during her TOD or provided any type of alibi, but from Heathcliff's notes, Skolnick's death was going to negatively affect Sanderson since his cash cow could no longer produce any milk. Therefore, he lacked motive for her murder. Still, I wished there was more information, and I hated that I missed the interview because of my meeting with the highly irrational Lynette Smidel. For future reference, I should only work one case at a time. Concluding my off-topic musing, I tried to get back on track by shutting my eyes and working the puzzle pieces out in my mind.

"Are you imagining what it's like to be me?" Heathcliff asked, interrupting my internal process.

"Scary prospect," I retorted, surrendering his chair.

"Anything turn up on the backgrounds?"

"Nada." He dug through his desk drawers, looking for a legal pad. "You're the consultant, so I'd like you to consult." His pen was poised over the paper, waiting for my brilliant assessment of the facts.

"Alvarez is a piece of work, and something doesn't sit right with Sanderson. When I spoke with Mr. Martin, he mentioned Sanderson tends to pop up a bit too frequently." He scrawled 'Sanderson – too often' on the page. Pain in my ass, I thought angrily. "Do we know who had something to gain from Caterina's death? Maybe she had a life insurance policy or left everything to someone in her will. Are you going to talk to the photographer, Jake Spencer, and see if they were intimate immediately preceding her death?"

"We're checking all those possibilities, and Spencer's coming in tomorrow morning. We also scheduled an interview tomorrow afternoon with the head of her modeling agency, a Yolanda Tate." He dropped his pen. "Any more brilliance you wish to instill upon me?"

"Did you see who slipped the drugs into the drinks?"

Smirking, he led the way to another room in the police station, filled with dozens of monitors, and hit play. Four different screens flickered to life. Each one displayed a different camera that was used for security at the event. "Have fun. I'll be at my desk, filling out paperwork, when you find the culprit." I glared at his retreating back. Hopefully, I wouldn't be here all night.

ELEVEN

I rubbed my neck and thought about the enticing prospect of getting a third, or was it a fourth, cup of coffee. The monitors continued to play, and as of yet, nothing struck as clue-worthy. Staring at the footage was making my eyes cross, and I feared that even if someone were to pull out a gun and mow down the entire guest list, I wouldn't notice at this point. I hit pause and got out of the chair, walking around the small room. Since the drugs were most certainly placed in the cosmos that Martin ordered for himself and Caterina, I decided to prioritize my viewing. I scanned the screens, looking for Martin's impeccable flair for fashion and showmanship.

Finally, I found him on monitor three, talking with a small group of people. I kept an eye on him as he moved around, appearing on monitor one and then monitor four. He was at the bar now, ordering a drink. It was scotch, given the shape of the glass and his affinity for the golden brown liquor. As he sauntered away, I spotted Caterina in the corner of the screen, drinking something from a martini glass and animatedly conversing with a man. Was that Jake Spencer?

I shifted my focus to her since she was now attempting to strangle the man by shoving her tongue down his throat. That was one classy broad. She released him just long enough to let him gasp for air, before grabbing his hand and pulling him out of sight of camera four. I scanned the other three screens, trying to find her. Where are you going? Briefly, I caught a glimpse of the two of them on the second monitor, before she dragged him into a room and shut the door. I paused the feed and recorded the timestamp to point out to Heathcliff.

About fifteen minutes later, Caterina and the mystery man, who I was now positive was Jake Spencer, exited the ladies room. Sex in a bathroom, could this woman get any classier? I immediately scolded myself for judging the dead. Having a sexual appetite and a spirit to party were not reasons someone should kill you.

Refocusing, I found her on monitor four, sitting at the bar alone. Martin reemerged on the screen with Richard Sanderson. The two seemed lost in conversation until Sanderson turned to the end of the bar where Caterina was seated. Despite the fact I couldn't see Martin's facial expression, I knew his looks all too well. He smiled or smirked and introduced himself. The two conversed briefly before another woman appeared. Seconds later, Sanderson was gone.

For the next thirty minutes, Martin flirted with the deceased. He finished his glass of scotch and motioned the bartender over, holding up his hand to indicate two. I glanced down at the timestamp and noted this as well.

I focused intensely on Alvarez as he lifted two liquor bottles in the air and poured the sight-measured contents into a shaker. He put the bottles down, adding something else to the concoction with a flourish. He shook the metal canister and poured the contents into two martini glasses. Martin and Caterina were oblivious since they were wrapped up in one another.

I tried to study Alvarez's expressions and actions, but the footage left a lot to be desired. He was watching the two with a level of disdain, and as he reached for the little plastic swords to skewer the lime, he stopped mid-skewer. Leaning forward in my chair, I was intrigued. Now would be the time for him to do something. He reached underneath the bar, out of sight of the cameras, and popped up a second or two later with two pre-skewered limes. Could the drugs have been on the limes?

The bar had a large array of fruits and numerous plastic implements. Why else would he retrieve two from below the bar? I continued to watch the footage as Martin handed one of the glasses to Caterina, and they walked off screen. By the time I located them in monitor three, the glasses were half empty.

Martin teetered slightly and took his jacket off. He strode off screen, and Caterina followed him. That must have been when he left the party to get some air. It was just after midnight, and I tried not to think about Caterina chasing after him like she was a puppy and he was her new chew toy. Her TOD was sometime soon after. The drugs probably hit him first due to the copious amounts of alcohol he had already consumed and his prescription painkillers. Jackass, my mind commented.

I rewound the footage to see what Alvarez was up to. He was still mixing drinks, but not once did he retrieve anything else from below the bar. Hitting pause, I rested my chin in my palm and tried to think. I sighed audibly and rewound the whole thing. Now that I had these few facts, the surveillance would have to be watched and re-watched for additional clues or personal interactions. After already spending too many hours staring at the footage, I couldn't bring myself to do it again.

Leaving the small room I had been exiled to, I found Heathcliff in the bullpen, chatting with a few other cops. He saw me coming and held up a hand, indicating that I give him a minute. Impatiently, I rubbed my eyes and waited.

"How was America's Rich and Fabulous?" he asked with a level of cynicism only public servants were capable of mustering. I shared the few key facts I witnessed, and he raised an eyebrow. "Guess we'll be bringing Mr. Alvarez back in tomorrow for a follow-up. Did you see anything else out of the ordinary?"

"We need to go back over the footage from the beginning to see if he acted suspiciously at any other time. And we need to determine who left the party and hung around the marina, waiting to kill our vic. Also, we should track Spencer's movements throughout the event." I rubbed my eyes again and looked at my watch. "But you need a fresh set of eyes on this."

"Careful, Parker," he warned, "you're starting to sound like a burnt-out cop."

Picking up my jacket, I asked, "Can I get out of here or do you need me to stick around?"

He assessed my words for a minute and then glanced at the group he was speaking to before my appearance. "Looks like the real detectives have work to do." He smirked slightly. "Guys, we're gonna be burning the midnight oil tonight since our consultant's got a hot date or something." He jerked his head toward the door. "Get out of here. I'll see you in the morning."

"Yes, sir," I teased, walking past the other cops who decided it'd be a good idea to catcall my exit. I raised my middle finger and continued out of the precinct.

*   *   *

The next morning, I parked down the road from the Smidel's house, planning to tail Roger to school before going to the precinct. The kid emerged a little before seven thirty, dressed in his school uniform, and got into a bright blue Lexus and peeled out of the driveway. At least I didn't have to worry about losing him amidst a sea of similarly colored cars, I thought as I maintained a decent distance, but his driving was erratic. Teenagers, I griped, slamming on my brakes as he pulled into a parking space in front of a diner.

He got out of the car and went into the restaurant. There were some spaces on a side street, and I decided stopping for breakfast wasn't a bad idea. Girl's gotta eat, after all. Entering the diner, I spotted him sitting in a booth with three other teenagers. I took a seat at the counter and ordered a black coffee and a scone. After the waitress brought my breakfast, I tossed a few discreet glances in their direction as I nibbled on the pastry.

Roger's dining companions consisted of two other teenage boys and a girl. The girl obviously favored the goth style. She wore dark eye makeup and dressed predominantly in black. A pair of fishnet stockings protruded from the tops of her boots to the bottom of her miniskirt. The other two guys seated with Roger were dressed in preppy clothing, designer button-up shirts and dark wash jeans. If they attended public school instead and weren't built like athletes, they would have the shit kicked out of them. High school, it's amazing anyone lives to see nineteen.

The waitress brought the check, not bothering to see if I wanted a refill, and I put some money on the counter. While I sipped the remainder of my coffee, the group devoured eggs, pancakes, and sausage. Checking the time, it was getting close to eight, but none of them seemed concerned about missing school or being tardy. I was more concerned about missing the Spencer interview than they were about missing homeroom. Finally, one of the two guys waved a waitress over, handed her what appeared to be a fifty, and the four of them got up from the table.

Counting to three, I waited for them to clear the door before following them outside. By the time I exited the diner, the girl was pressed against a vehicle, kissing one of the preppy guys, and the other kid was getting into the passenger's side of Roger's car. I continued past to the side of the building, paying them no attention as I got into my car and watched my rearview mirror for a flash of blue.

Ten minutes later, the Lexus whizzed past, and I pulled out of my spot, backed into traffic, and continued after him. Roger parked in one of the student spaces at Highland Prep, and I slowed down but stayed on the main thoroughfare, not wanting to arouse any more suspicion from the overzealous security guards. At least he wasn't ditching class, and he ate a decent meal to start his day. His mother should be proud. I drove to a cross street and executed a magnificent three-point turn before heading for the police station.

I was almost at the precinct when a thought hit me. "Dammit!" I slammed my palm against the steering wheel. My deductive reasoning skills were shoddy this early in the morning because it just occurred to me that Roger was the only one wearing the Highland Prep school uniform. His three breakfast pals were not dressed for school. Did they even go to Highland Prep? It was too late to turn around and see if Roger was still there, so I called his mother instead.

"Mrs. Smidel?" I asked. "This is Alex Parker."

"Yes, Ms. Parker," she sounded worried. "Is everything all right? Is Roger okay?"

"Everything's fine. We didn't have a very productive conversation yesterday, and I was wondering if you could provide a list of Roger's friends. Do they all attend Highland Prep?" I was trying to be smooth in my questioning. "The reason I ask is he stopped for breakfast this morning, but he was the only one in uniform."

"The kids like to change when they get to school. They don't want the uniforms to cramp their style." She let out an audible sigh. "Regardless, I will e-mail you a list of his friends later. I'm busy at the moment, but I will get it to you by this afternoon."

"Thank you."

I parked my car next to the out-of-service patrol cars and combed my hands through my hair, trying to get a grip on my current juggling act. Eventually, I went inside the precinct. It was time to start another fun-filled day.

TWELVE

The interviews today didn't take nearly as long as I expected. Jake Spencer admitted his romantic involvement with Caterina quickly before crumbling. As I watched Det. Heathcliff interview Spencer, I was surprised at how the man melted into a pile of blubbering, tear-wracked sobs. Either someone needed to give this guy an Emmy, or he wasn't the murderer.

"I'm her lover," Spencer sniffled. "I could never do that." He pointed to the crime scene photos on the table, turning puce and burying his head in his hands as he continued to sob. Heathcliff threw a glance at the two-way mirror, hoping someone, anyone, would come and rescue him from the weeping Jake Spencer.

"Mr. Spencer," Heathcliff's tone was cold, "try to pull yourself together. Do you think Caterina would want to see you like this?" The mention of her name sent Spencer into another tailspin of tears. "I'll give you a minute." Heathcliff gave up and exited the room.

"You really know how to crack a suspect,

Detective," I remarked as he came into the observation room and stood next to me, watching Spencer try to get his emotions under control.

"Why don't you go in there and give him the gentler, feminine touch, then?"

"Hell, no. I'm about as gentle as broken glass. Maybe we can just leave him in there until he gets bored and wanders out on his own." Heathcliff emitted a sound, which was supposed to be a chortle, before going back to conclude the interview.

"Mr. Spencer, I think we're done for the day. If we have any more questions, we'll be in touch, but stay in town," he warned, holding the door open and ushering Spencer into the hallway. That was one down, two more to go.

The second interview was with Yolanda Tate, head of the Tate Modeling Agency. She reminded me of an evil witch, cold and methodical. I also got the distinct impression she loathed men. How she managed to marry, I'd never know. Mrs. Tate was in her late forties or early fifties and had been a former model. As she aged out, she took over the business and opened her own agency. Maybe that was when her husband came into the picture.

"Ma'am." Heathcliff continued the interview, having already established the baseline of facts. Skolnick had worked for Tate for the last four years and was set to have a big spread in an upcoming fashion magazine in the fall.

"It's Mrs. Tate," the witch icily responded, staring daggers at Heathcliff. If a fight were to break out, I'd put my money on the ice queen.

"Mrs. Tate," he started again, undaunted, "can you account for your whereabouts Saturday morning from midnight until two a.m.?"

"Am I a suspect in Caterina's murder?" she

inquired. "Because quite frankly, I don't see why I should account for my presence to you." Her tone dripped disdain.

"Ma'am," I was positive he said it just to piss her off, "it's my job to investigate Ms. Skolnick's murder. Wouldn't you like to be cleared from any suspicion?" Maybe he was trying the carrot and stick theory.

"The news said some CEO was responsible. Why are you still looking into it?" It was my turn to glare.

"That was a mistake. The man in question was another victim, not the perpetrator."

She let out a harsh, awful-sounding laugh. "Mr. Detective, you can either arrest me or I'm leaving. There is no reason why I would harm the number one model at my agency. Her death has cost me thousands, and if you insist on continuing this pointless interview, I'd like my attorney present to witness the harassment."

"Bitch," I cursed. She would be a hard one to crack. Today's interviews were going just swimmingly. First, we had the blubbering boyfriend and now the evil ice queen. Next would be Alvarez and his misogynistic attitude.

Heathcliff cut her loose after she insisted on taking his badge number and speaking directly to his superior. When he returned to the observation room, he shut the door and slammed his fist into the wall. He forgot I was there and was looking for a moment of solitude.

"Don't worry about it," I offered my condolences, "the rich bitch ice queen probably just got her panties in a bunch. Moretti won't hold it against you, especially if he has to spend more than two minutes alone with her."

He graced me with a brief smile. "I say we break for lunch." He looked at his watch. "Alvarez is supposed to show up around two. In the meantime, wanna grab a bite and check out the crime scene?"

"Music to my ears, Detective."

*   *   *

We made small talk as we sat in the unmarked police car, eating our lunch and staring out over the pier. Our bonding required some give and take on both our parts, and I provided a brief overview of my short-lived career at the OIO, my current P.I. and security consulting gig, and how Det. O'Connell and I became unlikely friends.

Heathcliff was a third generation cop, following in the footsteps of his father and grandfather. And while he tended to come off as a serious, no-nonsense guy, I had seen a few cracks in that pristine business-only exterior. Maybe he wasn't such a bad guy to work with, after all.

"What about the ethical ramifications of working for James Martin and the police department?" he asked, bunching up the packaging from his lunch and tossing it into the takeout bag.

"It's a fine line. I made the same argument, but I'm a MT employee, no longer in the James Martin private security business. Plus, everything we figure out is going up the chain of command to you guys, not anywhere else." I didn't divulge the fact that I promised Martin I'd fill him in on who was responsible.

"It's good to know you can prioritize." I wasn't sure about that, given my two current cases and my unsteady personal relationship with Martin, but if I appeared on top of things, I was willing to go with it. "Ready to check out the yacht?"

"Definitely."

Following him down the pier, he held his badge up to the uniformed cop guarding the scene, and we ducked under the tape and climbed on board. The yacht was lavish, just like everything else Martin owned. I surveyed the main deck, vividly recalling Martin's retelling of the events. I surmised where he passed out on the floor and where he found the body.

"The assailant must have walked onto the boat, just like we did." Heathcliff pantomimed the most likely attack scenario.

"Martin was out cold, right here." I indicated the floor next to the bench seats. "Skolnick's body was discovered here." I pointed to the crime scene marker.

"There were no defensive wounds," he continued. "She was probably already passed out on the seats." I squinted into the distance, thinking. "What?"

"Based on everything I've heard and read, Martin blacked out first. So if I were Skolnick, I would try to revive the guy who just hit the deck."

"Maybe you're more altruistic than she was." But he didn't sound convinced. He knelt down. "Act something out with me." I gave him a skeptical look but played along. "I'm Martin, and I black out." He attempted to take a seat on the bench but missed and landed on the ground, the most plausible theory.

"I check to see if you're okay. Maybe I think it's a game you're playing." I flashed back to Skolnick and Spencer exiting the bathroom. "Perhaps you just want some mouth to mouth."

"But you're feeling woozy because you've been drugged too. You come over to check on me, but it hits you. What do you do?"

"Me or Skolnick?" I was getting confused with our role-playing game. "I would probably call for help while I still could. Or I would check on you."

"There's no way you would just lie down on the

bench above me?" I saw where he was going with this, and I shook my head.

"Did you find her phone? Or her purse?" Maybe someone positioned Skolnick on the bench above Martin.

"Neither." He stood up and glanced around the marina. "The cameras didn't catch anything, and the rope to tie the boat to dock was missing when the Coast Guard towed her in."

"You think the assailant tossed her phone and belongings?" I surveyed the main deck, trying to make sense of the scene.

"Could be, but we don't have the resources to drag the marina looking for them. I doubt it would help anyway."

"Have you checked her phone records? It'd be easier than dragging the whole damn ocean." The victim wasn't positioned in a particularly remorseful way. Her hands weren't folded, and her eyes weren't closed. Whoever murdered her wanted to make sure she was dead and escape as swiftly as possible. "Shit," I cursed. "Her eyes were open." The ramification hit us simultaneously. "She was still conscious when she was killed."

"Barely," he retorted. "Like I said, there were no defensive wounds, and look at this place," he gestured around the yacht, "no obvious signs of a struggle. Maybe the force of the attack woke her from her unconscious state."

The thought of waking up paralyzed to the terror of knowing death was imminent was an unbearable concept. I swallowed and leaned against the railing to steady my nerves. Don't get in the victim's head, Parker. "I don't think we'll get anything else from being here." I had seen enough and wanted to leave.

"Hang on." He disappeared into a cabin.

I studied the area from the building at the top of the pier, where the event was held, to our current position on Martin's yacht. We were about fifty yards away. There were some streetlights near the docks, but not much cover between here and there. Even in the dim light, the assailant would have been visible from the boat.

"Did you get lost?" I bellowed, and he emerged.

"Y'know, our murder weapon doesn't match any of the other pillows or cushions on this boat. Do you think our murderer brought his own pillow to the slumber party?"

"Did Martin verify it belonged on his yacht?" He shrugged. Apparently, no one bothered to ask. "I'm still having trouble determining if this was premeditated. The knife and pillow probably came from elsewhere, so was this planned? Or was it the perfect opportunity in the heat of the moment?"

"I could see it happening either way. But assuming Martin's innocent," he sounded skeptical, "then some planning had to go into the drugs and the killing."

*   *   *

Once we returned to the precinct, Heathcliff began reviewing the notes the other officers made regarding the video surveillance as he patiently awaited Alvarez's return. I was getting a bit antsy, anxiously drumming my fingers against the desk.

"Why don't you take the photos and ask Mr. Martin about the pillow?" he suggested. "Right now, you aren't being very helpful."

I obediently picked up my phone and dialed Martin's cell, but my call went to voicemail. He rolled his eyes, unimpressed by my dialing skills. "Fine, I'll ask in person," I relented.

When I arrived at the MT building, I went straight to the seventeenth floor. As I expected, Martin wasn't in his office. Instead, I unlocked my door and sat down at the computer. In the meantime, I could check to see if Mrs. Smidel e-mailed me. I printed off the list of Roger's friends and shut down my computer. Hopefully, Martin would stop by his office in between meetings or whatever it was he was doing. Finally, the elevator dinged, and he came bustling past, unlocking his office door.

Going across the hallway, I knocked on the doorjamb. "Do you have a minute? It's for official police business."

"Can I see your badge?" Four different folders were open on his desk, and he seemed to be moving in seven different directions at once. "Or can this wait?" For once, he was serious.

"It'll just take a minute, I promise. We need you to identify this pillow." He looked up to see if this was a pathetic attempt at a joke, and I held out the crime scene photo for his inspection.

"It's white, rectangular, and filled with stuffing." He raised an eyebrow.

"Is it yours? Did it come from your yacht?"

"Oh," his eyes darkened, "no. Everything is color coordinated, and all of the cushions and pillows are either square or round." He considered it for a moment. "But I'm not positive. The beds have memory foam pillows. Unless there were extras stored somewhere." He made a crappy witness, and I snatched the photo away before he admitted to shopping for pillows that resembled the one in the picture.

"That will be all. Thanks for your time."

"Lunch Friday?" he asked as I attempted to flee. I stopped in my tracks, closed his office door to prevent being overheard, and turned to him.

"Fine, and just so we're clear, this pillow definitely does not belong to you. Understand?" He wasn't a murderer, and I doubted anyone would question an unmatched pillow not belonging to his yacht. But his uncertainty wasn't helping to solidify his innocence.

"Okay." He caught my drift.

THIRTEEN

I called Heathcliff on my way back to the precinct, expecting to get his voicemail, but strangely enough, he answered. I relayed the message that the murder weapon did not come from Martin's yacht. In my mind's eye, I envisioned the killer waiting for the perfect opportunity while taking refuge on another boat docked nearby. It would explain why no one noticed the assailant, and as far as I knew, the individual hadn't shown up on any of the marina surveillance footage either.

"Your hunches, while creative, aren't going to give us just cause to get a warrant to search every single boat docked at the marina," Heathcliff chided.

"That's the problem with being on the job, all this 'just cause' bullshit." He ignored my comment. "Did I miss seeing you put the screws to that misogynistic prick?"

"Unfortunately, no. We've issued a BOLO on Alvarez. He didn't show up, and he won't answer his phone. A couple of uniforms went to his apartment and the bar where he normally works, but no one's seen him since yesterday."

"Great." I sighed. "Don't these people ever realize when you run it just reaffirms your guilt?"

"It's not that. They just believe we won't find them if they run," he surmised. "Look, there's nothing else for you to do today. Moretti wants a meeting with me and a few of the other guys working this, so I'll give you a call tomorrow and let you know when to come back."

"All right. Good luck with Moretti." Obviously, I was so incredibly helpful that I earned some free time of an unknown duration.

Rerouting to my office, I wanted to run backgrounds on the list of Roger's friends before heading to Highland Prep to tail him again. As I suspected, none of his friends had official run-ins with the law. There were no records, sealed or otherwise. I wondered if I could call in some favors and see if any of them had jackets without convictions, but that could wait until I knew more. I still didn't think there was anything going on with this kid, other than the fact he was a teenage boy who suffered a tragedy.

At Highland Prep, I meandered through the parking lot and noted Roger's blue car still parked where he left it this morning. I circled around to avoid the overly enthusiastic security guards, certain that they locked onto my vehicle with their spy cameras and were running my license plate number to find out who I was and how much money I kept in my bank account. To avoid any further altercations, I parked a block away from the school and waited for class to be dismissed.

Soon after, Roger got into his car, alone. I followed at a decent distance, realizing he wasn't going home. Eventually, he stopped at the park and carried a small rectangular box to the picnic tables. I could only hope he was about to do something illegal because stalking a teenage boy when you were no longer a teenage girl was ridiculous. I kept an eye on him but made sure my nine millimeter was loaded before clipping it into my shoulder holster. One could never be too careful when dealing with potential criminals, even if they were scrawny, high school students.

Roger took a seat at one of the empty tables. Next to him, a couple of people were playing chess for twenty a game. It was amazing the cops never bothered these swindlers.

Roger opened the box and flipped open an odd looking game board. It laid flat on the table, and he propped a cardboard sign next to it. He sat patiently, waiting for someone to play. This was not the way I envisioned he'd spend an afternoon at the park.

After five minutes, I approached the table. Luckily, he didn't know who I was, and as long as he didn't recognize me from the diner, we'd be okay.

"That doesn't look like chess to me," I commented, reading the sign. *Mancala, $5 a game.*

"That's because it's not," he replied snottily. "I mean, er..." He didn't expect a woman to speak to him since most of the chess players in the park were drunken, elderly men. His eyes roamed the length of my body, making it embarrassingly obvious he was checking me out. He smiled a big toothy grin and reddened. "It's better." Real smooth, kid.

"Fine, five dollars and you teach me how to play." I had to do something to figure out what was up with this kid.

"I'd be happy to teach you anything, babe." He was trying to be suave, but he was seventeen. It was a pathetic attempt, and I gave him a stern look.

"I'm too old for you. What are you? Eighteen?

Nineteen?" It was best to pretend I had no idea who he was. Play it cool, Parker.

"Close enough," he responded, setting up the small colored marbles in equal numbers on the wooden board. "How old are you? You must be in college, right?"

"Not even close," I remarked, trying to build some kind of rapport.

"Oh, come on, graduate school then. You can't be more than twenty-five." I scoffed, and he offered a big wide-eyed grin.

"Flattery will get you nowhere." I smiled. "So explain this game to me." He ran through the fundamentals concerning the game play and ways of winning. The object was to get the most marbles. It sounded simple enough. Carefully, I pulled my wallet from my purse, zipping up my jacket in the process in order to keep my holstered gun invisible, and handed him a twenty. "I just bought three games."

He looked pleased and quickly changed my twenty for a stack of fives, placing three of them separately on the table and adding equal amounts to the top. It took the first two games to figure out the finer points of strategizing, and I came close to beating him on the last game.

"Better luck next time," he intoned.

I leaned back on the bench and looked around. There were a couple of people waiting for a particular chess match to finish, but no one was waiting to play this odd game. This wasn't a practical way for a teenage boy to spend his afternoons.

"So how lucrative is this venture?" I asked, unwilling to relinquish my seat to the nonexistent line.

"You tell me. I just made twenty dollars in fifteen minutes."

"Touché." Standing up, I stretched slowly. "Are you out here every day? I've never seen you before."

"I'm here about four times a week after sch...class." He was still trying to pass for older than he was, and I let it slide. "It's easier than working a part-time job." I remained neutral, knowing damn well his mother would give him anything he wanted.

"It's an odd game to play. Have you ever considered chess or even checkers?"

"Nope, just this." His expression shifted, and he looked forlorn.

Cautiously, I pushed a little harder, hoping for something concrete that would put his mother at ease. "Why?" I offered my demure smile. "Is there some special reason, like you grew up on the streets and all you could afford to play with were rocks and egg cartons?" He was dressed too nicely for anyone to actually believe he was poor, and he laughed.

"No. My dad taught me this game when I was little. We used to play for hours on the weekends. Actually, we used to play right there." He pointed to a grassy area where some people were sitting with picnic baskets and blankets.

"That sounds nice." It was time to walk away. "Thanks for the game. Maybe I'll see you around." I strolled down the path and took a circuitous route back to my car, so I wouldn't seem quite so suspicious. There was nothing wrong with the kid; he was just lonely and trying to recapture missed memories.

*   *   *

Back at my office, I phoned Mrs. Smidel. It felt like I was ratting Roger out, but his mom was paying for an update on her son's activities. Now, she should be relieved that there was nothing greatly amiss with her kid.

"But, Ms. Parker," she protested, "that still doesn't explain the scratch marks."

"Mrs. Smidel, if he's spending his afternoons at the park, maybe he had a reaction to the flora and fauna. He's okay. He just misses his dad."

"We all do," she replied before hanging up.

It was time to focus on more serious business. I ran background checks on the suspects in the Caterina Skolnick case. Alvarez had a few DUIs and the stalking charge but not much else. Maybe if we could identify some of his known associates, we could determine where he was hiding. After coming up with no solid leads, I shifted gears to investigating the triumvirate: the agent, Rick Sanderson; the owner of the modeling agency, Yolanda Tate; and the photographer, Jake Spencer. On a sheet of paper, I diagrammed the interconnectedness of the group in relation to Skolnick, but inspiration failed to strike.

"Knock, knock," Agent Mark Jablonsky announced from my office doorway. I narrowed my eyes, suspicious of the reason for his visit. "I come in peace."

"Why are you here?" I inquired, pushing my diagram aside. It was almost seven, and time had flown by.

"Oh, come on, Parker." He took a seat in my client chair and made himself comfortable. "I thought we were friends. You've always been like the daughter I never had."

"Lucky me," I deadpanned, studying him. He was dressed in his usual wrinkled suit, and his gun and credentials were still clipped to his belt. "Didn't I make myself clear that I'm not coming back to the OIO again?"

"Don't worry, this isn't about that. Well, actually,"

he reached into his breast pocket and pulled out an envelope, "I wanted to deliver your check." I opened it, made sure it was correct, and stuck it in my top desk drawer. "Are you working the Skolnick murder for the police?"

"You know I am. After all, you called in a favor or two, I'd imagine." He smiled warmly but didn't offer an elaboration.

"How's it going? Is Marty cleared yet?" He was up to something.

"He's been cleared for the last," I thought back, remembering today was Wednesday, "four days. Didn't you see all the press conferences and news reports?"

"I've been busy," he replied, but I didn't believe him. He was well aware of the situation since Martin was one of his closest friends. "I just wanted to see how you were. We didn't part on the best of terms Friday night, and then all this crap happened Saturday. I wanted to give you a minute to breathe before checking on you."

"We're good."

He examined my notations and diagram. "Want some input?" He jerked his chin at the paper.

"It couldn't hurt."

"Tate and Sanderson both have boats docked at the marina, near the same slip where Marty keeps his yacht." I was amazed by his candidness. "I did my own checking after he called earlier to ask about pillows. That has to be the strangest conversation I've ever had." I shut my eyes and sighed. Martin needed to learn to keep his damn mouth shut.

"Did he tell you what I told him to say?"

"I know nothing," Mark responded. "But you know I've got his back, and when I don't, you do."

"I thought, after last time, the best way to keep him

out of trouble was to stay away from him, but it didn't work too well."

"This isn't your fault. He's had some shitty luck recently. Hell, maybe we should be thankful we aren't him. Then again, if I had a private yacht, there wouldn't be any dead bodies on it because I'd be sitting in the middle of the ocean away from all of this."

FOURTEEN

The next day, I threw on some workout clothes, found a windbreaker, and zipped it over my shoulder holster. I tailed Roger Smidel to school and hung around in my car, drinking coffee and catching up on NPR. Needless to say, I was bored. Heathcliff didn't call, and since Smidel paid for a week's worth of surveillance, she might as well get her money's worth. When school was dismissed, I followed Roger to the park and watched him set up shop at one of the picnic tables.

Getting out of my car, I hit the walking trails for a nice long jog. A little fresh air and some exercise couldn't hurt, and it would enable me to keep an eye on Roger. I was on my second lap before anyone approached the table. The man who sat across from Roger was elderly, in his late sixties or seventies. He played a few games before walking away. No one else approached, and the kid stayed there, all alone, for the next twenty minutes.

Completing mile five, I stopped within Roger's view

to stretch before calling it a day. He noticed me and offered a lopsided grin. "Hi, again," I greeted, walking toward the table. "I didn't expect to see you two days in a row."

"I told you I'm here most days," he responded. "Do you want to try your luck again?"

"No cash." I slapped my pockets to demonstrate my lack of wallet and pulled out my keys. "I just came for a run."

"How 'bout one on the house?"

Shrugging, I sat down. "You're not the best businessman if you're giving it away," I quipped.

"Maybe it's a brilliant sales tactic to get you hooked. I mean you did come back today." He was relentless.

We played a slow-paced game as I analyzed every move in order to prolong the possibility for useful conversation. Unfortunately, he was completely content to do nothing more than stare doe-eyed at me. After a close match, I stood up.

"I don't see how you win every time," I complained, even though I could have easily beaten him if I wanted to, but there was a possibility that was just my stubborn, competitive side talking.

"I don't always win," he said quietly. His comment left me intrigued, and I felt there might be a story there. "We've all been bested once or twice."

"When you lose, if you lose, do you pay the player back for the game?" Maybe a fellow mancala lover thought he had been cheated and was looking for revenge.

"Yep, full refund and bragging rights." He tilted his head to the side, apprehensively. It'd be best to escape before whatever was leading him to be wary turned into an actual thought.

"See ya around, kid." I waited in my car for a few

minutes in case anyone else showed up. But he watched my exit, so I couldn't stay too long.

As I put my car in reverse, two teenagers approached the bench where he was sitting. I didn't get a good look at them, and there was no realistic excuse to backtrack. Maybe they were his friends from school, and he wouldn't be alone the rest of the day.

*   *   *

Late that afternoon, I attempted to dress elegantly but still appear casual and headed for the Guillots' house. It was Thursday night, and I agreed to meet with Luc, Vivi, and Thomas for dinner. Maybe Vivi could shed some light on the intricacies of Mrs. Smidel.

Stopping by the liquor store, I bought a mid-priced bottle of red wine since one should always arrive with a gift for the host. I didn't know why or how certain rules of etiquette got stuck in my head, but it probably wasn't a bad thing that some aspects of my life were refined. Or at least I had enough sense to pretend to be refined.

I pulled up to the Guillots' estate. It was large and intimidating, even though it was only two or three levels, but it seemed to go on for miles in either direction. Why in the world three people needed such a large house was beyond me, but it was none of my business. I stood outside, staring at the ceramic fountain and holding my pathetic gift as I waited for someone to answer the door.

"Ma'am," a maid opened the door, "may I take your purse and coat?" I handed over the items, and Vivi appeared in the foyer to greet me.

"Alexis, how wonderful to see you again." She kissed both my cheeks, and I gave her the bottle of wine. "Thank you so much. How are you? I was delighted to hear we were having company for dinner," she practically gushed. Considering the fact I only met the woman a handful of times, Luc's assessment of her loneliness seemed accurate.

"I'm very well, thank you. How are you? Your home is lovely." She uttered cordial responses, ushering me into the living room and pouring a glass of wine.

"Thomas, Luc," she called, "Alexis is here." A teenage boy, probably fourteen or fifteen, slunk down the steps. "Where's your father?" she asked in French. I pretended not to notice as I sat primly on the couch, scared to death of spilling or breaking anything. Luc was in the middle of a business call with the Paris office, concerning some type of management issue. "Men." She rolled her eyes, and we spent the next twenty minutes catching up and making small talk until she asked the real reason for my visit.

"Do you know Lynette Smidel?" I inquired.

"Lynette, oui." Maybe if my name was something French sounding, I would have enough money to afford an estate and maids. "She's absolutely lovely. We're on the PTA together, but I must plead guilty." My brow furrowed, confused by her words. "She was in a bind, and I suggested you could solve the problems she's having with Roger."

"I appreciate all the work I can get," I said, much to her relief. "But I haven't found anything wrong. Roger seems like a great kid, a bit of a loner but sweet and smart. Anything you can tell me about either Lynette or Roger might be helpful." She nodded and nudged Thomas with the tip of her shoe.

"Ms. Parker, I've seen Roger at school." His English was less accented than his mother's, probably because he had been speaking it since he was four or five. Europe tended to favor teaching multiple languages, unlike the United States. "He is two grades ahead of me, so I don't know him very well. But he's often teased. He's a dork, and his friends are outcasts." She gave him a sharp look, and he sunk into the couch.

"I might have caught on to that." I winked, hoping he wouldn't get in trouble for his assessment. "Has anyone ever beat him up or made his life unpleasant?"

"No. No one says anything to him. It's more like they say it about him." Well, it was high school. This was to be expected.

"Thank you for the help, Thomas." I turned to Vivi. "Is there anything I should know about Lynette? Does she seem stable? Do you know any details concerning the death of her husband?" My conversation was starting to sound more like an interrogation than friendly chatter, and I made the conscious effort to turn off the ingrained federal agent instinct.

"He died of a disease. Something rare I never heard of before. She's been keeping busy with little projects in the school and PTA. She's worked on every single fundraiser since I started helping at Highland Prep."

Luc entered the living room and poured himself a drink, smiling brightly. "Alexis, so glad you could make it." I thanked him for his generous invitation, and not long after, the maid announced supper was ready. We ate mostly in silence, but I uttered as many compliments as possible. "How are things with James?"

"Um." I tried not to appear as flummoxed as I felt.

"The model on his yacht," he clarified.

"Oh," I recovered somewhat, "like I said, Mr. Martin's not responsible for any of it. I'm assisting the police. They have a few leads, but nothing significant has surfaced yet." He nodded solemnly, and Vivi opened her mouth with a question. But before she could say a word, my cell phone rang. "How incredibly

G.K. Parks

rude of me," I apologized, excusing myself from the table. "I hate to do this, but I need to take this call."

Once I was in another room, I answered. "Any news on Alvarez?" I asked Heathcliff.

"Still nothing. Moretti's assigned more guys to the case. The longer we go without answers, the harder it is to dodge the press and find the scumbag."

"Do you want me to knock down some doors, Detective?" I teased since I didn't know Heathcliff to beat around the bush. Something was up.

"We've come up with an idea, but you're not going to be happy about it. Do you have time to meet me at the precinct?" I shut my eyes. How discourteous would it be if I ran out the door right now? Etiquette would not be pleased with such action.

"Can you give me an hour?"

"Sure." He didn't make any snide remarks. Whatever he wanted, I wasn't going to like it. I went back into the dining room, trying to look ashamed.

"Is everything all right?" Luc asked. I suspected they heard my end of the conversation.

"Speak of the devil," I replied. "I hate to eat and run, but I have to leave for the precinct in a few minutes."

"In that case, we shall put dessert on the table." Vivi signaled the maid to clear the plates.

"I am so sorry about this," I said sincerely as the most delectable cheesecake was placed on the table before me, and I resisted the urge to inhale it or ask for a to-go box. "I always imagined working in the private sector would lead to more stable hours." Vivi made a noise and looked pointedly at Luc.

"Stability and reasonable hours don't exist anywhere," he offered. "Even in business, eight to four is never actually eight to four. I've been working long hours too. First, because of my new position at the company, and then filling in for James as he recovered from surgery, and tomorrow, he's out of the office, so it'll be another long day. But I can't complain," he looked unyieldingly at his wife, "it's all part of the job."

After dessert, I said good-bye to Thomas, who looked relieved to be able to slink back upstairs. Luc disappeared into another room to conference call for work, and Vivi insisted on showing me out.

"It was wonderful to see you, Alexis. Don't be a stranger. We'll have to do this again soon."

"That sounds great." I collected my belongings and opened the front door.

"Lynette's a lovely woman. I hope you can help her." She smiled warmly.

"I'll do my best," I promised.

FIFTEEN

Leaving the Guillots, I went straight to the police station. Immediately, upon entering, I noticed Heathcliff, O'Connell, Thompson, and Moretti all huddled around the corkboard.

"What? You needed a coach to call the plays?" I quipped as my heels clacked loudly against the tile floor. I probably should have changed before coming to the precinct in a red dress and unreasonably high heels.

"Damn, Parker," Thompson commented, "did you dress up just to demonstrate your willingness to..."

Before he could finish his statement, Heathcliff kicked him under the desk and gave him a dangerous look. I raised an eyebrow and waited for someone to explain what was going on. Either Thompson was planning to make a lewd comment or something strange was about to happen.

"You look nice," O'Connell complimented. Moretti went into his office, probably trying to distance himself from the three chuckleheads. "I'm sorry we ruined your evening. Were you out with anyone special?" I gauged his question, trying to determine if he was implying something. As far as I knew, he was the only person who had any idea about my history with Martin.

"Okay, what the fuck is going on?" I asked. Knowing looks were exchanged, but no one said a word. "Fine. I was gathering info on something else I'm working, but instead, I drop everything to come down here. No inappropriate comments," I snarled at Thompson. "And no hot dates with anyone special," I growled at O'Connell. "Detective Heathcliff, what the hell is so important for me to be here tonight?"

"Let's go in Moretti's office to talk." He threw angry looks at the other two detectives before escorting me into Moretti's office. "Are you trying to piss her off?" I heard him whisper to them. I rolled my eyes, and Moretti shook his head.

"Y'know, the reason we have to hire consultants is because of the brain trust we got working here," Moretti said, exasperated.

"Okay," Heathcliff was back to being his normal stoic self, "I know this started out as a bad joke, but we're not making any headway in finding Alvarez or getting enough hard evidence. We want to send someone inside to infiltrate Tate's agency. She has an obvious opening left by Caterina and is hosting an open call on Monday." Today was not the day to show up at the precinct in a dress.

"You can't be serious. I'm still waiting for the punch line." I rubbed my forehead, hoping this was a bad dream.

"You signed a waiver." Moretti produced the pile of paperwork I agreed to. "But you're a consultant, so I can't order you to do anything. You don't have to work this."

"I'm knocking on thirty's door, and I'm not a giraffe for god's sake. I'm 5'6 and not model thin."

"You're close to model thin. Hell, you're one missed meal away from model thin," Heathcliff offered, and I gaped at him. "You could probably pass for twenty-four or twenty-five. It's a little on the older side, but you won't be auditioning for runway. Maybe we can sell you as print ads or those girls that stand next to cars and boats."

"Showcase," Moretti offered.

I was horrified. This must be what it was like to enter the Twilight Zone. "Boys," I tried a different tactic, "I'm damaged goods. I have more scars than I care to count." I uncrossed my legs and moved the hem of my skirt up an inch to reveal the jagged scar on my thigh. The wraparound pink lines on my wrists and the white remnants of electrical burns on my chest were obvious enough on their own without having to point them out.

"Makeup or airbrushing can take care of that." Heathcliff had all the answers. He and the Three Stooges must have practiced the conversation, so they'd be prepared for anything I could throw at them.

"You said you wanted to track down the killer after our James Martin blunder," Moretti cajoled. "If you agree and give us the go ahead, we'll send you and a few of our female officers to audition at Tate's agency on Monday. We'll establish your cover story, complete with background and previous experience. You just have to show up and strut your stuff. It's our best chance at a solid lead. The more people we send, the more likely one of you will be able to infiltrate Tate's inner circle."

"Looks like I'm jogging home tonight," I muttered sarcastically. "And fair warning, I get incredibly bitchy when I'm hungry, so you might want to keep your

Kevlar on at all times." Moretti chuckled and called the techs to start creating a profile.

"You mean to tell me this is non-bitchy Parker I've been dealing with for the last few days," Heathcliff teased as we left Moretti's office. "God, I'm already scared."

"Careful, Detective," I jokingly warned, "you're right on the edge of clever banter. I'd hate to see you cross over to the dark side."

*　　*　　*

The next day, I put on a pair of jeans, sneakers, a button-up white linen blouse, my shoulder holster, and a leather jacket. Subconsciously, I was doing my best to scream out law enforcement instead of model. I wasn't particularly fond of undercover work since it relied too heavily on the unknown and not enough on tried and true investigations, but no one ever spoke openly to law enforcement. This was why undercover assignments were so important and why Moretti was using this tactic as a last ditch effort to get answers to Caterina's murder. It wouldn't have been as bad, except I didn't like being gawked at while dressed in skimpy outfits, preferring instead to blend in to the background rather than being the center of attention.

"Parker," Heathcliff handed me a file as soon as I walked through the door, "here's your alias. Make sure you have every bit of this memorized by Monday, the day of the interview."

"Can't we spend today and the weekend locating Alvarez and finding Skolnick's assailant so this," I held up the folder, "won't even be an issue."

"I like the way you think." He just crossed over to the dark side. "Feel free to enlighten me with your omniscient abilities." I remained silent. "Until that

- 116 -

happens," he continued, "go downstairs. The tech department has set up a photo shoot near the locker rooms. We need headshots, comp cards, and realistic previous experiences done for everyone, so we've hired some professional makeup people and wardrobe guys."

"Smile pretty for the camera," O'Connell called, and I gave him my smoldering look before turning back to Heathcliff, who nodded to the stairway.

"Walk with me, Nick." My voice was commanding, and a chorus of 'oohs' echoed through the squad room. O'Connell obediently followed, and once we were out of earshot and within the privacy permitted between the two sets of double doors, I stopped. "I thought you weren't allowed to work this case. What the hell is going on?"

"Martin was cleared. Even if he turns around and gives us the murder weapon, the DA won't touch him. It's kosher. No ethical quandaries to deal with. Plus," he made sure no one was coming, "the longer this goes on, the less likely we are to find Skolnick's killer. Everyone in major crimes and homicide is working this right now. Three words, joint task force."

"High profile case," I concluded. "That's why I have to shake my ass for some photographer."

"You're supposed to be a model, not a stripper. Ass shaking isn't required." I resisted the urge to sigh. "Hey," he glanced around again, "were you with Martin last night?"

"No. I was working something."

"Well, you looked hot for just working. No offense." He tried to redeem himself. "And for the record, I'm not saying *I* thought you looked hot. I was only practicing my observational skills and stating the obvious, or my wife would murder me."

"Oink," I joked, squaring my shoulders and

preparing to march into the torture chamber of flash photography. "By the way, if I get this gig, I wasn't kidding. You're going undercover as my flamboyant stylist, so give some serious thought to dyeing your hair neon pink." I grinned evilly and walked away.

The rest of the morning was spent with my blouse half to completely unbuttoned as the photographer took a dozen or so shots. Luckily, they didn't make me change clothes for every take. Some clown with the title of makeup artist painted me up, and I was forced to exchange my shoulder holster and sneakers for stilettos and other fashionable accessories.

After a couple dozen photos, I was permitted to leave. As I stood in front of the sink, washing off the pounds of gunk they applied to my skin and scars, I noticed a few of the female officers doing the exact same thing.

"Alex Parker," I introduced myself, "consultant." I got a round of head nods and a few returned introductions. "I take it we're all stuck in the same boat comes Monday."

"Oh yeah." Two women settled at the neighboring sink. "I'm Miranda Costas, and this is Shelly Taylor. You must be the ringer they brought in." The women laughed, amused by their assessment.

"Don't even joke. So have any of you been briefed yet?"

"I'm in vice," Taylor responded, "so they're letting us use the wardrobe, hoping something will make an impression."

"Shit," Costas remarked, "we make a ton of impressions. Just ask the dozens of johns we brought in last weekend."

"The goal is to flood Tate's office early in order to prevent any actual aspiring models from auditioning." Taylor said 'aspiring models' with such loathing that I was positive she was my kindred spirit. "That way, one of us will be hired to fill the vic's spot." She examined my appearance. "There's a pool on who it's gonna be. My money's on you, girl." And Costas agreed too vehemently for my liking.

"Hell," I pulled a few bills out of my pocket, "I'll put ten down that Det. O'Connell would get it before any of us if he'd shave his legs and put on a dress." There was a round of robust laughter that erupted throughout the women's locker room.

"I like you, Parker," Costas said, slapping my back on her way out. "You just made my day."

"Tell your friends, I'll be here all week." I was playing up the stand-up comic routine since I didn't want to deal with any more hazing, particularly from the female officers, after the guys had been making my life miserable since I started consulting for the police department.

Returning upstairs, we got back to business. I pinned my flow chart concerning Tate, Sanderson, and Spencer to the board. This led to a thorough analysis of public business records to determine how frequently Sanderson's models were hired by Tate and photographed by Spencer. With their combined set of skills, the three of them could probably take over the modeling world if they put their minds to it.

"Maybe they're all responsible for Skolnick's murder. It's insane how much overlap there is," Thompson remarked. "If you look at the models employed by Tate, almost all of them are represented by Sanderson."

"How does that make sense?" I questioned his reasoning. "Didn't Sanderson and Tate lose money because of Caterina's death?"

"I have Skolnick's will and insurance policy here," O'Connell offered, grabbing a few sheets from under the mountain of paperwork on his desk. "Her parents were the beneficiaries of her estate, but the insurance money is being paid to Tate's agency."

"Hang on," Heathcliff scribbled a note about the insurance and tacked it to the board, "who took out the insurance policy?"

"Tate," O'Connell replied, his brow furrowing.

I swiveled in my chair to study the latest tidbits of information we posted, but they made little sense. If Skolnick was scheduled for an upcoming, highly lucrative ad campaign, then now was the worst time to stage her death. Money wasn't a clear motive for either Richard Sanderson or Yolanda Tate, unless the insurance policy was greater than the projected gains from the advertising.

"Is there any solid information on the big modeling campaign Caterina was supposed to do in the fall?" I asked.

Heathcliff flipped through some pages but came up empty. "Looks like someone might have to get that information from the inside," he suggested, and I rubbed my eyes and stretched, ignoring the comment. It was no wonder we lacked leads; we didn't have enough facts to work with. "I wanna bring Spencer in for a follow-up. Maybe, by now, he's calm enough to answer questions instead of crying like a little bitch." I cocked an eyebrow, tossing him a warning look.

"Dammit." I noticed the time. I was supposed to meet Martin for lunch in twenty minutes. "I have an appointment. Call me if something surfaces."

"Why do I feel like we're working for you?" O'Connell asked as I picked up my purse and headed for the door.

"Oh, you will be soon enough," I threatened. "Shall I stop by the drugstore for neon pink hair dye or would you prefer purple?"

SIXTEEN

I was not dressed for the high-class restaurant Martin selected. Unfortunately, I didn't have time to go home and change. The reason he requested this meeting was still a mystery. Maybe he wanted an update on the Skolnick situation or just needed an excuse not to eat alone.

I entered the restaurant and was immediately met with a glower. Luckily, it was an off-hour time to rendezvous, just after the lunchtime rush, so the hostess didn't threaten me with the dress code. I gave her Martin's name, and she instantly toned down the haughtiness. At least he was good for something.

Martin was at a table for two, gazing out the window. Bruiser was outside, monitoring the situation from a nearby bench, eating a pretzel, and pretending to be oblivious to his surroundings. Maybe the hostess thought he was violating the dress code too and refused to let him occupy one of the many empty tables.

"I'm sorry I'm late," I apologized.

Martin turned away from the window and focused on me. "Notice anything different?" His smile was infectious.

His arm was no longer in a sling, and his final doctor's appointment must have been earlier today. The case of the mystery lunch meeting was resolved. If only everything else could be this simple.

"Um, you got a haircut?" I tried to keep my lips from curling up at the corners. "No, wait, you bought a new shirt. Am I getting closer?"

"Smartass." He smirked.

"So, you're okay?"

"I'm better than okay." Classic egotistical Martin. "The scar tissue's been removed, and the surgeon said the nerve damage has healed nicely. So my mobility won't be impeded by any more inflammation. I just need to rebuild some muscle mass, and the scar itself is streamlined now, in case you want to see it." He lowered his voice a little and added, "It shouldn't freak you out as much in the future." I caught his flirtatious tone.

"Looks like we're celebrating."

"Champagne?" He motioned to the server.

"No, this is just my lunch break. I have to get back to the precinct soon enough."

"Anything you care to divulge on the case?" he asked, switching to a more professional mindset.

I relayed a minimal amount of detail concerning our three persons of interest. The only official suspect was Alvarez, and he was in the wind. When I concluded my rundown and gave him even stricter instructions not to mention anything I said concerning the case to anyone, including but not limited to Mark, he eyed my salad suspiciously.

"Since when do you consider leafy things food?" He looked contemplative. "I've seen you eat salads before but with other things like steak, burgers, or pizza. But never just salad. Come to think of it, I've seen you put lettuce and tomato on top of pizza and call that salad."

"I was out of clean forks, so I had to get creative. And there's nothing wrong with trying to keep my girlish figure in check," I deadpanned, and he looked as if I just said the grass was made out of marshmallows. "By the way, that reminds me, what do models wear?"

"What?" He was clearly confused by my conversational skills. "Is this a trick question?"

"No." I angrily stabbed at some lettuce that wasn't cooperating with my fork. God, now I wanted a cheeseburger with fries and a shake. "You've dated like half a dozen models, or so you claim. How the hell do they dress?" I sighed. "It's for the job."

He put two and two together and leaned back in his chair, savoring the moment. The look on his face was disconcerting. "Oh, I so want pictures."

"I am armed, and since you're in perfect health, I'm not afraid to make you bleed."

"Depends on the person. It's about accentuating assets. I'd say stilettos, skintight pants, or short skirts, and something slim fitting with a plunging neckline but still slightly more conservative on the top." I sat there motionless, gawking at his highly detailed analysis. He was visualizing all of these things into some ensemble he had already picked out, and if left to his own devices, his mind would end up in the gutter.

"Right, so I'm guessing raiding the stockpile of outfits reserved for vice isn't the most effective plan."

"Models aren't hookers," he turned back to serious, "regardless of what you might think."

"If you say so. Any additional tips I can share with the other ladies?"

"What's the goal?" I pressed my lips together. He was a civilian with no clearance to be privy to the inner workings of an impending sting operation. I hedged, and he noted my reticence. "How about I instill upon you the few tidbits of information I have on the industry?" he offered. "First, open calls are almost always filled by individuals with representation. Chelsea would harp about how these nobodies believed they had a shot. Secondly, the biggest challenge is getting an interview or audition or whatever." He was confused by the proper terminology, which made me feel better since I was clueless on all of it. "Sometimes being outlandish or classily provocative may stand out more than a nice," we made eye contact, "cover story."

I put my fork down and pulled out the small notepad and pen I kept in my purse and made a note of his two suggestions. I'd discuss this more thoroughly with Heathcliff to see if there was anything the police hadn't already considered. Shutting my eyes, I shook my head slightly before opening them and letting out a small chuckle. I had come to the sudden realization I was a much more assiduous investigator than I ever realized because nothing else explained why I was trying so hard to give one of us, be it me, Taylor, Costas, or any of the other women in uniform, a realistic shot of infiltrating Tate's agency. I was dogged in wanting to identify Skolnick's assailant since someone had to do it, and Martin asked that I assist in this endeavor.

"I need to stop asking for your help," I commented, giving up on the green and purple leaves still on my plate. "You shouldn't be anywhere near this."

"That's funny since I asked you to help, or at least Ackerman did," he argued. "And I can't remove myself from this. It came to me." He reached for my hand, but I pulled away.

"I need to get back and run your helpful hints by the detectives, and then I have to tail a teenage boy to the park."

He laid some cash on the table and stood up, slipping on his jacket. "I didn't know you were into younger men." He guided me out of the restaurant, his hand coming to rest on the small of my back. I didn't say anything, but it felt awkward, just like most things with him.

"Separate case," I mumbled. "I'm," I paused, trying to determine the appropriate word, relieved, ecstatic, thankful, "glad you're okay." He brushed a strand of hair out of my face and rubbed his thumb across my cheek in the process. His faint touch served as a painful reminder of everything we lost.

"Think about where you thought we'd be, and let me know if we can ever get back there." He smiled sadly and leaned in, placing a gentle, lingering kiss on my cheek. "Stay safe."

"Always."

Once inside my car, I watched Bruiser trail Martin into his chauffeured town car. I took a deep breath and pulled away. Crisis averted. Good job, Parker. I attempted to congratulate myself on navigating the muddied relationship waters, but I didn't feel much like celebrating.

*   *   *

At the precinct, the dream team was tossing questions and theories around the room, along with rolled up scrap paper as they played a rather strange version of desk basketball.

"Working hard or hardly working?" I inquired, sitting across from Heathcliff.

"There's still no word on the whereabouts of Mr. Raymond Alvarez," O'Connell offered, tossing a paper wad into the trashcan beside me.

"Spencer claims to be in the middle of a job, but he's offered to come in bright and early tomorrow morning. He even managed to contain the uncontrollable sobbing over the phone," Heathcliff condescendingly added. "Funny, I'd imagine someone that distraught wouldn't be able to work. How can he see through the viewfinder with all those tears cascading down his face?"

"Maybe it's supposed to make the photos more artistic," Thompson mocked.

"Okay, so I just came from a brief meeting with Martin." I might as well let the cat out of the bag. "I thought he might be able to provide some tips on the modeling world." The guys looked intrigued.

"Did he use to model? Is that how he started making his millions?" Thompson asked, but I disregarded his question.

"I'm guessing none of you have dated any models," I continued. "Apparently, the chances of getting selected depend greatly on representation and a flair for the dramatic. Something needs to be done to get attention in a positive way."

"And here I thought you were completely opposed to the possibility of this undercover assignment," Heathcliff remarked. "But we aren't as stupid as we look. Well, I guess I can only speak for myself." He threw a glance at the other two guys. "Moretti has a team making calls to all the agents in town, looking for some assistance on this thing, but we can't force them to play along. And there's been no word yet if any of them will be promising."

"How many officers are you sending undercover on Monday?"

"Eight. Nine if we count you," Heathcliff replied. "It's too many for one agent to accept, and all we can really do is threaten to look into their business practices. It's a hard sell. They're afraid of getting a bad reputation and losing their current clients or the willingness of agencies to hire the models they represent."

"You know what I still don't understand?" Thompson interrupted. "If it's a modeling agency, why do the women need to have individual representation too?"

"Don't ask me. I was just hired to sit around and look pretty," I responded.

We spent the next hour spit-balling ideas and theories. Hopefully, Spencer would provide something useful during tomorrow's interview. Skolnick was killed almost a week ago, give or take several hours, and the police still had no solid leads. Alvarez was our best bet but only if he could be found. For all any of us knew, he could be drinking mai tais in the Bahamas at this very moment.

"Let's take a break," Heathcliff ordered. "We're not getting anywhere, and we're two minutes away from someone suggesting she was suffocated by a UFO disguised as a pillow."

"Shit." I forgot to share Mark's insight. "The pillow didn't belong to Martin, but Agent Jablonsky did some digging into the marina's records. Sanderson and Tate both have personal watercrafts docked at the same pier. Since the pillow had to come from somewhere, it could be one of theirs."

"Yeah, we know," O'Connell said, "but it's too circumstantial to warrant a warrant." He looked proud of his play on words. "Thompson and I are going to check into a couple other things that have found their way to my desk since we are taking a break, right?"

"Go ahead," Heathcliff dismissed them. After they left, he let out a sigh. "You should take off too. Whenever Moretti gets a verdict on the modeling representatives, I'll give you a call." His brow knitted together. "Do you think Martin could use his influence to do us a favor?"

"The only connection he has to the modeling world besides some ex-girlfriends," although I suspected they were more brief hook-ups than relationships, "is his passing acquaintanceship with Sanderson." Something crossed Heathcliff's eyes, but he didn't speak. He only nodded, deep in thought. "But if you want to ask, I'm sure you have his number."

"I doubt Martin has any exploitable resources," he was lost in devising a plan, "but if that changes, it'd probably mean more coming from his company's security consultant."

The last thing I wanted to do was ask for a favor, but we were running out of time and options. "Keep me apprised." I put my jacket on and left the building.

SEVENTEEN

I was at the park, sitting in my car and staring at the picnic tables where the grungy chess players and a lonely teenage boy sat. I couldn't solve Roger's problems. Life had dealt him a shitty hand, full of loneliness and tragedy. The only compensation he had was his family's wealth. Although, when it came down to it, we all had misery and hardships to face. Sadness and loss were the great equalizers everyone could relate to. I tried to ward off the melancholy as my mind returned to the task of disentangling the intricacies of the modeling world.

About an hour had passed, and no one approached Roger. I wondered why he would choose to sit outside for hours on end in the hopes of finding some type of human interaction. He had friends. I saw him eat breakfast with them. Why didn't he just hang out at the mall or movies or whatever it was teenagers did nowadays. "God, you're getting old and out of touch, Parker," I said to myself. I was also becoming senile since I wasn't only speaking to myself out loud but mocking my own age. Maybe I needed to make more friends and not the imaginary kind.

Slumping back against the headrest, I played with the radio for a while. The sun was preparing to set, and I wondered how much longer Roger would sit at the table before going home. I had gotten distracted making a list of potential model-appropriate clothing choices and completely missed the appearance of two dangerous looking men who were now seated on the bench in front of Roger.

As soon as I noticed them, I opened my car door and waited. The two clowns wore leather and chains, but the most troubling aspect was the shift in Roger's body language. Instead of being outwardly open and friendly, he was cowering and leaning away from them. The change in his posture was foreboding, and I knew he'd run.

I just unzipped my jacket for easier access to my holstered weapon when Roger took off in the opposite direction of the men. He was moving fast, and the two goons gave chase. Fuck. I slammed my car door and pursued. Whatever was going on wasn't good. As I attempted to follow through the wooded areas, the cause of the red scratches on his neck and arms became apparent. Damn low-lying tree branches, I cursed.

The two leather-clad men caught up to Roger and knocked him to the ground. They were some distance ahead of me, but Roger's panicked cries carried through the park. Upon reaching a clearing, I stopped dead in my tracks. The three of them tussled as Roger attempted and failed to fight off his assailants. One of the men, probably not much older than Roger, had gotten a tight grasp while the other man, also a teenager, proceeded to hit him.

"Hey. Leave him alone," I ordered, my voice deadly.

The punk turned to face me, temporarily stopping the assault.

"This isn't your problem, lady. Get out of here," he sneered.

"I asked nicely. The next time I ask, it won't be so nice." On brute force alone, I was outmatched, so I pulled my gun and steadied it on the little twerp. He might come off as a badass, but he wasn't bulletproof. "Let him go. Now," I growled.

The hitter put his hands in the air and stepped back, shocked to see a weapon aimed at him. The other punk released Roger but studied me with intrigue. He wasn't afraid, and I wasn't sure how things were going to conclude. After all, I was pointing a loaded nine millimeter at a couple of unarmed teenagers. There was a very good chance I was going to jail. The ridiculous nature of the situation was not lost on me.

"Be cool. We were just messing with him. No harm done." The hitter was already edging back to the trail.

"Remember what we said," the other one warned, not so quietly in Roger's ear, before the two ran off in different directions.

"Who the hell are you?" Roger's eyes went wide, and he looked more afraid of me than the guys who were knocking the shit out of him. I holstered my gun and listened for the sound of sirens.

"I work with the police." It was true enough. "Are you okay?"

"Can I see your badge or something?" He seemed unsure. "I thought you said you were a graduate student."

"You said that. I just didn't bother to correct you. And I'm a consultant, not a cop, but I can show you my private investigator's license." I tried to keep him calm since I didn't want him to run off until we had a chance to chat. "Come on," I jerked my chin toward the parking lot, "we don't want your friends to return." He was still uncertain but agreed to follow me.

"Were you going to shoot them?" he asked quietly. The sight of my nine millimeter made him tense, and I reminded myself most people weren't used to seeing firearms in person.

"I wasn't planning on it, unless they gave me a reason. I'm glad they didn't." He nodded. "Are you okay?"

"Yeah. I'm tougher than I look." He wanted to appear strong and masculine. "Then again, you are too," he added. Apparently, my attitude and gun deflated his machismo.

"Who are they, and what did they want from you?" He hesitated, trying to determine if I was one of the good guys. I needed to do something to earn his trust, and saying his mom hired me wouldn't work out well for any of us. "I'm on your side. Y'know, I really do work for the police department, but if you want to make sure this is on the level, call the precinct. Anyone in major crimes will vouch for me. Ask for Lieutenant Moretti or Detectives Heathcliff, Thompson, or O'Connell. I'm Alexis Parker, by the way." I smiled encouragingly.

He dialed information and got the number; then he waited for someone to answer. Finally, he asked to speak to one of the four men I had volunteered. After being put on hold and shuffled around, he nodded thoughtfully at the reply to his question.

"He wants to talk to you." He handed me the phone.

"Parker," I said in order to appear much more professional and no-nonsense than usual.

"What the fuck is going on now?" O'Connell asked.

"Why is some guy asking about you? He sounds like he's twelve."

"Nick, there was a situation at the park involving two adolescent thugs. If you could send a squad car to keep an eye on things, I'd appreciate it."

"What are you doing at the park?" he asked, but I interrupted before he could continue further with his line of questioning.

"Thanks for your cooperation, Detective." And I hit end call on Roger's phone, handing it back to him. "Satisfied?"

"I guess." He shrugged. "I don't want to get anyone in trouble. I'm just going home."

"Roger," I said his name, stopping him in his tracks, "do you like cheeseburgers? I've had a bitch of a day, and I'm starving. C'mon, it's my treat. I owe you some honesty, right? We can eat and talk. I'll drive." I wasn't taking no for an answer. So he got in my car, and we headed for the nearest diner. Once inside and waiting for our orders, I broached the subject again. "Do you know the guys that were assaulting you?"

"Maybe. They used to go to my school." He swallowed and stared at the napkin, fidgeting with the fold.

"High school, right?" I wasn't playing dumb anymore. "I hated high school. There were the popular kids and the outcasts. You had to be one or the other, and it branched out into different sects with the smart kids and the jocks and the druggies. Horrible times." I was hoping to find common ground.

"Yeah," he sounded wistful.

"All I can tell you is that once you're finished, it doesn't mean a damn thing, except for the losers who do nothing with their lives afterward." I smiled slyly. "You don't strike me as one of those."

"I'm not. After I graduate, I'm going to MIT. I've already been accepted on early admission."

"Congrats, but the two punks at the park don't seem to be the MIT types. How come they were harassing you?" I was slowly circling back around.

"I'm not supposed to be on their turf," he sounded disgusted. "They chase me off every week. One of these days, they'll get tired of it and leave me the hell alone." This made no sense, and I knew I was missing something important.

"Did you encroach on their mancala racket?" I asked, feigning serious. The server brought our food, and I was momentarily distracted by having something greasy, fried, and full of fat in front of me. Heaven. It was a short-lived euphoria as Roger began speaking again.

"No. I don't know what their problem is, but I'm not going to let them push me around." He was adamant. "I've lost enough. I won't let them take anything else." My focus shifted away from the cheeseburger.

"I promise to keep your response completely confidential," I said solemnly, "but I need the truth. Do you understand?" He nodded. "Are you involved in any illegal activity at the park? Maybe selling drugs or buying drugs?" He paled. "I work for the police department. If you are involved, you can be a confidential informant. Your name can be left out of it. You won't get in trouble." I was making up the most believable cover story possible; hopefully, the kid had seen a few cop shows on television and would buy it.

"I've never done anything, but I know people who have. A lot of times, I hear them talking in the hallways about buying some study aids, like around finals."

"Study aids?" I tried my best to remain professional

by daintily picking at the fries, resisting the urge to swallow them whole.

"Ritalin mostly, some Modafinil, Adderall, things like that," he whispered as his eyes darted around the room. "Anything to get an edge in order to pull an all-nighter."

"Okay." When did caffeine and sugar go out of style? Then again, there was always speed and other methamphetamines. Apparently, it came down to pharmaceutical grade versus street quality. Obviously, I needed more elaboration.

"The park, that's where they go to buy what they need," he finally filled in the blanks. "I was with Ka-" He stopped and regrouped, fearing he ratted on someone. "I was with some people from school, hanging out one day, when they had to make a quick stop."

I picked up my cheeseburger and took a large bite, chewing slowly. The longer I remained silent, the more likely he would continue to talk. One of the best things about civilians was they tended to ramble when faced with awkward silences. Instead, he silently watched me eat with a level of disbelief and utter shock. Teenagers didn't fall into the category of normal people, unfortunately.

"So," I wiped my mouth with a napkin, "the thug-wannabes from today are the dealers."

"How'd you know?" For someone who was granted early admission to MIT, he lacked basic common sense skills.

"I'm smarter than I look. But if you're not selling, what's it to them if you hang out at the park?" He remained silent, picking at the food on his plate. I couldn't make him talk, and I couldn't prove his involvement in anything illegal. "Are you going to eat that?" I asked, pointing to the pile of fries sitting untouched on his plate. He shook his head and pushed the plate away.

"How come most cops are pudgy because they eat donuts all day and you're scarfing down fries like there's no tomorrow, but you're definitely not overweight?" he commented, much to my chagrin.

"Because I don't sit around eating donuts all day or fries, usually. I'm trying out this diet thing. It's a stupid idea, and I've been dying for fries and burgers ever since." I laughed. "Clearly, we all do stupid things sometimes."

"Do you think those guys will give me a hard time again?" Perhaps my own human imperfections gave him a bit more courage to talk about his current dilemma.

"It depends." I tried to convey the severity of the situation with the use of eye contact. "Why don't they want you at the park?"

He shrugged again, but he knew the answer. I waited him out. Although, I might have had better luck watching paint dry. After an eternity and the last of the fries, I paid the bill. He wasn't going to crack.

"Maybe you should call your mom since you're late getting home. She's probably worried sick," I suggested.

He let out a bitter laugh. "I'm sure she hasn't even noticed I'm gone. She stays so busy, running from one thing to another. She can't sit still. She's been like this since my dad," he swallowed, "since he passed."

"I'm sorry. I'll give you a ride back to your car." I felt like a complete failure since I didn't figure out what was wrong with the kid or determined the severity of the situation at the park. I didn't know how to fix his life or make it easier. His mom tried by hiring me, and all I could tell her was that some drug dealing bullies liked to chase her son off and knock him around. "Have you ever considered self-defense classes?" Turning into the parking lot, I shut the engine and made one final effort to get him to open up.

"I'm not the athletic type," he quipped. "I know it's hard to believe with all these bulging muscles."

"Look, I get that this place means something to you. I also understand not running from a fight or rolling over and letting people walk all over you, but unless you tell someone what is going on, no one can help you. It'd probably be best to stay clear of those troublemakers."

"I'll be okay. I can take it." He was filled with righteousness, and it would probably get him hurt or worse.

"Take this." I handed him my card. "Do you remember those four names I told you earlier? If anything happens or if anyone comes after you, you can call me or one of those policemen."

"Thanks, Alexis," he double-checked my name on the card, "but I'm a big boy. I can handle myself."

After he got safely into his car, I signaled for him to go ahead. He was out of the parking space and down the road before I turned the key in the ignition. Blowing out a breath, I tried to come up with some feasible options, but none of them were practical under the circumstances. What was I supposed to do now?

EIGHTEEN

I wanted to have something concrete to report before I informed Mrs. Smidel about the situation at the park. I was hoping to earn Roger's trust and gain his cooperation instead of having his mom destroy all of it. She would do what she felt was best for her son, but I didn't see how forbidding him to go back to the park would help. The most likely scenario would involve Roger going even more often just to defy her, and right now, the two thugs were a concern, especially in the wake of pointing a gun at them. The stakes had been raised, and if they came back, they'd be prepared. They would either be frightened and tone down their illegal activities or seek back-up. The back-up might come in the form of some of their big, strong friends, or it might be a concealed weapon.

"I thought I told you to go home," Heathcliff commented as I walked over to his desk.

"I need your help," I admitted, filling him in on Roger, the thugs in the park, and the illegal prescription drug 'study aids'.

"You might have better luck talking to someone in narcotics," he replied, but I knew he'd help as much as he could. "What are you going to do about the kid? Are you planning to tell his mom what's going on?"

"I don't know." I sighed. "If the thugs are left alone, the same thing or worse is bound to happen. If they get arrested, what happens once they get out? They used to attend Highland Prep. They must come from money, so I'm assuming they don't have a rap sheet. With no priors and a decent bank account, they'll get a slap on the wrist and be released, and then they might decide to retaliate. What am I supposed to do?"

"You've got yourself a conundrum." He leaned back and slowly swiveled from side to side. "If you're smart, you tell his mom and let her figure out what to do."

"She'd come running back to the police station, throwing around unsubstantiated allegations and demanding someone do something."

"On second thought, I'd rather this be your problem than mine." He smirked. "Wouldn't it be easier to convince the kid to stay away from the park?"

"Tried and failed. He's obstinate. He's dealt with a lot, and this is his breaking point. He's unwilling to compromise."

"It looks like the only thing you can do is convince the adolescent miscreants to reconsider the location for their illegal activities. If they stop selling in the park, they won't have a reason to bother the kid."

"What should I do? Have a sit-down and make them an offer they can't refuse?"

He considered my point for a minute and picked up the phone. "It's a public service to get drug sales out of the park. Mothers go there with babies, and dogs chase Frisbees. I'll put a call in to narcotics and see if they can come up with a better solution to your problem." I was about to reiterate my worries concerning the lack of rap sheet and retaliation for being arrested, but he read my mind. "This isn't a big deal. Unfortunately, we worry more about crack, meth, and heroin than some kids popping Ritalin. It's society, what can I say. But the narco guys are some badasses. I'd know since I used to be one of them." He grinned. "They'll get some UCs to move into the territory or threaten to, and it'll scare the punks off. It always does. The only time that doesn't work is when we're dealing with serious dealers."

"Thank you." I was grateful for the help.

"In the meantime, do what you can to keep the kid clear of the park. Homicide already has enough to worry about." I couldn't tell if he was joking, but either way, it was an incredibly morbid statement. "Also, give Martin a call and see if he'll introduce you to Sanderson. Maybe with enough cajoling, you can land Sanderson as an agent since all roads lead to nowhere."

"Just me? Or all nine of us?"

"Just you. Frankly, you're our best bet, and since Sanderson's still a person of interest, we can't risk tipping him off by asking for cooperation through official channels. We're not in the business of letting people get away with murder."

"Right." I tried to formulate a cover story for Martin to use since he didn't need to be dragged further into this, but we had no choice. "Thanks again." With any luck, narcotics would provide a quick-fix to Roger's problem, and Sanderson would be the perfect in for the newest model at Tate's agency.

*   *   *

I dialed Mrs. Smidel while I rummaged through my closet, pulling out clothing options to wear. She answered after four rings, and we briefly exchanged pleasantries.

"He has those weird scratches again," she whispered. "Have you discovered anything? I'm not paying you to sit around and do nothing."

"Mrs. Smidel," I began patiently, "the scratches are from running through the park. There are a lot of low-lying tree branches and shrubbery."

"Why in god's name is he running through the forest?" A door slammed shut, and I figured she was seeking some privacy. Now was the moment when I had to make a decision on what to tell her.

"Ma'am, there are a couple of kids at the park who appear to be a bit brutish." I was downplaying the scenario.

"Brutish," she repeated. "Are you going to do something about them? They should not be allowed to walk around being...brutish. Maybe I need to go back to the police."

"I have already spoken to the police department. We are working to resolve this issue quickly." I was being as diplomatic as possible. "In a few days, they will no longer be present at the park. However," I had to think of what to say, "it would be best if Roger has something else to focus on for the time being. Perhaps a trip to visit MIT or a weekend getaway might be particularly convenient right now. Maybe the two of you could spend some quality time together as a nice change of pace."

"You've spoken to Roger?" she practically screeched.

"Yes, ma'am." My voice was calm, even though she was pushing my buttons. "He's lonely. But don't worry, he doesn't know that you hired me. We just randomly bumped into one another and got to talking. That was it."

"I see." Her remark was clipped. "I will consider your suggestion. Please notify me once the brutes have been removed."

"As you wish." I hung up and resisted the urge to throw my phone. She was a worried parent, but she was also an absent parent. She thought removing danger was the only way to help her son when, in actuality, the only thing he wanted was someone to talk to who listened. "Rich assholes," I griped.

Speaking of, I needed to call Martin. It was Friday night, and Sanderson needed to believe I was a model in dire need of representation before Monday morning. The timeframe sucked. I doubted anything would get done, but Heathcliff wanted me to try. I went into the living room and found the file folder on my alias, Lola Peters. That was one hell of a stripper name if I'd ever heard one, but no one consulted me. How ironic.

"I didn't expect to hear from you so soon," Martin sounded overjoyed by the prospect of my call.

"The police department needs a favor, and they're too afraid to ask." My tone was irritated, bordering on cynical. They made the mess and expected me to clean it up.

"Anything I can do for our friends at the precinct." His tone matched mine. "Do they want me to confess to murder since they've done such a great job so far?"

"No. They'd probably just show up at your place and ask that one in person. I know you've only met Rick Sanderson a few times in passing, but how well do you actually know him?"

"Not well at all." He was agitated by answering the same thing repeatedly.

"We need someone to convince him to represent a new model. She has a decent résumé, even if she isn't entirely up to snuff." I flipped through the background history fabricated by the tech department.

"Who?" His curiosity distracted him, and the bitterness left his voice.

"Lola Peters," I was reading the file for the third time, "she's done some advertisements, a bit of catalog work, some car shows."

"Never heard of her." He was still clueless. It might have been cute if I wasn't wondering if he had paid any attention to the brief synopsis I gave him at lunch about the undercover sting. "Do you have some stats on her?"

"Why? Planning to start your own modeling agency?" I quipped. "Or are you just looking for another date?"

"Alex," he was trying to be patient, "if I call Sanderson, he's going to ask."

"Five foot six, one hundred and twelve pounds, brunette, blue eyes, supposed to be twenty-four." I paused, suspecting he was making notes. "I didn't think you knew Sanderson well enough to call him yourself."

"I can try. I don't have any other connections in the business to offer."

"You can't tell him it's part of a police operation. He's still considered a person of interest."

"Okay. Will she know who I am and why I vouched for her, just in case Sanderson asks?"

"I guess so," I snickered, "considering you and I need to figure out what my cover story will be. I don't want you getting dragged deeper into this, so I'm thinking she's a niece or cousin of one of your employees, asking for a favor. That way, you can remain an innocent bystander. The timing is still suspicious as all get out, but we need to have this happen before Monday."

"Do I get to retroactively count you as one of the

models I dated?" At least the dots connected for him.

"Seriously, I don't want you to be familiar with Lola at all. Call Sanderson, but you're asking for a favor for someone else. Whatever you decide, keep it simple, and tell me what it is once it's said."

"All right." He had all the notes he needed. "I'll call you back in a few minutes."

While I waited for Martin to phone with the news that Sanderson rejected his request, I rifled through the clothing piled on my bed. If the vice squad's outfits wouldn't hit the mark, then I'd have to figure something else out. Surely, somewhere in this pile was the perfect interview outfit.

I decided to forgo a skirt because the scar on my thigh could easily be a deal-breaker this early in the game. In the recesses of my closet was a pair of black leather pants from some undercover assignment when I was full-time at the OIO. To add to the ensemble, I found some black spike heels with silver studs. Now all I needed was an appropriate top.

My phone rang, and I grabbed it. "Are you free tonight?" Martin inquired. I couldn't tell if he was being his lothario self or if this was Sanderson related, so I waited for additional details. "Sanderson's hosting a party at his place, and if he likes what he sees, he'll sign you tonight."

"Where's the party?"

"I'll give you the address." He rambled off the information. "I told him I'd have to relay the message to your uncle in accounting, and he'd give you the message. Rick said the party will be going on until three or four a.m., so at least you have plenty of time."

"I need to call Heathcliff or Moretti and get approval." I was making a mental list. "Thanks for this," I added.

"I know you're busy," he spoke quickly, hoping I

wouldn't hang up on him midsentence, "but I forgot to give you some paperwork from Ackerman today at lunch. It's just an employment release form since you signed with them but didn't actually work for them. I said I'd take care of it and bring it by in the morning."

"Good thing I called." I wondered what he planned to do had I not called but realized I probably didn't want to know. "I'll be home for the next hour or two, working out details and finding something to wear. Can you have Marcal or a courier bring it by for me to sign?"

"Sure."

NINETEEN

Heathcliff got approval and gave the go-ahead on meeting Sanderson, but I didn't have high hopes of a positive outcome. I wasn't a model. I never aspired to be a model, and with the exception of half a decade worth of classical dance classes as a child, I never desired to be tall, svelte, and coordinated. By the time I turned fourteen, my interests had shifted, and my life had taken more turns than I cared to recount.

I was in my bedroom, wearing the black skintight leather pants, the spiked heels, and a black bra as I circled through the pile of blouses and tops that were now scattered all over my room. My doorbell rang, and I grabbed a sweatshirt before answering it. I looked through the peephole and opened the door.

"Hey there, Bruiser." I smiled at him as Martin entered my apartment. "Want to come in and join the party?"

"I think I'll wait in the lobby," Jones said, retreating toward the stairwell.

"My building has a lobby?" I asked Martin who

sauntered past and was seated at my counter.

"You know, the area on the ground floor where the mailboxes are," he responded so casually that I wondered if he spent his free time stalking me.

"Uh-huh." I went to my desk and found a pen. "You didn't have to bring this over personally. On the phone, I specified using a courier."

He had a mischievous grin. "Sorry to disappoint, but I had to see what you were wearing." He made an obvious show of checking me out. "You need to reconsider the top. I said conservative, but that's just ridiculous."

"No shit." Uncapping the pen, I read through all the legal stipulations, making sure I wasn't giving them permission to cut out my brain or anything like that before signing and dating the bottom. "Was that it?" He flipped through the pages, finding one final tabbed spot to sign.

"And now you're free from all legal hassles and no longer granted any privilege pertaining to me." Strangely enough, this was a good thing.

"Great." I went into my bedroom and shut the door. "Help yourself to a drink. I haven't moved the liquor cabinet since the last time you were here," I called. It felt strange for him to be back in my apartment. Maybe I was the one who needed the drink. "Hell, make it two." Taking off the sweatshirt, I continued evaluating the pile of clothing in order to figure out what to wear.

"What?"

Our communication skills were even more impaired than usual on account of my bedroom door being in the way, so I opened the door halfway and hollered into the main room, "I said make yourself a drink. Then I said make it two, but that's probably not the best idea since I have to woo Sanderson. Maybe I should pack a flask and force feed him hundred and fifty proof liquor until he's too drunk to disagree. What do you think? Overkill, right?" I was rambling. "Never mind. Just ignore me."

Martin appeared in the doorway, holding a glass of scotch. "Oh, sorry." He turned away.

"Screw it," I muttered. "It's nothing you haven't seen before." I pinched the bridge of my nose, trying to come up with a solution. "Get in here and help me figure out what to wear."

He assessed my pants, shoes, and bra. "Maybe you should just go like that," he smiled slyly, and I gave him a dirty look. "I'd sign you."

"Either help or get out." I was annoyed with him, the situation, and my lack of wardrobe choices. He began sifting through the assortment of tops. "Do we know Sanderson's sexual orientation?" I inquired as Martin did a wonderful Tim Gunn impression.

"I have no idea." He held up a cream colored cashmere sweater. "Try this." I felt like a four-year-old whose parents had to pick out her clothes. I put the top on and waited for a reaction. He adjusted it at the shoulders, so the v-neck plunged deeper than usual. He cocked an eyebrow and smirked, very self-satisfied.

"Well?" I was tired of feeling like a dress-up doll.

"Classy sex kitten." I glared at him and went into the bathroom to look in the mirror.

There was a fine line between sexy and slutty, and I didn't trust his judgment. It wasn't as bad as I imagined, but the two burn marks on my chest were impossible to ignore. Why didn't anyone take my protest about being damaged goods seriously? A modeling agency wouldn't hire someone who was covered in remnants of the occupational hazards of her day job. There wasn't enough makeup in the world to erase what I'd been through, but I searched the bathroom cabinets, looking for concealer and foundation anyway. Thankfully, modeling was only skin deep.

"Goddamn scars," I cursed. Martin appeared behind me, watching with a level of fascination often reserved for predators in the wild who were about to pounce on their prey.

"Do you have any long necklaces?"

"Jewelry box on my dresser."

I didn't even bother to ask what he was thinking. To be perfectly honest, I was taken aback by his overall fashion sense and stylistic attitude. Sure, he came off looking perfectly coifed and polished on a daily basis, but he probably spent years perfecting that talent. Dressing me should not come this easily to him.

He came back into the bathroom, holding a long silver chain with a simple circular charm at the end. Brushing my hair to the side, he slipped it around my neck and fastened the clasp, letting the charm fall just below the v of my shirt. I went to adjust it, but he grabbed my hand.

"The silver will draw the eye. No one will even notice the slight discoloration left." His voice trailed off. The event responsible for those particular scars wasn't something either of us wanted to revisit; it had been part of the impetus that broke us apart.

I looked in the mirror again, judging the veracity of his statement. My eyes immediately went to the pinkish white marks on my chest, but I knew what to look for. After all, they were my scars. Also, I wasn't a guy, so he was probably right about where the eye would be drawn.

"My god," I teased while applying an absurd amount of makeup, classy but still outlandish, "you need to be a guest judge on *Project Runway*. Are you sure you're into women and not just dressing them?" Maybe he had some kind of strange fetish I wasn't aware of.

"You could just say thank you." He left me to my own devices as he went in search of the scotch he abandoned somewhere in my bedroom.

When I emerged a half hour later, my hair was wavy, my eyes were smoky, and my skin looked as flawless and young as some cheap drugstore makeup could manage. Honestly, I'm not sure I would recognize myself. "What do you think? Am I up to snuff?"

He turned from his place at the counter and smiled, mesmerized by the transformation. "Goddamn." His curse was low, sultry, and full of something that instantly sent chills through my body. He met my eyes, and in the green depths of his irises, I could see something that could only accurately be described as loss. "If he doesn't want to represent you, Ms. Peters, then he must be blind."

I snorted. "Lola Peters, what a name. Maybe you should have been at the station today, explaining the difference between hookers, strippers, and models."

He smirked and put his glass in the sink, grabbed the paperwork off my counter, and edged toward the door. "Good luck." He winked. "One final suggestion, don't wear the shoulder holster. It will ruin the entire effect."

I laughed good-naturedly. "Thanks for the tip." I followed him to the door. "If I weren't painted up like a drag queen, I'd probably ask for a good night kiss, but it'd take turpentine to get the paint transfer off your skin." I was playing with fire, and he cocked his head to the side, assessing me for a moment to determine how serious I was.

"Pity," he examined my reaction closely, "I ran out of turpentine this morning."

"Maybe next time." I opened my front door. "Tell Bruiser my building doesn't have a lobby." He tossed his patented smirk over his shoulder and left.

* * *

It was almost midnight by the time I arrived at Sanderson's house, a large estate in an exclusive neighborhood. How come it suddenly seemed like everyone else owned mansions? I had a tiny apartment comprised of one large multifunctional room, a bedroom, and a small bathroom. On the plus side, cleaning it didn't take more than a couple of hours. If I had a mansion, it would have to come with an entire staff of maids and butlers. Apparently, Sanderson's came with parking attendants, cater-waiters, a DJ and impressive sound system, and a myriad of people. Or at least he hired them for the party.

Lola's résumé, comp card, and headshot were folded neatly in my purse. All I needed to do was locate Sanderson. After asking a dozen or so guests to point me in the right direction, I found him sitting outside by the heated pool, watching amused as some bikini-clad women played volleyball in the water. This seemed to answer my question regarding his sexual orientation, despite his dark, perfectly styled hair. And even from behind, I could tell the price of his clothing coincided with the price of his house.

"Mr. Sanderson," I interrupted, giving him my most captivating smile, "Lola Peters. I believe you were expecting me."

"Rick." He gave my appearance a quick assessment. At least he wasn't an ogler. "Let's step inside and see if we can't find someplace quiet to chat." He guided me through the house and up the spiral staircase to the second floor. He opened a door to a large room, the purpose of which I couldn't quite discern. "I use this for photo shoots," he explained. "It's easier than having to book a studio." I tried to appear in the know and up to speed on such things.

"Here's my headshot and résumé." I pulled out the documents and smoothed the creases before handing them to him.

"Why are you in such a hurry to find an agent?" he inquired, sitting on one of the only three pieces of furniture in the room. With the door closed, the thrum from the music downstairs was muted, and I wondered why he soundproofed the room.

"Well," I tried to look anxious and a little desperate, "Mr. Sanderson."

"Rick," he insisted, and I smiled graciously. I would have preferred to be able to call him suspect, but that was Alex's hang-up, and right now, I was Lola.

"Rick, I haven't worked around here," I gestured to my résumé, "but I heard the Tate Modeling Agency is having an open call on Monday. I've been dying for a chance like this all my life," I gushed, making a mental note that dying wasn't an appropriate term but made for a wonderful pun anyway. "Independent representation is my best chance to make this happen, especially since I'm not getting any younger. Plus, my uncle is always bragging about how he works for some hotshot who's dated a ton of models, so this felt like kismet. He asked around and," I tried to look humbled by being in the presence of such an important agent, "here I am."

"Here you are." He looked momentarily wolfish before going back to pleasant professional. He studied my résumé for a few moments. "Twenty-four," he commented as I stood quietly, waiting. "5'6," he scrutinized my physique, "with legs like those, you've gotta be taller than 5'6."

"I'm cheating." I indicated my heels, and he scrunched his face and considered things for a few minutes.

"Let me think about it," he said, eyeing me once more. "Is this your current contact information?" He indicated the police provided cell phone number and fictional address.

"Yes."

"I'll make a decision before Monday." He stood, stepping uncomfortably close. Maybe if it wasn't painfully apparent he was soft and out of shape, I'd feel uneasy being in a soundproofed room with him. But he didn't pose a threat, and I was clearly being dismissed. Or maybe this was the part where I was supposed to offer to sleep with him in order to get his representation. I couldn't be sure since I wasn't a model, and Martin kept insisting they weren't prostitutes. But Rick seemed sleazy enough, or maybe he just had to assess and reassess my qualifications based on a purely professional basis. Once again, I couldn't be sure, so I tried not to jump to conclusions. Lola was naïve when it came to these things, I decided. "Please stay and enjoy the party."

"Thank you." He led us out of the room and down the stairs.

Quickly, I disappeared into the throng of people, checking to see if I spotted anyone familiar, like Alvarez. An hour later, my head was pounding from the loud music, my feet were aching from the horrible heels, and if one more guy hit on me, there would be bloodshed. I went outside and waited for the valet to bring my car around and drove home.

Free from the torturous world of models and

parties, I called Heathcliff and left a message that Sanderson would probably be a bust, but someone needed to keep an eye on Lola's voicemail, just in case. Then I scrubbed the layers of gunk off my face and went to bed. I needed to make some kind of decision about Martin. The attraction was still there, buried under anger, resentment, and fear. However, our constant problem was also still there. My life was precarious, but then again, so was his.

TWENTY

The next morning, I decided to forgo witnessing Spencer's second interview at the precinct, and instead, I went for a nice long run at the park. Every little bit of exercise and toning couldn't hurt, and it provided the perfect excuse to see if Roger was staying out of sight. I looped the trail a couple of times. But the brutes weren't around, and neither was Roger. I finished mile five and headed to my car.

After a shower and a very unsatisfying whole grain breakfast bar, it was time to do some actual investigating. I got Alvarez's home and work address from the police file and went to see if an extra set of eyes could locate the bastard faster than the BOLO, which no one paid attention to. What was the point of being on the lookout when the guy couldn't be spotted?

I parked a few blocks from his apartment building, wishing I had gotten more information, like the make or model of his vehicle. His apartment was in one of the less gentrified areas of the city. The building was dimly lit, dank, and a little eerie. Of course, this was my imagination getting the best of me. The hallway was empty, but the muffled sounds of people arguing and a television blaring could be heard in the background. I knocked on his door, instinctively reaching into my jacket and placing the heel of my hand on the butt of my gun. Old habits die hard.

"Ray," I called, "it's Tammy from down the hall. I got some of your mail by mistake." No response.

I watched the shadow underneath the door to make sure there was no change in the light patterns. Then I waited a few minutes and tried again. Glancing down the hallway, I reached into my purse and pulled out my lock picks. Even though I was consulting with the police, I wasn't a cop, so reasonable cause wasn't a necessity.

Carefully, I worked the picks into the lock, making sure not to leave any obvious tool marks or other signs of a break-in. The lock popped open, and I stowed my picks. The hallway remained clear, so I stepped inside.

"Ray," I called again. If he was home, I could always lie and say the door was open, but the apartment was empty.

Putting on a pair of gloves, I quietly checked each room. There was no sign of Alvarez. The place was a mess, unmade bed, clothing strewn about, dirty dishes in the sink. There was no indication he left without planning to return. On his dresser was an envelope with cash, his watch, and some expensive looking jewelry. He wouldn't have left without the money. Obviously, wherever he was, he was coming back.

I let myself out of his apartment and relocked the door. My next stop would be Patty's bar, his regular job. Maybe someone there would know where he went. Checking the time, I wondered if it would be open yet. If it was the typical Irish pub, they should be serving lunch right about now. That idea was overwhelmingly appealing, and I realized my diet was doomed. Thankfully, I wasn't really a model.

I was half a block from my car when someone fell into step behind me. I made the conscious effort to continue walking at the same pace so as not to tip off my tail. My need for a plan was assisted by the alleyway ahead, and I ducked into it, unclipping my nine millimeter from its holster. But I kept the gun against my thigh, just in case I was wrong. My tail, a man about six foot one and a hundred and eighty pounds, turned into the alley after me, and I tensed.

"Police," he identified himself, pulling a chain from around his neck and lifting his badge from under his shirt. "Ma'am, I need to–" He noticed my gun and pulled his. "Drop the weapon," he commanded. His stance wasn't very good. His elbow was raised too high, and his hands were unsteady. His footing was off too. I raised my non-weapon hand and slowly knelt down, placing my gun on the ground before standing back up.

"Easy there, sport," I said soothingly. "I'm Alexis Parker. I'm a consultant for the police department." The guy looked uncertain. He seemed skittish, but he managed to steel his nerves long enough to reach down and collect my weapon. I must be much more frightening and intimidating than I ever imagined, and I liked it, as long as it didn't get me shot. "I'm going to reach into my purse and show you my license and permit. Don't shoot," I said it slowly but jokingly.

Luckily, it made the officer realize he had yet to holster his own weapon. No wonder these mooks couldn't locate Alvarez. They were still too green to even have proper procedure memorized. I handed him my credentials and waited as he radioed for confirmation.

"Sorry about this, ma'am," he apologized, handing back my wallet. "We were told to keep an eye out for anyone suspicious."

"Have you seen anyone suspicious besides me?" I took my offered gun, checked the safety, and reholstered it.

"It's been quiet for the past couple of days."

"Okay, keep up the good work, Officer." The sarcasm in my tone was faint, and by the wide grin that erupted on his face, it had been completely lost on him. I rolled my eyes and walked back to my car. That little incident warranted a corned beef sandwich from Patty's since it'd be a shame if a whole grain bar turned out to be my last meal.

I drove to the pub and found an excellent parking space right out front. Parallel parking, I fed the meter before going inside. The room was brightly lit to make it appear more afternoon-friendly and give the alcoholics a nice place to drink where they wouldn't feel any self-loathing for being piss drunk at noon. To be fair, not everyone in a pub on a Saturday afternoon was a drunk. There were quite a few families sitting at the larger tables and booths, enjoying a relaxing weekend.

I found a spot at the corner of the bar, so I could monitor the entire room, and asked the bartender for a menu. I ordered a corned beef sandwich with boiled potatoes on the side and a pint. They wouldn't think I was a cop if I was drinking at noon with the rest of the lot at the bar. As always, pub food was delicious, but there went any chance of eating dinner, I thought sadly. Normally, I wasn't this much of a foodie, but knowing I wasn't supposed to have it made me absolutely ravenous. It was a good thing I wasn't an addict; I'd end up dead on my first day out of rehab.

Ordering a second pint, I curiously examined the

walls. There were a few photos from various events pinned behind the bar, and when the bartender returned with my refill, I pointed to one of the pictures. "Who's that guy?" I asked, playing at some game I was making up as I went along.

"Ray," she responded. I was grateful the bartender was female, so I could play the slut card easier. "He works here."

"Damn," I whistled, "I wouldn't get much work done if he was here." She wiped the counter while I dithered on. "I think I've seen him before. He works nights, right? I haven't been here in a while, but it might have been last week, maybe the week before. Time has a habit of slipping away." I could multitask and play the out-too-often-drinking card simultaneously with the looking-to-get-laid card.

"Probably last week." She seemed more comfortable talking to me than the old men sitting on the other side of the bar who had been hitting on her every chance they got. "Ray's got another job bartending special events and parties, so he hasn't been here lately."

I made a tsk sound. "What a shame. I may be shallow, but I like my bars to have fine men and good beer." She giggled.

"He's supposed to work Monday, ten to close. I'm sure he'd love for you to stop by." She went to refill a pitcher, and I laid a twenty on the counter and left. Maybe I ought to consider raising my consulting fee.

* * *

At the precinct, O'Connell and Thompson were working on something at their desks. Heathcliff wasn't in, and Moretti's office was dark. I stood alone, assessing the board. I wrote a note, 'Alvarez scheduled at Patty's: Monday 10PM until close', and pinned it to the cork, checking to see if anything changed.

"What are you doing?" Thompson asked.

"Spending my Saturday locating our suspect," I retorted. O'Connell finished whatever he was doing and spun around in his chair. With two sets of eyes focused on me, I either needed to make a run for it or give them an update. "I went by Alvarez's place. From the looks of things, I'd say he's still in town. He left too much behind to have taken off. So I dropped by Patty's, and one of the other bartenders said he hasn't been around much because he's been working private parties, but he'll be in Monday night."

"What'd you do, torture people for this information?" Thompson looked skeptical.

"No. I ordered a few and asked some friendly questions. It's nice when you don't have to play by the rules and follow protocol all the time."

"Is that why Officer Wade radioed dispatch about some chick that pulled a gun on him?" O'Connell asked.

"Newcomers these days need to be better trained," I argued. "He follows me into a dark alley, scares the shit out of me, and then I have to remind him to holster his own weapon." I sighed for effect. "I bet it was the first time he ever aimed his piece. His hands were shaking so badly I was afraid the tremor would be enough force to cause his weapon to discharge." I was playing up the entire situation as a distraction tactic in case either of the detectives wanted to ask why I was in Alvarez's apartment building for an extended amount of time.

"You should write that down on a comment card," O'Connell suggested.

"First, you should make a complaint about the lack of comment cards," Thompson interjected.

"The two of you should take your act on the road. Get a tour bus and go city to city with your routine." I was feeling snarky since a little gratitude for the tip would have been nicer than the sass I was getting. "Did anyone get my message about Sanderson?" I asked, shifting gears.

"No calls to Lola's number," O'Connell replied. "How did your evening go?" I gave him a brief overview of Sanderson's indifference. Even though Martin wasn't able to pull any strings for us, he tried. "Heathcliff's off the rest of the day after Spencer's interview turned out to be a bust. Thompson and I are working a separate homicide, so unless you plan to solve the case or apprehend Alvarez, you can have the day off too. Just try not to scare any more of our recent recruits. Although the hiring freeze has been lifted, we still can't afford to lose men."

"Fine. If something turns up, let me know."

*　　*　　*

The rest of the weekend was spent at the park or at home, and no one called with any additional information on either the Skolnick case or the Smidel case. It was Sunday evening, and apparently, there hadn't been any calls to Lola's phone. Furthermore, Alvarez hadn't been apprehended, and no additional leads had been discovered. Tomorrow morning, the attempt to infiltrate Tate's agency would go into play, and if that failed, then the authorities would have to devise another plan. But on the bright side, I didn't spot Roger or either of the leather-clad assholes at the park, and I'd logged over a dozen miles on the trails since Saturday afternoon. Maybe it wouldn't completely counteract the fries, burgers, corned beef, and beer I had consumed, but at least I could say I tried.

Just as my consultant role began to seem pointless, Moretti phoned with information concerning the impending undercover operation. The fact that the lieutenant took the time to call made me realize this was our last chance to get answers. If all nine of us were rejected, it would be difficult to get enough evidence or cooperation to break the case. Whoever killed Skolnick had done a great job to cover their tracks and cast dispersion. Luckily, the police wouldn't reconsider Martin a suspect, but public opinion might differ. The ABC law firm might just have to deal with a civil suit, and the repercussions could be detrimental to Martin's company and his well-being. So we needed to get to the bottom of this.

Monday morning, I got up two hours before the scheduled briefing in order to do my hair and put on an astronomical amount of makeup. Wearing the same outfit I wore to Sanderson's, I hoped Tate would be more impressed by Lola than Rick was. At the precinct, I picked up a more formal version of Lola Peters' résumé, photo spread, comp card, and the fabricated catalog ads. On my way out, Heathcliff handed me the cell phone that matched Lola's contact information and wished me luck. I was going to need it.

Arriving twenty minutes early to the open call at the Tate Modeling Agency, I didn't expect to find a flock of tall, blonde, and sickly thin women taking up all the seats in the reception area. I gave my résumé and information to the secretary sitting behind the desk and wandered through the mess of silicone and stilettos. Miranda Costas was sitting on the arm of a couch, looking incredibly out of place with a short pink miniskirt and cropped top. She apparently raided the vice closet, and Taylor was on the other side of the room, similarly dressed and looking uncomfortable. At least when I was rejected, most of my dignity would remain intact.

I leaned against the wall with my hand on my hip, recalling all of Martin's suggestions. I needed to do something outlandish. Glancing around the room for inspiration, I noticed a few of the blonde bimbos tossing dirty looks my way. There was a very small part of my psyche that loved the ego boost.

Spotting a wireless camera stuck to the ceiling just above a large bookcase, I ran through the reasons for it to be there. Maybe it was for security or to monitor the animals while they were in the wild and not on their best behavior. Either way, it gave me an idea.

Sauntering to the bookcase, I stood a decent distance away to ensure I was caught on camera and dug through my purse until I found a compact. I put the compact on one of the shelves and pretended to double-check my appearance. Next, I readjusted my sweater, as Martin had done Friday night, pulling the v down so it barely concealed my bra, and then I classily readjusted my cleavage, smiled at the camera, and blew a kiss. What the hell, it was definitely outlandish. I sashayed back to the wall and waited.

Someone came out of the closed hallway next to the reception desk and asked the secretary something. Papers were shuffled around, and the next thing I knew, I was summoned to the back for an interview. As I hurried past, I caught a glimpse of Costas, and she stared with utter fascination and awe. Lola Peters was a beguiling creature to witness.

TWENTY-ONE

"Ms. Peters?" Tate asked, staring at her computer screen and not bothering to look up.

"Yes." I stood awkwardly as the receptionist shut the door. "It's such a privilege to meet *the* Yolanda Tate. You've always been such an inspiration to me." Before this case, I never heard of her, but my flattering words drew her attention. She stood up, tearing her eyes from the monitor and examining every aspect of me.

"Well, of course. That's how it is for all of my girls," she stated matter-of-factly, striding toward me with an unwavering gaze. No detail of my physique would go by unnoticed. "You could stand to lose another five pounds, maybe ten." She continued her evaluation. "At least your posture is confident, not that you have any reason to be so sure of yourself. You're not quite what I'm looking for." She scowled. "What caused those two scars on your chest?"

"Burns," I replied. The question caught me off-guard, and since I wasn't prepared, I answered truthfully. She narrowed her eyes at the discoloration as if it was a personal affront to her. Join the club.

"That's preferable to a botched boob job. I assume you're all natural since you're barely average." She was still making her assessment, and I tried to exude as much calm confidence as I could muster, even though I was rapidly beginning to feel uneasy with her unyielding stare and negative commentary. "Twenty-four." She circled like a shark that smelled blood in the water. "Older than the girls I normally hire, but you have great skin, no signs of sun damage or wrinkles. I'm sure you moisturize." Every compliment was masked in an insult or vice versa. "Do you use drugs?"

"Never," I responded, facing forward as if I were trying to infiltrate the Marine Corps.

She stopped circling and stood towering over me. She was probably five foot ten, but she was wearing stilettos too. So she was a good four or five inches taller. Reaching out, she brushed a wave of my hair back and tilted my head to the side, looking for something. Maybe signs of a facelift or graying at my roots.

"You're older, shorter, and heavier than I would like." She stepped back but continued her inspection. "I noticed your stunt in the waiting area. Clearly, you're confident and tenacious." We stood silently in the midst of our own little standoff, waiting to see who would break the silence first. "I like that."

"Thank you." I had no idea how things were going or if this was considered normal for modeling interviews.

"Don't thank me. I haven't done anything for you, yet." And the silence returned. After she completed her evaluation, she spoke again. "If I were to give you a chance, at least I wouldn't have the hassle of dealing with a representative since you have no agent. However," she returned to her desk, "Rick was kind enough to send an e-mail strongly encouraging me to give you a second look." I was surprised by this fact but held my face in a neutral position.

"He's not representing me," I added for affirmation to her previous statement.

"You're lucky he isn't." She made eye contact briefly, and her words seemed ominous. I filed that thought away. "Is this your comp card and most recent photo spread?" She indicated my portfolio which was on her desk.

"Yes." I returned to my clipped speech since she was a woman who liked succinctness. She flipped through the pictures so swiftly I doubted she even had time to process them.

"I'll tell you what, Lola, I'll keep you in mind for the next two weeks. If any work comes up that requires someone of your particular body type and features, I'll see what you can do. If not, at least you'll be able to say you had the opportunity to be considered by the great Yolanda Tate." This bitch really thought she was something.

"Oh, Mrs. Tate, thank you so much," I cooed, faking excitement with every fiber of my being.

"Please," she gestured to the door, "see yourself out. And tell Peggy to send the next girl in." I exited her office, strode down the hall, relayed the message, and headed outside. I had no earthly idea if my interview was a success or just another dead end. Confused as hell, I got into my car and returned to the precinct.

* * *

"How'd it go?" Heathcliff asked the moment I

stepped foot in the squad room. "Are you starting a new career?"

"It was brutal." I exhaled, taking a seat. "I swear it was akin to being slapped in the face after being complimented."

"Did you slap back?" He sounded worried.

"No. I honestly don't know what happened." I relayed everything Tate said while Heathcliff did his best to listen without staring down my top. I wasn't making his life any easier since I was leaning down to take off my shoes. I had packed a change of clothes and put a sweatshirt on over my low-cut top so he could concentrate on the case instead of worrying about not looking at me. After all of Tate's vicious comments, I wanted to change out of my Lola Peters get-up, but we were in the middle of a conversation. The next best thing was to layer up since taking off my clothes in the middle of the precinct wasn't professional.

"Sanderson sent her an e-mail," he repeated. He searched his desk until he found the incorporation documents for Tate's agency. It was frightening how much information was considered public record. "Apparently, he not only has some input on who she hires, but he's also a partner in the business."

"Really?" I picked up the paper and read it myself. "Doesn't it seem odd that a model's personal representative also owns part of a modeling agency? Is it just me or is that double-dipping?"

"It might be, but I don't think it'll bring us any closer to finding Skolnick's killer."

I left him to update the board while I dragged my bag into the women's locker room and finished changing into a pair of jeans, a sweatshirt, and tennis shoes. Even though it was Monday, I was all set for casual Friday. When I went back to the bullpen,

Moretti was standing next to Heathcliff, admiring our updated handiwork. I stood on the other side, waiting for brilliance to strike.

"Assuming you don't get the job," Moretti turned to me, "are there any other sources that can provide solid information? Maybe your pal, Martin, might be of some use?"

"Not in the least." I shook my head for added emphasis. "His ties to this world are incredibly limited. He couldn't even ensure an agent for Lola." Moretti sighed and went back to his office.

"Maybe we'll get eyes on Alvarez tonight," Heathcliff said, flicking the note I left about Patty's pub with his forefinger.

"Hopefully." Sitting at the empty desk across from Heathcliff's, I pulled out my notepad. "You haven't been very forthcoming, Detective," I criticized. He looked confused, so I soldiered on, reading from my list. "Did you ever determine where the knife originated?"

"It was one of the knives the caterers brought for the event. It was used to slice and dice the fruit. The mold taken from the wound track matched the knives stocked by the catering company, but the actual weapon was never recovered. Forensics checked all of them for blood, but we didn't get any hits." He opened the crime scene report. "The stabbing didn't kill her, but we've been through this a few times by now. She was suffocated."

"I know. It's just nice to have all the pieces in front of me. Since she was suffocated, did you ever ascertain where the murder weapon came from?"

He was getting frustrated with my twenty questions, but we were almost at a dead end, so the only thing to do was reassess everything. "CSU ran it down. It's a generic pillow. There's nothing fancy about it, so it could have come from anywhere. The only trace on it was Caterina's DNA and some makeup transfer. The pillow and linens were brand new. It was never slept on or used, and it won't lead to our killer."

"He's going to get away with it, isn't he?" I steepled my fingers and leaned my chin against them, trying to weave the unconnected strands into a tangible thought.

"Prayer won't change anything. Let me see if I can get a printout of the report we made concerning the surveillance feed. You remember, that was the night you left me high and dry." Who replaced no-nonsense, tight-lipped Heathcliff with this talkative guy?

"Forget it. I need to watch the damn thing again to follow my own leads. It's just how I work." He ushered me into the same small, cramped room from before, flipped on the monitors, and entered something into the computer. "Care to join me?" I asked, and he checked the time and pulled up a chair.

After four hours of watching the footage on fast forward, I noticed a few important things. Namely, Jake Spencer never ordered a drink, even though he spent a good portion of the night at the bar, waiting for Caterina. I rewound the tape and watched Spencer mingle throughout the course of the evening, talking to a few different women while he wasted time. An hour into the event, he took a seat at the end of the bar and spoke briefly with Alvarez.

"Freeze it," I exclaimed.

Heathcliff hit pause and assessed each of the four monitors. From the grainy footage, it appeared Spencer was in the midst of a clandestine hand-off with Alvarez. Either that or they were just shaking hands for the hell of it.

"I see it," he remarked. "I don't know what it is, but I see it." He made a note of the monitor number and timestamp, so the IT team could print an enlargement. "Do you think he gave Alvarez the drugs to slip to Caterina?"

"Maybe."

I reached over and hit play. Even though I watched the footage repeatedly, I didn't see any other strange behavior from anyone near or around Alvarez. The bartender never acted suspicious with anyone else or at any other time, except when Martin placed the order for two cosmopolitans.

"Isn't it weird that no one else ordered a martini all evening?" he asked. "We've seen this over and over again. Shit, I can probably tell you every drink ordered based on the glasses used. Wine, champagne, whiskey, shots, beer, but no martinis, except for Caterina."

"Are you sure?" I looked at him skeptically. It made no sense why that would be the case.

"Watch. We'll do it on fast forward, but see where the martini glasses are stacked?" He pointed to the screen. "Keep count." The party progressed at ten times normal speed, and he was right. Only Caterina's drinks were served in martini glasses.

"What are you thinking? The glasses were laced?"

"I didn't consider that, but I doubt it. She had how many before she was drugged? Three?" He did some quick rewinding. "Three. She would have been on the floor if the drugs were already on the glasses." The wheels were spinning, but I wasn't sure what he was thinking. Finally, he spoke. "If no one else was drinking martinis, they must have known what was going to happen. Maybe the order for two cosmos was what signaled the dosing."

"But there were tons of guests at the party. It was a charity event, not some all-inclusive modeling gala."

"Then Alvarez came up with some excuse not to use

the glasses or serve martinis."

"The Rohypnol must have come from the lime wedges that were pre-skewered behind the bar," I reiterated.

It would have been possible for Spencer to give the drugs to Alvarez. Then Alvarez could have slipped the packet into his pocket, and once the timing was right, poured it onto the limes and dropped them into the glasses so no one would be the wiser. It was a hard sell to prove without substantiation by one of the guilty parties.

We went back to viewing the surveillance for anyone who left the party early, and Heathcliff went to get the surveillance tapes from the marina cameras to use as cross-reference. While I waited for him to return, I gave my eyes a reprieve from staring at the monitors. We were getting closer, but we weren't there yet.

After another hour, we had created a list of guests who left the event prior to Skolnick and Martin's departure and had made enough phone calls to verify our list was reasonably accurate. The good thing about dealing with affluent people and pseudo-celebrities was they were easy to identify. There were only two names I recognized on the list, Yolanda Tate and Richard Sanderson.

TWENTY-TWO

"Okay." I was trying desperately to rub the kink out of my neck. "We have a list of fifteen or twenty people who left the party prior to Caterina's departure which took place at 12:11 a.m., according to the timestamp."

Heathcliff wrote numbers next to the names, perhaps to simplify things or because he couldn't count in his head. I wasn't sure which was more likely at this point. "Now the fun of cross-referencing begins." Sarcasm bled from his words as he pulled up the marina surveillance footage, and we stared at the screen.

It was a little easier identifying and crossing out individuals this way because we could just match up timestamps and see who left the premises and headed for the parking lot. We had knocked out about half the list in twenty minutes when my phone rang.

"Yours or Lola's?" he asked, not tearing his eyes away from the screen.

"Mine," I replied, fishing out my phone. The caller ID read L. Smidel. "Sorry, this might be important." I left the room before answering with, "Parker."

"I thought you said this issue was resolved," she shrieked. "Roger came home today with a black eye, went to his room for a few minutes, and took off again. I have no idea where he went or what caused it." Shit.

"Have you tried to call him?" I asked, grabbing my purse and keys.

"Of course, but he won't answer. I hired you to watch my son and make sure he's okay. Do you think any of this is okay?" She was back to screeching.

I shook my keys at Heathcliff's back until he turned around, and then I gestured that I was taking off. He nodded, unenthused by my sudden need to depart. "Do you have any idea where he went?" More screaming ensued. "Did he take his car?"

"Yes." Her worry and irritation were barely held in check.

"Are you at home?" I got in my car and headed for the Smidel residence.

"Of course. Where else would I be with my son missing?" I chose to believe that was rhetorical.

"I'll be there in a few minutes. Luxury cars have anti-theft tracking systems, so we'll call the company and locate Roger." She needed a clearly thought out, simple plan. I hung up and drove at breakneck speed to her house. Luckily, I didn't get stopped.

"How could you let this happen?" Her barrage of questions and accusations resumed as I entered her house.

"Ma'am," I was using my respectful, calm, federal agent voice, "I need you to get the phone and call the company, so we can locate Roger's Lexus. Can you do that?"

She obeyed and retrieved the number. After dialing and being shuffled around, I handed her the receiver, so she could give the pertinent security information to the woman on the line. Then I fudged on a few of the details and got the GPS coordinates for Roger's vehicle. I wrote them down and thanked the woman for her assistance.

"I will find Roger and bring him home," I promised, "but first, may I look around his room?" My tone was commanding but respectful. There should be an award for professionalism when dealing with shrieking, hysterical mothers.

"I don't see what wasting time snooping through his private life is going to accomplish." She was irate, but I stared unyieldingly until she gestured up the stairs to his bedroom.

Going inside, I made some quick observations. Roger had recently been in his room, but there weren't any helpful hints to discover what he retrieved. His room was meticulous with the exception of his dresser. One of the drawers was open, and his clothing was shoved to the side. Maybe he retrieved a gun, a stash of drugs, or some cash. Then again, it was possible he just wanted to pick up a clean pair of socks. Since there was no way to know for sure, I'd be walking into the situation blind. Roger always struck me as a good kid, but those jerks at the park were not. Back down the stairs, I went out the door, yelling over my shoulder, "I'll bring him home."

After entering the coordinates into my GPS, I hurried to Roger's location. I wasn't surprised to end up at the park. Finding a spot next to his car, I pulled my nine millimeter out of the glove box and grabbed an extra clip. I hooked it into my shoulder holster and threw my jacket on.

Slowly, I inspected the blue Lexus. There were no signs of anything awry. His car was just a car with no visible drugs, weapons, or paraphernalia for either.

The doors were locked, and the windows weren't broken. I took the lack of blood and damage as a good sign. Obviously, he must have come to the park willingly. Could this be nothing more than teenage rebellion blown out of proportion?

My eyes darted around as I meandered past the picnic tables, checking for any sign of Roger. He wasn't at his usual table with his mancala board, and I asked a few of the chess players if they had seen the kid. They shrugged, annoyed by my interruption.

Following the trail that wound through the park, my eyes roamed the area, and I listened for any sound that might lead to him. After I circled back to the picnic tables without discovering his whereabouts, I was running low on options. Either he was picked up from the park and wasn't here, or I'd have to venture away from the path to find him. Wherever he was, did he go willingly? Dammit, Parker, one step at a time.

I was making my way through the trees and shrubs when I heard a girl crying. Placing my hand inside my jacket, I followed the sound to a clearing. The two assailants were back, and I ducked behind a tree in order to assess the situation. If they were armed and holding Roger or the girl hostage, then surprising them would only cause matters to escalate.

The two brutes from Friday were standing to the side. One of them was holding a baseball bat, and the other was yelling at Roger. Roger was cowering on the ground, attempting to plead his case while the girl from the diner crouched near a tree trunk next to the boy I had seen her kissing that morning.

"I told you to stay away from here," the thug with the bat bellowed. "But you can't follow simple directions, can you?" He hit the ground for emphasis.

"I brought you the money," Roger insisted. "I'm not going to say anything. None of us will say anything."

The girl nodded between sobs. "Why won't you just leave us alone?"

"You should have thought about that before you ruined our business," the weaponless brute threatened. "Not only did you fuck with something that you know nothing about, but you brought some chick cop down here too." My bad, I thought. "That stupid bitch must have reported us because two days later we're getting hassled by a few lowlifes. They claimed to be dealers, but I've seen one of them before. They're the goddamn po-po." He stalked the ground in front of Roger. "You've ruined everything, you sniveling piece of shit. Now we have to figure out what to do with you." He looked to the batter to reinforce his threat.

"I promise we won't say anything," the girl cried. "Just leave us alone. You can take your business somewhere else. No harm done."

"No," he growled, "we were set up here for a reason. And since we have to deal with the consequences," he sneered viciously, "so do the three of you."

Analyzing the situation, I spotted two hostiles. One was armed with a baseball bat, and the other appeared to be weaponless. The actual clearing was an open area with no cover. However, its surroundings were heavily forested with numerous trees and shrubs. I had to move to a more practical vantage point since I could only reasonably grab one of the thugs, and it would make more sense to take down the batter.

Quietly, I unzipped my purse and pulled out the few plastic zip-ties I always kept with me and slipped them into my back pocket. Dropping my bag on the ground, I circled around the clearing, searching for the perfect position. The two ruffians were still talking amongst themselves, trying to determine what to do with Roger and his two friends.

Moving from tree to tree, I got behind the unarmed hooligan. By all accounts, he was the ringleader. I pressed my back against the trunk, hoping to remain undetected while I searched for my next cover position. Unfortunately, the boy from the diner spotted me and stared wide-eyed in my direction. Thanks a lot, kid.

One of the two brutes would eventually notice the kid's gaze, so it was time to move to plan B. Take down the leader and hope his minion didn't bash my skull in. Running out of time, I took a deep breath, exhaled, and broke cover. I dove onto the weaponless brute and pinned him to the ground, using surprise and a carefully placed knee.

"You don't want to fuck with me today," I warned. My gun was in my hand, and I pressed it against the kid's temple. The batter took a couple of steps forward, and I shifted my aim to him and used my forearm to apply direct pressure to my hostage's neck. "Drop the goddamn bat before I drop you." Wow, I was amazed at how menacing I could be. Dieting really did make me a bitch. The guy dropped the bat and considered running. "I wouldn't," I threatened, jerking the gun and indicating he should kneel on the ground. He crouched low, unsure of what to do.

Flipping the leader onto his stomach, I zip-tied his wrists and ankles in case he decided to make a run for it. He cursed and bucked but didn't get off the ground. Carefully, I approached his buddy. The batter was in the throes of fight or flight. His eyes darted back and forth as he bounced on the balls of his feet. Either he was going to make a break for it, or he was going to make a move for the bat. I steadied my aim on him, and he focused on my eyes. Whatever he saw reflected in them must have frightened him because he raised his hands above his head. I shoved him face first to the ground and bound his wrists and ankles too.

"Y'know, I asked you guys to leave this kid alone, but you just couldn't listen. Didn't your parents ever teach you to respect authority? Or your elders? Jeez." I was annoyed but thankful they complied. The last thing I wanted was to fight or chase the punks through the park. This was easier. I took a deep breath and holstered my gun. Roger's friends, the girl and boy, were considering escaping this little soiree, so I focused on them. "Don't even think about it." And they slumped back on the ground. Now what was I supposed to do with five teenagers?

"Who the hell are you? We have rights," one of the two brutes insisted.

"Yes, you do, but I'm not a cop. So we're calling this a citizen's arrest. And when the actual police arrest you, they can worry about your rights because I don't give a shit. You think dragging some kids into the middle of nowhere and threatening them with bodily harm makes you the victim of some deranged vigilante?" I snorted. "Wow. You're seriously delusional. Are you using the crap your selling?" Leaving my two subdued hostages on the ground, I crossed the expanse and retrieved my phone, dialing 911. I relayed the information to dispatch, which was sending some patrol cars to deal with the situation. "While we wait for the actual police to arrive, we're going to play a little game. It's called whoever tells the truth gets to go home without being arrested." I looked at Roger. "You go first."

"Alexis," he began, "I...er...we...you see." He was tongue-tied.

"Wrong answer." I shook my head. "You," I pointed at the girl, "what's your name?"

"Karen," she said uncertainly.

"Good," at least someone was cooperating, "what's

going on here, Karen?"

"Those two guys wanted to hurt us, but you saved us. We're the victims."

"Not quite what I was looking for." I turned to the boy next to her. "C'mon, you're a big strong guy, talk to me. I'll let you guys go home if I can get a straight answer." He looked ashen, and I suspected he was a bigger baby than the rest of the lot. Inside two minutes, he'd be sobbing and begging for his mama.

"A few weeks ago, we came here," Roger spoke up, "because a friend wanted some study aids." I raised my eyebrows and waited for him to continue. "We interrupted these guys in the middle of–"

"Shut up if you want to live," the batter threatened, and I gave him a friendly kick in the ribs.

"Continue," I urged Roger, who was still uncertain about defying the batter. "These clowns can't hurt you," I insisted.

"Bitch," the one I hit retorted. Fortunately for him, I heard sirens fast approaching. Our sharing time was coming to a close.

"They were in the middle of a buy or something," Karen volunteered. The impending threat of jail time softened her resolve to keep quiet. "We spooked whoever it was, and ever since then, they've been threatening us. Roger's been paying them every week to make up for their supplier's loss, but they keep telling us it isn't enough."

Before I had time to process the severity of the situation and the implication of her words, I heard the announcement and felt a presence surround the opening. "Police." I put my hands in the air, and the three teenagers followed suit.

"Thanks for the prompt arrival. I called in to report these two." I indicated the two bound thugs on the ground.

"We normally don't find our perps pre-cuffed," the lead cop commented.

"Alex Parker, police consultant at your service," I offered. "My gun's holstered at my side, and my credentials are in my purse." The cop took my weapon while another one rifled through my wallet, looking for my information.

"Let's take this downtown and get everything sorted out at the precinct," he told the four other officers. "You'll have to come with us, ma'am."

"Yeah, I figured as much. But can we skip the handcuffs?" I had issues being bound that I had yet to shake and scars to prove it.

"It's policy, ma'am." The responding officer looked at Roger's bruised face, the two teenagers I potentially falsely imprisoned, and the girl crying. Being handcuffed was the least of my worries.

I put my hands behind my back, cringing as the metal tightened and clicked into place. The officers escorted our motley crew to the parking lot just in time to see Detective Heathcliff pull up in his unmarked car.

"Sanchez, unhook her," he ordered, much to my relief. The officer escorting me released the cuffs, and I immediately rubbed my wrists out of sheer paranoia and a bit of PTSD. We watched as the kids were loaded into the waiting police cars. Roger and the other boy were put in the back of one cruiser. The girl got in a separate car, and the two punks were placed in a third car. "We'll meet you back at the precinct. Don't worry, I won't let this one escape. She's your collar," Heathcliff assured them as they pulled away.

"My hero," I sighed. His gaze shifted to my wrists, which I made the conscious effort to stop rubbing.

"I take it the kid didn't listen when you told him to stay away from the park." He handed me my purse off the hood of his car, where the officer dropped it. Unfortunately, he didn't leave my nine millimeter.

"His mom called and said he came home with bruises and abruptly left, but she didn't know where he went. I found him here with his two friends, and the reprobates from Friday were back with a baseball bat."

"So you decided to arrest them?" He sounded amused. "You realize you're not a cop, right? As far as I know, you were never a cop."

"Not a cop," I agreed. "I told them we'd call it a citizen's arrest."

"How'd that go?"

"About as well as could be expected. It seems Roger and his friends interrupted a drug deal or maybe a meet with the supplier. I'm not sure which, but it cost someone a pretty penny, and they've been shaking Roger down ever since."

He glanced at my car. "Are you all right?" His focus shifted to my wrists and then back to my face. I nodded. "Okay. I'll follow you to the station."

"Why? Are you afraid I'll make a break for it?"

TWENTY-THREE

My first foray into the wild world of teenage drug sales could have gone better. Although after being questioned by a few of the detectives from narcotics division and getting my ass handed to me by Lt. Moretti, I was free to resume my role as consultant on Skolnick's murder. Maybe I wasn't as expendable as I imagined. Thankfully, I wasn't arrested for assault with a deadly weapon. Sometimes, it was nice to have friends in the right places.

"I told you she can be a handful." I heard O'Connell's voice all the way from the stairwell. "Like a tornado, lots of damage and fallout, but when the pieces come together, she'll leave your head spinning." I opened the door and walked into the squad room where Heathcliff and O'Connell both turned to gawk. I had no idea what O'Connell was going on about, but I hoped it wasn't me.

"Are you done playing with narco?" Heathcliff sounded annoyed. I was definitely in the doghouse.

"I think so. You guys in major crimes are so much

more fun to be around." I was trying to behave, but Heathcliff fixed me with a hard stare and didn't comment further. He handed me a notepad with a list of names of those whose whereabouts had yet to be ascertained after they left the party.

"Re-watch the surveillance footage and see if you can eliminate any more persons of interest. When you're done, see who's left, and if it isn't too late, start checking into alibis," he commanded. "I'm going to Patty's to locate Alvarez."

"He knows you, and if he spots you, he might make a run for it."

"Don't think for a second you're going down there. Not after what happened today," he berated.

I shot a look to O'Connell, who nodded almost imperceptibly, before picking up the notepad and heading into the other room. O'Connell would either offer to check into Alvarez himself or argue the reasons why Heathcliff shouldn't. In the meantime, I wasn't giving the police department any more reasons to consider throwing me in jail. As it was, my weapon was stuck in evidence until tomorrow.

I settled down with the list and played the footage again. My mind wandered, and I hoped Mrs. Smidel was informed of her son's trip to the precinct. I was tempted to call her with an update but dismissed the idea. He was seventeen and still a minor, so the arresting officer would have to notify his mom. Plus, I was in enough hot water right now, and my week of being in her employ was basically over. At least Roger and his two friends were okay.

I rewound the feed and started over. There were five names remaining on the list. By the time I finished examining the footage, it was down to four. Every one really does count. I tried to bolster my own morale which hit rock bottom after all the negative feedback I received today, but it wasn't working. Giving up, I went into the bullpen and found Heathcliff still at his desk. Thompson and O'Connell were gone, probably at Patty's. Silently, I wrote the four names on a sheet of paper and tacked it to the board.

"Tate and Sanderson we know," he read the names, "but who are the other two?"

"I performed a quick search. Valerie Yves and Monique Webber are models at Tate's agency. All four of them disappeared down the pier instead of back toward solid ground, but the camera loses sight of them. All I can say is they each left alone." I checked the time. "It's too late to call without raising a few alarms, and I didn't think you'd want to scare off any of our suspects." He barely acknowledged my comment as he typed something into the computer. Maybe he was waiting for an apology. "Thanks for getting me out of trouble today. I appreciate it."

He stopped typing and examined me for a moment. "What's your deal, Parker?"

"I don't have a deal. I just got caught up in a secondary case, and one of the thugs had a bat. Apprehending them seemed like a no-brainer."

"Everyone's got a deal." He continued to stare, and I reconsidered my earlier judgment of his interrogational skills. When I provided no forthcoming answer, he grabbed my elbow and dragged me into one of the empty interrogation rooms.

"Really? You're going to interrogate me? Unbelievable."

"No," his tone didn't change, "but I thought you might be more apt to talk in private."

"I'm sorry, okay?" I was annoyed. "I got wrapped up in trying to get the stupid kid out of trouble. Did anyone even notify his mom? I haven't heard a word. Was he arrested?"

"He and the other two were scared shitless, but their parents were all called. And if they cooperate, they'll be fine. The two you apprehended are a different story." At least he supplied a couple of answers. "Why aren't you a fed anymore?"

"It doesn't matter, does it?" I was being guarded.

"It does if I'm working with someone who has a death wish. You went into an unknown situation alone. You take on two guys by yourself, and if I didn't hear the call over the radio, you might be in lockup right now. Do you have any idea what they do to cops in lockup? Especially the pretty ones. How can you have such disregard for your own well-being? If you get sent in undercover at Tate's agency, are you going to be just as reckless?"

"You think I'm pretty?" That wasn't the part of his speech I was supposed to latch on to, but it was the least serious response I could come up with. His cold gaze didn't waver. "O'Connell would have gotten me out," I retorted. "At least I think he would." Heathcliff shook his head, assessing me. "I'm not some suspect you get to interrogate, Detective."

"What's with your wrists?" he asked, staring at my scars and ignoring my protest. I shot daggers at him, but he didn't back down.

"Maybe I'm just into bondage." He returned my look. "Not that it's any of your business, but you get abducted, hung by your wrists, and electrocuted repeatedly, and then we can have this conversation again. I'm still breathing, so obviously, I'm not that willing to roll over and play dead." I stormed out and slammed the door.

In the squad room, I inhaled a few times to calm myself down. I wasn't sure if my erratic breathing and pounding pulse were the result of rage or the beginnings of a panic attack, but right now, we were working. There wasn't time to waste on either of these pointless emotional reactions. I used the board as a distraction and tried to make sense of all the papers, names, dates, and information, but it was a jumble. I wanted to go home.

Instead, I sat at the empty desk and began conducting background checks on Valerie Yves and Monique Webber. Ten minutes later, Heathcliff came into the squad room and sat across from me at his desk. I wondered if I didn't play well with others or if others just didn't play well with me.

"Who are you checking into?" he asked.

"Yves," I responded, not looking up from the screen.

"Okay. I'll look into Webber. If we split it up, we'll get finished in half the time."

"Fine." My tone was neutral.

An hour and numerous searches later, nothing even remotely suspicious surfaced concerning Valerie Yves. She was a naturalized American citizen originally from Canada. She had been employed by the Tate Modeling Agency for the last eighteen months and had done a few fashion magazine covers but nothing too extensive or impressive. On a whim, I typed her name into an internet search engine and skimmed through the first page of entries, but no warning bells blared.

"Yves looks clean. We'll have to question her about the party, but she doesn't have a record. There's nothing of any real interest here."

"Webber apparently changed her name, and I'm having difficulty tracking her from before. It looks like she might have some sealed records, but they might be someone else's." He tossed the pen onto the desk.

"We'll worry about it in the morning. Maybe our computer savvy officers can check into it." I stared at him. Why was he trying so hard to be talkative now? There wasn't anything left to say. "Thompson and O'Connell are at Patty's. That was a good call you made."

"Uh-huh."

"Want to call it a night?"

"Whatever." I turned off the computer and grabbed my stuff.

"Hold up," he halted me in my tracks, "I'll walk you out." I held my tongue instead of telling him where to go. Once we were outside the police station, he sighed. "I'm not good at interpersonal communication."

"People who use words like interpersonal never are." The snarkiness was back, and he chuckled slightly.

"I just want to make sure you take the necessary precautions. I won't be in the field with someone who takes too many risks and doesn't have my back. There are a million stories circulating about you, Parker. I know rumors are rumors, but it's nice to know who I'm working with."

"Don't fret," I remarked. "I don't even have a gun anymore. And no one around here trusts me to do more than watch surveillance and tack up photos, so you're not alone. I'm sure Moretti doesn't plan to send me on patrol."

"Funny," he leaned against my car as I unlocked the driver's side door, "O'Connell just got through saying how impressive you are."

"Oh yeah, I'm so impressive I was almost arrested today. Maybe you're right, and you shouldn't work with me. Why don't you tell Moretti he needs to find someone to replace Lola?"

"Parker," he got off my car and stood in front of me,

"I'm trying to apologize for overreacting earlier. I thought you might be suicidal with those scars and taking on a group of thugs in the park by yourself, but I was wrong. Are you gonna stop breaking my balls?"

I raised my eyebrows, considering his question. "Probably not." I winked and got into my car. "If they bring Alvarez in tonight, give me a call. I want to be here for that."

"You got it." He shut my door and tapped the side of my car.

TWENTY-FOUR

I poked around in my refrigerator, looking for something to eat. After my long day, first interviewing at Tate's, then running through the surveillance footage, and finally dealing with Roger's fiasco, I didn't have time to eat. One day pretending to be a model and I was already starving myself, albeit unintentionally. Finding some cold cuts and bread, I made a sandwich.

Today was rough, and I wanted to hear a friendly voice to commiserate. Briefly, I thought of calling Mark, but he was apt to point out my obvious flaws instead of letting me vent. I checked the time and phoned Martin. It was a little before eleven, and he should still be awake.

"Alex?" he asked, and I automatically smiled because of the worry in his voice, even though I shouldn't care that he cared.

"Hey, I'm sorry to call so late."

"It's okay. I was up, reviewing some merger information. What's going on?"

"It's been a long day." I tried to come up with a

legitimate reason for calling. "A really long day." My head sunk into the couch cushion, and I shut my eyes. "Do the names Valerie Yves or Monique Webber ring any bells?"

"I don't think so." He sounded thoughtful. "Should they?"

"I don't know. We're tracking leads, and they both left the party prior to you and Caterina. So it couldn't hurt to ask."

"Are you okay?"

"Yeah, I'm fine. Pretending to be a model is hell. Those girls really go through the wringer." I sighed. "I'm just tired, but as usual, there's no rest for the wicked. I should let you get back to work, but thanks for your time."

"Maybe one of these days you'll call, and it won't be business related."

"Maybe." I disconnected and lay on the couch. Kicking my shoes off, I closed my eyes. I was too emotionally drained from Tate's interview, the situation in the park, and Heathcliff's accusations to do anything other than sit in the silence and let my mind go blank.

I had been asleep for forty-five minutes when my phone rang. Picking it up, I regarded the display. "Alvarez was a no show," Heathcliff stated. "He called in sick last minute. I think he's gone. Hell, he might have left the state or even the country by now."

"I doubt it," I mumbled. I had gotten into enough trouble today, but there were a few details to divulge regarding Alvarez's apartment. "Did you get a warrant to search his apartment?"

"Yes, but I didn't do it personally. The report said they found no evidence of where he might be." Apparently, some idiots conducted the search.

"There was an envelope of money on his dresser,

along with some personal effects. He wouldn't leave town without them. What is the woman's name who has a restraining order against him?" I heard papers being shuffled.

"The order of protection was taken out by Linda Reynolds. How do you know what's on Alvarez's dresser?"

"A little bird told me," I responded, putting on my shoes. "Do you have an address for Ms. Reynolds?"

"Yep. By the way, I like the way you think." He was still on his best behavior.

"I'll be there in twenty minutes, if you can wait. Do you think they'll relinquish my gun back into my custody if I ask nicely?"

"We'll convince them. I'll see you soon."

*   *   *

It was after midnight, and Heathcliff and I were in an unmarked police cruiser, staking out the apartment leased to Linda Reynolds. He pulled some strings and got my firearm back without too much hassle. It was once again in my shoulder holster at my side. The lights were off in the apartment, but someone was still awake because the television kept flickering through the window.

"It's late," I stated the obvious. "Maybe we should come back tomorrow."

He hedged and looked as if to say *this was your idea.* "Go ring the doorbell and ask her to lower the TV." I opened the car door and got out, silently shutting it.

I was standing in front of Linda's front door, not liking his suggestion. Mussing my hair and streaking whatever mascara might still remain from this morning, I banged loudly on the door. "Chester," I bellowed, "you son of a bitch, I know you're here." I slurred my words and kept hammering away at the door. "Let me in, you bastard." Knocking over the potted plant on the stoop with a loud crash, I continued making a racket until someone came to the door. "Who the hell are you?" I spat, pretending to be a drunk, jealous girlfriend.

"This is my house." The woman standing in front of me was pissed. "There is no Chester here, and if you don't leave immediately, I'll call the cops."

"Chester," I screamed, pushing my way inside. "Chester?" A couple of toddler toys were in the corner, along with a highchair and changing table. My wailing should have triggered some crying, but I didn't hear anything.

Linda picked up a golf club and held it menacingly. "Get the fuck out of my house, skank."

I pretended to burst into outrageous sobs, apologizing profusely and insisting I had the wrong address. Thankfully, I made it out the front door with my skull still intact. Shuffling down the block and out of sight of her apartment, I crossed the street and went back to Heathcliff's parked car.

"You didn't like my TV story, did you?" he inquired as I flipped the vanity mirror down and combed my fingers through my hair and wiped the streaked makeup off my face.

"It didn't sound believable. Plus, this way, I got inside the house. She has a kid. Probably not very old, a few months or a year, but it's not there now."

"You think it might be Alvarez's?"

"It could be his, or the baby daddy could be the reason she needed the OP. Who knows? But I'm guessing, after my little stunt, she'll call her significant someone to come over and keep an eye on things."

"We're going to be here awhile." Resigned, he

settled into his seat.

We had been sitting in the car for almost an hour, staring into the monotony. Nothing changed. The television flickered, but no one showed up at Reynolds' place. I leaned my seat back and took off my jacket, using it as a blanket. If I closed my eyes for a few minutes, I wouldn't miss anything.

"The next time we do this we need to remember the snacks." I exhaled. "Or a really large thermos of coffee. Or both. Yeah," I considered the possibility of dunking a few cookies into a warm cup of coffee, "definitely both." He laughed, but his gaze never left the apartment. I never met anyone who could concentrate for such an extended period of time. "Wake me if something exciting happens."

I turned on my side, facing the door, and shut my eyes. Despite the fact I was rapidly approaching being awake for twenty-four hours, I couldn't sleep. Maybe my forty-five minute nap ruined any hope of sleeping, or the car seat was too uncomfortable, or the nagging at the fringes of my mind wouldn't let me rest. I sighed and adjusted the seat back into an upright position.

"Don't you need your beauty rest, Lola?" he mocked.

"Lola would probably be awake, running five miles and then doing yoga or something equally energetic and stupid," I grumbled, staring out the windshield, but there was still no sign of life at the apartment. I closed my eyes again and considered broaching the subject of my current mental turmoil. Without opening my eyes, I asked, "Why don't you have a partner?"

"What?" I caught him off-guard which seemed a fair turn of events after earlier.

"The desk across from yours is empty. You've been

sidled with me on this Skolnick thing. What gives?" My eyes remained closed, and I wondered if he was examining my facial expression or shooting death glares. Most likely, he was still staring at the apartment. He swallowed and cleared his throat.

"My partner took a leave of absence to find herself or some New Age bullshit like that." He sounded morose. "She came back a few months later, and we were assigned to a joint task force assisting in a child abduction case. There was a ransom demand and a trade-off." His words sounded rehearsed or memorized, like he repeated them too many times. "The deal went south, and we recovered the body. Two days later, she didn't report to work, and when I went to her place, I found her in the bathtub with her wrists slit." I opened my eyes and turned to him, but he didn't look at me. He just stared out the window.

"I didn't know." My mouth went dry. "I'm sorry." He didn't say anything more.

At least I understood the reason for his earlier confrontation. O'Connell should have warned me before I blundered around like an insensitive bitch. We stared in silence at the apartment until the sun came up, and a second team relieved us.

"Can I buy you breakfast?" he asked, his stoicism faltering slightly in the light of day.

"I thought you'd never ask."

*   *   *

We were in the back corner of a pancake joint. Heathcliff ordered steak with eggs and black coffee. I ordered a decaf coffee and a blueberry muffin. He scoffed at my meal.

"Is this the meal you're skipping in order to be model thin?" he teased. It was a relief we were back in a friendlier pattern, and he loosened up. Last night, we both made incorrect assumptions and mistakes.

"No." I picked at the crumbs on the muffin wrapper. "This is my pre-bedtime snack." I shut my eyes briefly and pushed back against the seat. "How are you still wide awake? We've been up for twenty-four hours."

"I'm used to the long hours." We finished eating and returned to the precinct. I went straight to my car, ready to go home and crawl into bed.

"What time do you want me back?" I asked.

"I'll check if there are any new developments, and then I'm going home too. Unless something occurs, take the day off. You've earned it."

Not needing to be told twice, I went home, changed, and hit the hay. I had no desire to wake before dinnertime. Unfortunately, the universe has a habit of conspiring against me. It was noon when the ringing phone interrupted my dreamless sleep.

"Hello," I asked, holding the phone to my ear. There was no response, but the ringing continued. In my sleep deprived state, it took another two rings before I realized it was Lola's phone that was beckoning. I jumped out of bed and lunged for the bothersome device, answering it milliseconds before the voicemail cut in. "Hello." I tried my best to sound awake.

"Ms. Peters, please hold for Mrs. Tate," a woman said as music filled the dead air space. Just what I wanted, someone to call and put me on hold.

"Ms. Peters?" Tate's voice replaced the horrible, pre-recorded cacophony.

"Yes, Mrs. Tate. What can I do for you?"

"Thursday evening, a party is being held in memoriam to one of my former models." She was nonchalant. "It will be an opportunity to show off the new faces at my agency, or more accurately, in your case, a possible new face at my agency. There will be backers and business types present. This is an excellent chance for you to network, and hopefully, someone will make a request for you to advertise their product." She was selling a memorial as a great business prospect. Ice queen wasn't an accurate enough term to denounce her level of coldness. "My assistant will text you the details. I would suggest wearing your most flattering dress." She hung up before I even said a word.

I dropped the cell phone and picked up my home phone, dialing the precinct. I relayed the news to Thompson, who just happened to answer. The police were going to infiltrate the catering crew and wait staff in order to get an inside look at the suspects. More than likely, the same crowd who attended Caterina's final event would also be in attendance on Thursday. After relaying the news, I climbed back into bed and tried to return to my previous sound asleep state.

I just drifted into unconsciousness when, once again, the phone interrupted the peacefulness. I cursed at whatever deity was amused by the insanity of my life. At least, my phone was ringing this time.

"Parker," I answered.

"You said you would bring Roger home. Instead, he was arrested." Mrs. Smidel was rightfully angry. "I asked you to keep him out of trouble, and you let him get arrested. Arrested. How could you let that happen?" I wondered how many more times she was going to use the word arrested.

"Ma'am," the bored annoyance I was only capable of when exhausted was creeping into every syllable, "I've been assured if Roger cooperates, he will be fine. No record. No further incidents. Nothing. Quite frankly, getting arrested was one of the more positive outcomes that could have happened yesterday afternoon."

"I don't see how that could be," she snippily replied. "How can you think having a criminal record is a good idea? His college admission could be rescinded. His entire future could be jeopardized." She was screeching again, completely appalled by my actions.

"Ma'am," I was considering hanging up, but feared she'd keep calling until I heard her out, "I don't know what Roger told you, but I tracked him and his friends to a clearing in the park. The two brutes were threatening them, and one of them had a baseball bat."

"I thought the brutes were removed."

I pulled the phone away from my ear as she continued to scream. Maybe I could take the battery out and take my home phone off the hook. Then she'd probably hire another private eye to find me, so she could scream in person.

"I will make sure Roger's name is cleared," I paused, sensing her displeasure, "pro bono. I have some useful contacts, lawyers, friends in the DA's office, cops, whatever. It will be fine. In the meantime, I strongly advise you to tell Roger to cooperate with the police should they need anything from him. The situation isn't as simple as you'd hope. He ended up involved with some shady characters, but it's being resolved."

"But." She couldn't articulate a sound argument, but she wasn't easily dissuaded either.

"I'll be by late this afternoon to discuss things further. Expect me around five." I hung up, got into bed, picked up the extra pillow, held it over my face, and screamed. I put the pillow down and turned on my side, desperate to go back to sleep.

My mind was wandering in a few different directions as one thought wisp faded into another. Did Caterina scream when she was suffocated? Did anyone hear it? If there were four other people somewhere on the pier or on a boat docked at the pier, then why didn't any of them come forward? I was drifting off again when the phone rang a final time.

"I give up," I growled, answering with a very pleasant, "what the fuck do you want?" My question was met with silence, and I was afraid to see who I yelled at. After a moment, someone cleared his throat.

"I'm sorry," Martin offered, sounding sheepish. "Um..."

"No, I'm sorry." I audibly sighed. "That long day turned into a long twenty-four hours, and dozens of harassing phone calls later, well, you get the point." I was embellishing.

"Three things," he began. "First, I did an internet search last night for those names you mentioned. I don't know them, but you have to see what I found. Second, Martin Technologies needs you to evaluate some new security hires. Jeffrey Myers will be gone for six weeks because of rotator cuff surgery and well," he hesitated, probably afraid I would yell more profanities at him.

"Kinda falls under my job duties." I dropped all resentment and bitchiness, trying to sound professional. "What time are you finishing up today?"

"Four."

"Okay, I'll be there at four to pick up the job applications for a thorough review, and you can show me whatever it is then. Is that all right?" I searched my closet, looking for something to wear.

"I'll see you later. Sorry I called."

"I wish you were the only one. Or the first one."

TWENTY-FIVE

I made a pot of coffee and sorted through everything that needed to be done. I dialed Fletcher's number since I needed legal advice and a sound game plan to pass along to the incorrigible Lynette Smidel.

"Jack Fletcher," he answered pleasantly.

"Mr. Fletcher, it's Alex Parker. I'm in need of your legal expertise, and Ackerman, Baze, and Clancy are supposed to be one of the best law firms in the city." I was laying it on thick after my bailing on their request.

"You don't think my job is completely pointless?" he joked.

"Of course not." He probably didn't believe me. "This is a purely hypothetical situation, unless of course my client expresses an interest in hiring you or your firm, and you agree to take this individual's case." Even on my best day, legalese had a habit of making my head spin.

"All right," he sounded intrigued, "shoot." I ran through Roger's entire situation or as much of it as I was aware. Fletcher made the appropriate affirmative sounds to indicate he was paying attention. When I was done, I waited patiently for his evaluation. "No previous record, upstanding member of the community, and valuable information for the police. It shouldn't take much to strike a fair deal and have any record of this either sealed or expunged."

"Okay. If I were to pull a name out of a hat, should it be yours or do you want to recommend someone else who specializes in criminal cases?"

"I can handle it, and given our recent run-in with the police department and DA's office, they might still owe us a favor or two for not filing suit against them."

"Sounds good. I will pass your card along to the appropriate parties. You have my work address, right? Just send the bill there." At least I worked on resolving one issue.

I finished the remainder of the coffee, hoping that replacing the bulk of my blood with caffeine would help me get through the day a little easier. I decided to start at the MT building, stop by the Smidels, and then go to the precinct. Maybe I could take tomorrow off since today was a bust.

Once I arrived at the MT building, I went straight to the human resources office, hoping to pick up the pertinent applicant files while I waited for Martin to finish for the day. Unfortunately, HR didn't have the files. Bored, I made another cup of coffee. There was a good chance I would never sleep again.

Standing in front of the coffeemaker, I took a few long sips from the mug and stared in the general direction of Martin's opaque glass wall. When my phone rang, I jumped. Jittery wasn't a good thing, so I put the mug down and answered the phone.

"You busy?" Heathcliff asked.

"I'm about to be," I replied. "I have to deal with

some consulting stuff, and then I'm supposed to reason with a screeching banshee of a woman. What's going on?"

"We have eyes on Alvarez. He's at Reynolds' apartment. Back-up's on the way, and when they arrive, we'll move in and take him."

"It's about damn time. What'd you want from me?"

"Just thought you'd enjoy watching him get booked and questioned again. After all, it was your idea to check out his old lady's house."

"I'll swing by after I deal with everything else, so don't wait on my account. By the way, did you hear the news about the memorial that Tate's hosting?"

"Yes, Moretti's been on the phone with the party planner and catering company. We want to get some UCs on the inside, but since we can't rule out the hired help as suspects, it has to be approved from the top. This whole thing is a total shit storm."

"I don't see why murderers can't just wait at the scene of the crime, holding the weapon with a video of the act."

"Keep dreaming of a perfect world," he retorted before hanging up.

Actually, a perfect world wouldn't have murderers or criminals. What would I do in a perfect world? Maybe I'd be a painter. Hell, who was I kidding, I'd be bored to death.

As I returned my phone to my purse, Guillot exited Martin's office. He nodded on his way down the hallway. I checked the time and knocked on Martin's door. Promptly, he buzzed me in.

"You summoned," I teased.

He glanced up from behind his desk, his brows furrowing in concern. "Are you all right? You look like hell."

"Thanks, I try." I glared at him. "Did HR lose the," I

stopped midsentence, noticing the stack of applications on the corner of his desk, "never mind." I picked up the heap of papers and flipped through them. There were maybe twenty in the pile. It wouldn't take long to narrow it down. "What are you looking for? Top five? Top three? Anyone who can do the job and doesn't have a criminal record?"

He considered his options. "Top five, by the end of the week."

"No problem." I'd find time to sort it out. It's not like I needed to sleep or anything. "You said there were three things. One down. What are the other two?"

"Come here." He scooted his desk chair over, making room so I could stand behind his desk. "I won't bite." He grinned mischievously, and I ignored him and went around the desk. "Like I said, I searched for Webber and Yves, just to verify I don't know them."

"Sure, makes sense." I was flashing back to his ramblings about the pillow. Single word answers were perfectly appropriate. Why did he qualify every word that came out of his mouth?

"There are a lot of humdrum details, pictures, ads, et cetera, et cetera." He was basically summarizing the same results I found online, so I stared at him, waiting for the point. "But I happened to stumble upon this and thought it might be relevant to your investigation."

He clicked a link, and a video opened on the computer. Valerie Yves was on screen with Rick Sanderson. The quality left a lot to be desired, but as the video played, I was extremely relieved the quality was crap.

"You need to warn a person ahead of time." I grimaced as Sanderson disrobed. Amateur pornography at its worst. "Did you watch this?" I was appalled by the entire thing for too many reasons to even count.

"Not the whole thing. Trust me, I don't want to see that. Any of that." He got up from behind his desk and went to the wet bar. "No wonder he wears nice suits. He's trying to hide all that sagging flab." He cringed and swallowed a shot. "Want a drink?"

"Maybe to wash my eyes out," I retorted, "but no."

I commandeered the vacant chair and hit play. It had been brought to my attention, so I was condemned to evaluate it for clues or who knows what else. It played on. The camera moved from time to time, indicative of a third person acting as amateur filmmaker. The upload date was the day after Caterina's murder. It might just be a coincidence, or this was where a few of the remaining four names on our list disappeared to after the party. No one else ever appeared on screen, but I couldn't help but stare at the pillow on the bed. A pillow might just be a pillow, or it might be a murder weapon.

Forwarding the link to the police department, I dialed Heathcliff and told him to check his e-mail. The boys in blue could watch, re-watch, mock, fast forward, rewind, and otherwise dissect the entire thing before I got there. I saw it once, which was already one too many times. It might be a lead on the origin of our murder weapon, but much more still needed to be determined. For all any of us knew, this could have been filmed months earlier and only hit the internet that day. When I concluded the call, I closed the browser and stepped away from the computer.

"That's what he was wearing the night of the party," Martin said from his seat on the couch. "I remember because we were both wearing similar designer suits, and he commented that the dark blue shirt I had on was a better choice than the pale green he was wearing." Again, I wondered about his obsession with clothing but kept my mouth shut.

"I don't want to know how you stumbled upon that." I gestured at the computer. "Thanks for telling me though. The IT guys employed by the police department can probably determine when it was created and things of that nature. Maybe it'll lead to the break we need." I took a seat next to him. "I know you want updates on the case, but things are moving in a million different directions. Everyone has something to hide, but the things they're hiding might be completely unrelated to Caterina's murder." I stared at the ceiling and blinked, trying to make sense of this new piece of evidence.

Martin brushed my hair behind my shoulder, and I turned and looked at him expectantly. "Was Rick's party anything like that?" His voice had an edge, and I snorted.

"No, but maybe I left too soon." I turned sideways on the couch and faced him. "I have to get out of here in a minute and deal with another client. What was the third thing you wanted?"

"I received a call this morning. It was an invitation to a social engagement in lieu of Caterina's passing." His eyes showed disdain and anger. "Can you believe that?"

"Lola got the same invite, except hers was more along the lines of 'this is a great career opportunity to strut your stuff to potential backers and advertising firms'." I narrowed my eyes, trying to figure something out. "Does your marketing department hire models for whatever it is you create and sell?" Martin Technologies was so vast. I had no idea exactly what it designed.

"Depends on the product or technology. At conventions and expos, we hire a few to showcase our latest developments, but we don't advertise in the traditional commercial sense."

"Okay." Were all the previous guests invited to the memorial, or was Tate only inviting possible backers and clients? From what I remembered, she thought Martin was guilty, so it was strange he was invited. "Any idea why you received an invite?"

"Do you think I'm being targeted again?" His expression was neutral, and I couldn't tell if he was being serious. Obviously, I had been away from him for so long I couldn't pick up on his slight nuances anymore.

"I have no idea, but the police are using it as a sting. Well, information gathering opportunity would be more accurate." I doubted anyone would be arrested at the party. "My advice as your security consultant is to stay the hell away. You've already been mixed up in this once. There's no reason to risk a repeat performance."

"Noted." His green eyes were still searching my face. "Are you okay? You sounded off when you called last night, and well, you do look like hell, if hell was a gorgeous, intelligent woman." I gave him my 'cut the crap' look. "We're friends, or at least we were for quite some time." He could be relentless. "I'm here if you need anything, even if it is just to talk."

I gave him a warm smile and stood up. "I'll be okay, and we are friends." I picked up the stack of applications, dreading my next destination. "Friday afternoon?" I indicated the papers.

"See you then."

*   *   *

I had sat through Mrs. Smidel's ranting for the last twenty minutes. Roger was next to her, looking embarrassed by his mother's outburst. I was sitting opposite the two of them, trying to keep from yawning. When she finished, or at least stopped for an extended amount of time to catch her breath, I relayed the information Fletcher gave me.

"I know this seems unfathomable," I was working on being sympathetic, "but Roger," I looked at him, "you got yourself into hot water. I don't need any of the actual details. You've put me in an awkward position because I'm consulting with the police on a major crime, but I don't want to risk losing your trust either." Mrs. Smidel looked as if she were about to begin another barrage, so I pushed ahead. "Here is the name of an attorney who is familiar with the situation. Let's just say he has a few favors he can call in on your behalf." I offered the card to her, but she remained completely still, staring at it as if it were a venomous snake.

Roger took the card and gave me an impish grin. "Can he help Karen and Oliver too?" he asked. I assumed Oliver was the boy from the park.

"He'll do everything he can, and that's one of the questions you can ask when you contact him. He's expecting your call." I stood, hoping to escape without having to endure any more screeching. "Do you have any other questions, or is there anything else I can do?" I wasn't used to dealing with non-corporate or non-law enforcement clients, so I didn't know how to conclude business.

"I still don't see how you let this happen," she hissed, and Roger rolled his eyes.

"Mom, just shut up. Alexis is trying to help." I knew I liked the kid. He walked me to the door. "Thanks. Can I call and let you know how things go?"

"Talk to Fletcher first. He'll let you know what you can and can't tell me. In the meantime, stay out of the park and keep your head down. I don't want to get arrested again because I have to save you and your friends." I winked and left before his mom could verbally abuse me anymore.

Two down. One to go.

TWENTY-SIX

The police station was abuzz with new information. The Skolnick case had gotten new life breathed into it with the apprehension of Raymond Alvarez and the discovery of the amateur pornographic film starring Richard Sanderson and Valerie Yves. As I headed toward the back corner of the room that housed Heathcliff's desk, I was amazed at how lively everyone was. The energy in the room was palatable and upbeat. It felt good to no longer be stuck in the mud.

"You're missing all the fun," O'Connell yelled on his way to the interrogation room. I fell in step behind him and followed to the observation room.

Set up in interrogation room one was Ray Alvarez. Thompson and Heathcliff were taking turns questioning him, and I came in at the tail end of the interview. A few minutes later, the interrogation was concluded, and an officer escorted Alvarez to a holding cell.

"Anything?" I asked O'Connell as we stared into the now empty room.

"Alvarez admitted to being paid off to dose Caterina's drink." He spun around to face me since nothing exciting was happening on the other side of the two-way mirror. "He claims he needed the extra cash to support his kid. Seems he knocked up Reynolds, and the two have only reconciled in the last couple of months."

"The need for an extra income and someone else to babysit tends to have that effect," I commented. "Who paid him? Was it Spencer?"

"It's refreshing to find a hopeless romantic," he quipped. "And yes, Spencer was responsible for the hand-off, which you uncovered on the surveillance tape. But Alvarez says Spencer was just delivering the message."

"Message being drugs?"

"Right on the nose," Thompson answered, having caught the last bit of conversation as he entered the room. "Supposedly, there was a note attached. It gave Alvarez a location to pick up payment for his services. I'm on my way to bring Spencer in."

"I'll tag along," O'Connell offered. "Heathcliff should be in interrogation two with the LT, if you want to watch." I went across the hallway and into the next observation room connected to the second interrogation room. Inside, Heathcliff and Moretti were questioning Linda Reynolds.

She wasn't connected to Caterina's murder. The only thing Reynolds was guilty of was spawning with a misogynistic asshole. No matter how hard they pushed and threatened, she didn't crack. She didn't know where he got his money or what he was involved in. She was simply trying to make ends meet and was more than willing to take any assistance offered by the deadbeat bartender.

Finally, Heathcliff asked about the restraining

order and any instances of domestic abuse. As predicted, she claimed it was all a misunderstanding. There were no 911 calls or hospital records to disprove her insistence that Alvarez wasn't abusive. Originally, she just wanted him to leave her alone, but nine months later, the story changed. She didn't want her child to grow up without a father and the monetary support one could provide. Despite all of Alvarez's flaws, he took care of the kid a few nights a week, and his parents did an excellent job spoiling their only grandchild.

Moretti had no choice but to dismiss her, but he warned her if there were any other run-ins with the law, her parental rights may be reassessed by the state. It was the scariest threat the police could make against a new mother. She crumpled in on herself, but she still didn't have anything useful to give us.

"Are you gonna read me in?" I asked as Heathcliff opened the door, surprised to see me.

"Nice of you to join us, Parker." He held the door, and we went to his desk. "Reynolds is clean as far as we can tell. She seems clueless. And Alvarez is his pleasant self. We have him in holding until we figure out what exactly to do with him. We're waiting as long as possible before we book him as payback for the week spent tracking him down. According to Reynolds, Alvarez stays with his parents when he's babysitting, so he's allegedly been there the entire time."

"Someone's investigative skills are slipping," I teased, earning myself an icy look.

"He's insisting Jake Spencer gave him the drugs and a message to lace Caterina's drink. The envelope of money the bird told you about," he looked at me curiously, "is what he was paid for drugging her. He's a real brain trust, though. He believed the drugs were recreational, and he had no fucking idea they would be used in the commission of her murder. Regardless, if the DA wants to push, they can pursue felony murder charges."

"Brilliant defense." Alvarez's stupidity pissed me off. "With logic like that, he could have poured cyanide in her drink."

"Be thankful it was only a roofie or else we'd have two bodies in the morgue." That one hit too close to home, and a shiver traveled through me. I needed to get over my hang-up when it came to Martin's safety. "Sorry." He reconsidered his statement after watching the blood drain from my face.

"Thompson and O'Connell are bringing in Spencer now." I was moving the story ahead. "Any updates on the amateur porno I sent you?"

"Tech's working on determining the IP address, so we'll have the physical location where it was uploaded from. Hopefully, we'll get a date and time of its creation too." He exhaled. "It'll take some time and patience, and Moretti's warned us not to rush the tech department. Apparently, we've been looking over their shoulders too often." He adopted a sly grin. "However, from a preliminary evaluation of the video and background noises, it was filmed on a boat."

"Sanderson's?" That vile video might just get me excited, after all. "Did you see the pillow?"

"Oh, yeah. We're hoping it will be enough for a warrant." It was a relief that we were finally making progress. "How'd you find the video?"

I laughed bitterly. The last thing I wanted was to implicate Martin or bring him back into the investigation, but there was no use in hiding the truth. "I didn't. It was brought to my attention after I questioned someone about his familiarity with Tate's models."

"James Martin?" Heathcliff asked, even though he knew the answer.

"Yep. Just so you know, he was also invited to Tate's event this Thursday. I don't like it."

"You don't have to like it." The wheels were turning in his head, causing an uneasy feeling to settle in the pit of my stomach.

I didn't know why I was suddenly apprehensive, but my gut reactions tended to be right more often than not. Before I could determine the cause of my nervousness, Moretti opened his office door and barked at us to join him inside.

"Parker," he gestured to the empty chair in front of his desk, "normally, I'd be pissed by some outsider showing up my police force, but you've been helpful here, so thanks." I remained silent, waiting to see where this was going. "I've made arrangements for O'Connell, Thompson, and Jacobs to go undercover Thursday night as caterers. Obviously, Lola will be making an appearance. I wish some of our vice girls made the cut in order to back you up, but needless to say, we'll have people around. We need you to discover everything you can regarding Spencer, Alvarez, Sanderson, and that woman in the video. What's her name?"

"Valerie Yves," Heathcliff supplied.

"Yves, right." Moretti looked determined that answers would surface. "Someone's bound to know something. All we have right now is Spencer passing the drugs to Alvarez. We still need to determine if he was acting alone or on behalf of someone else. Since he didn't pay Alvarez straight out, he might have passed the drugs along on behalf of a third party, and we still don't know who suffocated and stabbed the vic." He shifted his gaze, and I hoped my turn was over. "Heathcliff, you've been the face of this entire investigation, so you're coordinating things from the surveillance van. With any luck, IT will get some useful information from the porno, and we will ascertain the filming location, maybe see if anyone else gets implicated, and track down the origin of the goddamn murder weapon."

"Aye, sir," he agreed, and briefly, I wondered if he served in the military or if he was just this polished and stiff from taking police work too seriously.

"Okay, kids, get back to work," Moretti dismissed us. His brief speech was strange, but maybe this was his way of keeping his staff up-to-date.

Heathcliff and I spent the rest of the night waiting for the tech team to give us some hard evidence. In the meantime, Spencer was brought back to the police station for his third interview. At last, we had something substantial to throw at him. Heathcliff was annoyed to think he'd have to deal with more tears and regret, but Spencer manned up, much to Heathcliff's relief.

As Nick and I stood in the observation room, watching the interview, he asked, "Are you up for some undercover work?"

"I'm overjoyed," I replied sardonically. "How 'bout you? Are you renting a tux to pose as a caterer?"

"I'm bartending since it doesn't look like Alvarez will be working this one. The LT also thought it'd be a good idea to ensure the safety of all the guests this time. Just imagine the news article, *guests poisoned during police operation.*"

I couldn't help but laugh, despite the morbid, gallows humor. "Good call." We fell silent when Heathcliff slammed his fist on the table, causing Spencer to jump in fear. He'd break. I was sure of it. "Do you think the internet porn is going to be any help?" I turned my back to the two-way mirror and faced O'Connell.

"Our murder weapon is in plain sight, so it ought to be enough to get a warrant once we determine the location of the film or the identity of the person who uploaded it. Unfortunately, we can't go after Sanderson straight out, or he might claim to be an unknowing participant, and his team of lawyers would be all over us."

"I hate how manipulative affluent people can be."

"Hey," his voice was sharp, "be thankful. If Martin didn't have resources and friends in high places, this case might have closed two weeks ago with him in lockup. The system might be flawed, but at least this time an innocent guy isn't taking the fall."

I lowered my voice and double-checked there was no surveillance equipment set up in the room. "He didn't do it, and he never should have been brought in as the murder suspect. But it was his yacht, and now, after he found the film on the internet, if I didn't know him or the circumstances, maybe I'd..." I didn't finish my thought. He wasn't guilty, but his helpfulness could get him into trouble. I wanted Nick to reassure me this was not the case.

"Any of us could have found the porno. Don't start playing defense attorney in your head. That's the DA's job. Not yours."

"Damn law school fucked me up more than I care to admit."

He chuckled. "I tend to overlook the fact you were a federal agent with your fancy ass background. I always think of you in a gritty, get your hands dirty way."

"Thanks," I gave him a genuine smile, "I appreciate that."

Heathcliff barged into the room, slamming the door. O'Connell and I turned and watched him stalk the enclosed space for a few moments, getting his anger in check. "Son of a bitch won't answer any more questions without his lawyer. I'm done."

"Good, he's scared," O'Connell offered. "Let's stick him in holding until morning. His lawyer won't show up this late." It was one of the tricks of the trade. We couldn't touch Spencer without his attorney present, but maybe he would rescind his request after a few hours downstairs. "Just make sure you keep him isolated and away from Alvarez."

"No shit," Heathcliff growled, still miffed.

*   *   *

We were updating our theory board when the tech department phoned Heathcliff's desk. The background noise and subtle vertical camera motion were both indicative of a water-based location, such as a boat or yacht. The file was created Saturday morning at 1:01 a.m., possibly minutes before Caterina's murder. The only hitch was the IP address was heavily encrypted and beyond the capabilities of the local PD. They would have to farm out the work to a federal agency or the larger state investigative unit if they wanted a location.

"Time just isn't on our side," Thompson muttered.

"I'll make some calls." Propping my legs on top of the desk, I was tired, aggravated, and now I had to call the OIO and beg for a favor.

"Jablonsky," Mark answered.

"Hey, Mark." I tried to sound pleasant, particularly since I hadn't been very nice to him recently. "Do you owe me any favors?"

"Nope." He was playing hardball. "If you want something, you're going to owe me. What do you need?" I explained the internet video situation.

"Sounds like you're in a jam."

"Can you help or not? Keep in mind the reason I'm working this." Maybe I could pass the favor owing off to Martin since it was his fault. I sat silently, waiting for a response, and Heathcliff motioned to tone down the bitchiness.

"If it were me, I'd help," Mark offered. "But you're asking for Bureau resources on a local police thing. It's above my pay grade. You'll have to talk to Director Kendall."

"Fuck me," I griped and heard an amused snort from someone nearby. "Is he still there?"

"No. He left at five when most people go home since he doesn't have to stay in the office, catching up on paperwork."

"See, that's reason number four to join the private sector." I let out a frustrated sigh. "I'll call first thing in the morning. But if he can't help, we'll be forced to source this out, and it could take weeks. Can you at least put in a good word or pave the way?"

"Of course," he sounded genuine. "Call at eight-thirty so I'll have time to grab a hold of him."

"Thanks. I guess I owe you." I hung up and relayed the information to my police brethren. They all seemed optimistic. I would have been more enthused if I knew we'd get a positive response without a quid pro quo.

I spent the rest of the night in the police station, ironing out every new detail, charting the new connections, and seeking new leads and suspects for Skolnick's murder. The paperwork for a warrant on Sanderson's boat was already in the works, but we wanted to rule out any uncertainty to avoid looking like we were fishing for evidence. There was so much information going in too many directions that I couldn't wrap my mind around any of it. The outside noise was blaring too loudly for my rational thoughts or gut instincts to be heard over the information overload.

Pressing my cheek against the cool surface of the desk, I tried to recall who decided to pin strings connecting suspects to evidence as an overlay on our theory board. The spider web pattern was making me dizzy. We had fleshed out as much as possible in the last twelve hours, but we were still missing the biggest parts of the puzzle.

"I take it you didn't get to sleep in yesterday," Heathcliff commented, putting a steaming mug of coffee down next to me.

"Did you?" I picked it up and inhaled.

"Probably more than you. It's seven a.m. Just another hour and a half until your scheduled call. After that, go home and get some sleep. You're working tomorrow night, and you need to look like a believable twenty-four year old and not a re-animated corpse."

"It's not tomorrow night. The party is Thursday night."

"Today's Wednesday," he said patiently.

"Right."

I sighed, drank the rest of the coffee, and otherwise remained useless for the next hour and a half. At eight thirty, I called Director Kendall and requested his assistance. He graciously offered the use of Bureau resources, but it was too easy. This would come back to bite me in the ass at some point.

"We'll send our tech staff to deliver it and offer to assist on the information recovery," Heathcliff insisted. "Now go home."

TWENTY-SEVEN

It was mid-afternoon when I awoke. Sleep had given my subconscious time to process everything, and the comforting gnawing returned, reassuring me we were getting closer to putting the pieces in order. I lay in bed, staring at the ceiling and thinking about the facts.

Why would Jake Spencer want to drug his lover? Obviously, Caterina had a voracious sexual appetite, based upon their brief interlude in the ladies room, so why slip her a roofie? Spencer was absolutely miserable during the first two interviews when confronted with the crime scene photos, but he gave the drugs to Alvarez. Was Spencer jealous that Caterina would pick someone else up at the party? But dosing the drinks wasn't an appropriate form of revenge because it left numerous unpredictable variables. We had proof Spencer handed the drugs to Alvarez. Hell, we even had Alvarez's statement and the envelope of cash, but Alvarez wasn't the killer since he was working well past the time of death. Who else had motive?

Both Richard Sanderson, porn star extraordinaire, and Yolanda Tate left the party at an appropriate time to kill Caterina. The cash in the envelope would have been pocket change to either one of them, but they stood to lose a lot by her death. Sanderson was her agent and making a cut from her work. Tate, on the other hand, insisted she was out thousands on the upcoming scheduled photo shoot Caterina had booked, but there was also the insurance policy. I didn't have the actual numbers in front of me, but maybe Tate would break even or profit because of Caterina's demise.

I got out of bed and took my time getting ready. I rummaged through the kitchen, preparing an extremely late breakfast or early supper. At this point, there wasn't much of a difference. As I pulled some silverware from the drawer, my mind drifted to the knife used to stab Skolnick. It could have been grabbed off of a tray or from the kitchen by any of the guests or servers. Without finding the actual blade, there would be no way of knowing who took it.

Everything rested on the pillow. Assuming the pornography was filmed prior to Skolnick's murder and the pillow in the video and the murder weapon were one and the same, then the assailant had to be Sanderson, Yves, or our mysterious filmmaker. Picking up the phone, I dialed the OIO and requested to speak to one of the techs assisting the local police. I asked if they had narrowed the time of the actual filming, or if they could get any angles or reflections which might indicate the identity of the off-screen third party. Since I owed a favor, I might as well get as much as I could out of the trade. Unfortunately, they were still processing the footage, and it would be at least several hours, if not days, until they had something usable.

I ate while working on a list of suspects, motives, and opportunity – the holy trinity of crime. From the list we compiled, only four individuals had the opportunity to commit the crime, but the reason for the killing left a lot to be desired. I needed to start at the beginning and work forward. Lola would have to find out everything she could about Jake Spencer's connection to Caterina Skolnick. This was where everything began, and with any luck, it would lead to our culprit. It also wouldn't hurt to get as much juicy gossip as humanly possible on Valerie Yves and Monique Webber just in case. After all, Yves was on film with Sanderson, and we still hadn't pinned down the whereabouts of Ms. Webber, if that was her actual name.

Once I finished eating, I went back to the precinct. Surely someone had some insight to share. The squad room was much more subdued. Moretti's office door was closed, but through the blinds covering his small window, three other people could be seen inside his office. O'Connell and Heathcliff were nowhere to be found, so I took my usual seat at the vacant desk and waited for Thompson to get off the phone.

"Do you have anything on Monique Webber?" I asked after he hung up.

"Yes." He passed me a printout. "Nothing conclusive. She's a small town girl who moved to the big city to start a modeling career and changed her name to something more marketable. No criminal record. Whatever Heathcliff was looking at was for a Monica Webber, not Monique. Damn auto-correct." Thompson wasn't normally the type to deliver a soliloquy, and I wondered what provoked it.

Moretti's office door opened, and Heathcliff came out, glancing at me as he shut the door behind him.

"What are you doing here?" he asked in a not-so-friendly tone.

"Brilliance has struck." I was undeterred by his brusqueness. "Our assailant has to be one of the four who left the party. And I've been considering what Spencer's motivation was for drugging his lover, but nothing I've come up with makes any sense."

"His lawyer showed up this afternoon for the official interrogation," Heathcliff began, walking to the coffeepot and remaining next to it, so I had to turn around to face him. "Looks like the hotshot photographer's been around the block a few times, and he wants to make a deal."

"For what?" What valuable piece of information would he have?

"We're still working out the finer points, but it's my understanding he can implicate someone else as passing the drugs to him."

"What the hell is this, middle school?" My good mood was rapidly turning into frustration. "It wasn't really mine. It was his." I rolled my eyes.

"Did you want to go upstairs to narcotics and see if they've made any progress on your other case," Heathcliff offered out of the blue.

Something was up. Everyone was acting off. I swiveled in my chair to glance at Thompson, and as I turned, Moretti's office door opened, and I caught sight of a familiar tailored overcoat still inside. O'Connell emerged and met my eyes. His expression was guilty as sin.

"Parker," he acknowledged, scurrying behind his desk, perhaps afraid I would explode, but I was preoccupied, staring at Moretti through the still open door as Martin shook his hand.

"We really appreciate your help, Mr. Martin." Moretti led him to the door. "Our people will be covering the entire event, so your safety will be guaranteed." Martin nodded and stepped out of the office. He didn't even have time to register my presence before I was out of the chair.

"Mr. Martin, a word. Now," I barked, storming to the double doors. In the precinct, there weren't many places that afforded privacy, so the small area between the two sets of double doors would have to do.

"Ms. Parker," he sounded professional, acknowledging my command as if it were only a request and following me.

I waited for the doors to close and spun around to face him, glaring through the window at any nosy onlookers. "What the hell are you doing?"

"Lt. Moretti called." His eyes danced ever so slightly. I think he was enjoying irritating me. "The police department has requested my assistance. It seems they think I might be instrumental in identifying the assailant. Looks like I'll be at the memorial tomorrow night, after all."

"You're a civilian." I tried to keep my voice low. "You can say no. You should say no."

"What fun would that be?" He smirked. "It'll be fine. Cops will be crawling all over the place, and you're going to be there."

"I'm working undercover." I spoke slowly to aid in his comprehension since he clearly had the mentality of a two-year-old. "Did you not hear me tell you to stay away from this?"

"But you don't work for me." He cocked an eyebrow up. "Remember?" I paced the small space in front of him. He was back to unilateral decision-making and being completely unreasonable.

"Why are you doing this?" From past experience, I knew arguing wouldn't help.

"The police are hoping it might jog my memory. Maybe I've forgotten an important detail, or I might recognize someone I failed to remember. They're confident they're close." I never should have admitted he discovered the internet video. "Am I wrong to assume the reason they're this close is because of you?" He smiled, watching as I accepted defeat.

"Take Bruiser with you and do not leave his sight. Not even for a second."

"Okay, no problem," he responded nonchalantly.

"Promise me. Please." I hated pleading with him.

"All right, Alex. I promise." His tone shifted to something softer. He narrowed his eyes, tilting his head to one side and assessing me. Not giving him time to complete his analysis, I turned on my heel and went back into the bullpen. Some of us still had work to do, regardless of the monkey wrenches being thrown into the mix.

"Were you going to tell me?" I asked Heathcliff. "Or were you going to let me be surprised tomorrow night just to see how well my undercover act works with some added stress and additional guests?"

"You're consulting here. You don't need to concern yourself with that situation." He gazed at the doors, making sure Martin left, and I threw a glance at O'Connell, who immediately avoided my eyes.

"Whatever," I huffed. "I called the OIO this afternoon and asked if they could check for a reflection that might provide us with an identity for the camera operator. Optimistically, they'll have the IP and everything soon." I tried to focus, even though I felt betrayed. "There isn't much to do in the meantime. Tomorrow evening, I'll try to dig up some dirt on Spencer, Webber, Yves, Sanderson, and Tate. Are there any other miracles you need me to work in my spare time?" I was feeling particularly bitter and sarcastic at the moment.

"Seems you've pretty much narrowed it down to our most likely suspects," Heathcliff complimented. "Now all we need is something concrete or enough substantiated information to obtain warrants to get the hard evidence. Maybe Mr. Martin will turn into a valuable asset if he can recall repeat guests or seeing someone do something he might have dismissed or forgotten. Worst case, he could confront Sanderson about the adult video and see what shakes loose since he's not a cop but just a curious internet searcher."

I bit my lip to prevent my forthcoming response. Swallowing, I got up from the chair. "Clearly, you have things under control, so I'm going home."

*   *   *

My actions were on auto-pilot as I drove to my office. I wasn't paying any attention, and when I pulled into the parking lot, I wondered how I got here. I went inside, checked the mail and messages, and sat behind my desk. It was dark out. Somehow, it was almost eight, and I suspected sleeping through most of the day had something to do with the lack of daylight hours.

Since I was here, I might as well get some work done. Retrieving the MT security applications from my car, I began reviewing them by entering names into the criminal databases and checking other pertinent job and career claims. Half of the applications were thrown into the nay pile based on lack of experience. Since no one had a criminal record or murky past, I had to base my decisions on skills and experience. Was military service a preferential factor? It indicated familiarity with weapons, tactical training, and an ability to obey orders. Maybe Martin should enlist so he could learn how to listen to other people and follow directions.

I continued reading and rereading the applications, slowly whittling the list down one applicant at a time. There were seven left when my phone rang. "It'll be fine," O'Connell said. The radio was playing in the background, and I imagined he was on his way home. "I would have warned you, but I didn't find out what the LT planned until ten minutes before Martin showed up." I rubbed the bridge of my nose, trying to think of something to say. "Are you still there?"

"I don't know what I'm supposed to do, Nick. I can't pretend he isn't there, but I can't ignore everything else in order to keep an eye on him. He shouldn't be there. Honestly, what good will it do?"

"It might shake any remaining suspicion off of him," he responded quietly. "Just think of the press coverage afterward. Millionaire CEO helps catch killer, details at eleven." He adopted an announcer's voice.

"I've seen him almost bleed out." My voice shook slightly. "How can I not worry about him being targeted by Skolnick's killer? Even if we're getting closer to pinpointing the killer's identity, we still don't know who it is. Anyone could do anything to him tomorrow night. It doesn't matter how secure the place is or how many guys Moretti has working. You know that, and I know that."

"Alex, if you don't remember, I know exactly what went down the first time. I was the one who radioed the paramedics and secured the area, so they could work on him. We both had his back then, and tomorrow night, everything will be fine. I'll be at the bar, and as long as he takes a seat and keeps drinking, you won't have anything to worry about. He's important to you, and I won't let anything happen to him."

"I feel like I constantly owe you." My voice contained the hint of a smile.

"I'll add it to your tab," he teased. "We're close to ending this. I can feel it."

"Me too. I just wish it'd be over before tomorrow night." Maybe some of Martin's initial paranoia rubbed off on me, and I was acting irrationally. But until the murderer was apprehended, I didn't want him schmoozing with any potential suspects. Too bad no one ever took my advice seriously.

TWENTY-EIGHT

I was sifting through my closet again. It was a memorial of sorts, so black was the most appropriate color choice. It was also slimming, stylish, and one of the predominant colors I owned. I found my classy little black dress and tried it on. It was a basic spaghetti-strap number which fell at an angle around mid-thigh. The only downside was I needed to imitate a makeup artist to cover up the nasty scar on my left leg which became visible whenever I sat down.

Two hours later, I was ready to go. I had enough makeup caked on to make clowns envious, but I could pass for twenty-four to the slightly inebriated. My hair was curled and clipped, allowing the long brown locks to cascade down my back. The insanely high heels I selected made my legs look long and might convince the same inebriated person I was tall enough to be a short model.

Packing an extra set of clothing, tennis shoes, and toiletries into a duffel bag, I wanted the option to change and wash up once the evening was concluded.

With any luck, a few arrests might be made or enough evidence would surface to serve a few warrants. This meant there was a good chance I'd end up back at the precinct, working through the night, and I didn't want to do that in a skimpy dress and heels. The guys already teased me enough about being a model.

Stowing the bag in the trunk of my car, I drove to the police station, planning to have a taxi take me to the party. It might appear suspicious if a model wannabe arrived in a homely subcompact, especially since it was an open bar. But in the meantime, I had a briefing to go to.

Moretti ran through the basics. Jacobs, Thompson, and O'Connell would be positioned inside. They were lucky enough to be given earpieces and radios, so anything I had to report would go through one of them. Heathcliff and Moretti were going to be parked outside in a nondescript surveillance van. The nondescript part always made me chuckle since it was in and of itself a description.

The goal was to evaluate the guests for suspicious behavior or activities and hopefully uncover something useful. Realistically, it was an experiment in fishing, and James Martin might just be the bait. With any luck, between Bruiser and O'Connell, the fish wouldn't get the opportunity to harm the worm.

"Everyone clear on what's going on?" Moretti asked, and there was a round of nods and affirmatives. "A back-up team will be on standby in case anything goes haywire." He looked at me when he said this. "However, since Jake Spencer and Ray Alvarez are still in custody, neither of them had the opportunity to clue in our other suspects, so no one should realize anything is off. Good luck, guys."

"I'll see you there," O'Connell called, climbing into his personal vehicle. I watched him pull away and saw

Thompson and Jacobs get into the same car, forming the bond of the cater-waiter.

"You look nice," Heathcliff complimented, checking the equipment in the van. "Do you have an actual game plan?"

"Wing it and hope no one dies."

He stopped what he was doing. "Are you still pissed?"

"Not so much." It wouldn't do any good to hold a grudge. "I just hate being stuck between a rock and a hard place."

"We didn't know it'd play out this way," he offered. "Nine times out of ten, your corporate boss wouldn't be involved with your law enforcement gig. It's just a fluke, but remember, we're in the business of catching criminals. Prioritize accordingly."

"Story of my life." I snorted and used Lola's phone to dial the cab company. "I guess I'll walk a block and grab a taxi. Do you think Lola's gonna be safe in this neighborhood?"

"She'll be fine. Alexis Parker's watching her back." He winked and shut the van doors. Game on.

*   *   *

Lola arrived on time to the party. As I walked into the banquet hall, I was immediately greeted by the large-scale, blown-up photo of Caterina Skolnick covering the front wall in the foyer. It was from one of her most successful modeling campaigns, and the eight foot enhancement reminded me of the 1958 poster for *Attack of the Fifty Foot Woman*. I stood mesmerized by Skolnick's beauty and the sheer size of the image.

"Ms. Peters, I see you made it." Tate's voice permeated the air with icicles as she circled me.

"Classic choice. I approve."

"Thank you." I tried not to sound annoyed.

"Well, don't just stand there like an outsider. Let's get you networking." She led me inside and briefly introduced me to various partygoers as we made our way to the back of the room.

O'Connell was behind the bar, doing his best *Cocktail* impression as he poured a martini into a glass for an older gentleman. I wasn't sure where Thompson or Jacobs was, and I had yet to locate Martin. He was generally very punctual, but it was a Thursday night. Weeknights were a workaholic's wet dream.

"Girls," Tate said it with such force she could have been a ballet teacher calling the dancers to the barre, "Val, Monique, Bettina, Carmen, Seline, this is Lola. I'm still deciding if she's cut out for this lifestyle." Her tone didn't sound convinced or enthusiastic. "Introduce her around if you get a chance."

The group of barely twenty-somethings was all ridiculously tall. They wore trendy dresses with short skirts, low-cut tops, and stiletto heels. If we threw the lot into the pool, there were a few that would have no fear of drowning due to the floatation devices strapped to their chests. It was painfully obvious I didn't fit in with this crowd, but for some reason, I was invited. With any luck, tonight would be the last time I'd have to blend in.

"Hi." I smiled, recognizing Valerie Yves and Monique Webber from the surveillance feed, but the others I couldn't place.

They all silently judged as they sized me up, and then they seemed to reach a collective conclusion. Maybe they shared a single, unified brain, and Tate was their queen. Talk about hive mentality.

"Kinda short and athletic looking, maybe you could

get some workout ads for sports equipment," one of the women offered. "Monique, why don't you take her to make the rounds?"

"Whatever." Monique wasn't happy being nominated, and the other four quickly dispersed. Was cattiness a qualification for modeling? Maybe my friendliness would ruin my cover story.

"Don't worry about it. I'll make my own introductions." It wouldn't be easy getting information from an unwilling participant. "I wouldn't want to be stuck with some newbie either."

"Who do you know in this industry?" she asked, leading us in an indeterminate direction.

"My uncle works for some CEO, Martin something or something Martin. I don't know," I shrugged, "but he put a word in with Rick Sanderson, and then he put a word in with Mrs. Tate."

"You know Ricky?" She instantly warmed at the mention of Sanderson. "Isn't he just the sweetest thing?"

"An absolute doll. I only met him the one time, but he's such a great guy." I forced the disgusting, disturbing images out of my mind.

"He's been my agent for years. I worked a lot of jobs solo, like catalog ads and stuff, but a few months ago, he got me on at Tate's. It's been one callback after another. I think, between the two of them, they must know everyone."

"Awesome." That was a twenty-four year old thing to say.

Monique introduced me to a couple of marketing and advertising people we passed. Mostly, they nodded and stared, but no one offered either of us a job or their business card. Maybe that's not how things were done. She didn't find any of this strange, but she seemed a little airheaded and naïve.

"Did you know Caterina Skolnick?" I asked as we neared the larger-than-life photo.

"No," she looked up at the picture, "we were both at Tate's, but our work schedules never overlapped. Maybe I passed her in the hallways once or twice when we got new headshots or press pictures made, but that was about it. We never really connected."

"Wasn't she dating that guy?" I paused. "What's his name? The photographer. Super cute, um..."

"Jake," she offered. "You might want to stay away from Jake. He dates a lot of the girls. Well, like all of us."

"Oh." That caught me by surprise, and I wasn't sure how to play it off. "Did you and he ever?"

"Three times." She thought back, grinning at the memory. "There is something incredibly irresistible about him, but he's trouble." She was back in gossip mode. "I hear he can be a real heartbreaker, but it's totally cool if you're just looking for a hook-up."

"I'll keep that in mind." I spotted Valerie Yves going into the ladies room. "Be right back. I want to touch up my lip gloss."

Taking a spot in front of the sink, I washed my hands and pretended to assess my appearance in the mirror. Yves emerged from the stall as I was drying my hands with paper towel. She scowled and sidled up to the adjacent sink.

"You look out of your element," she commented, scrutinizing my appearance. "Parties aren't your thing?"

"Not this early in the evening," I supplied.

"Want a hit?" she asked, opening her purse and pulling out a small vial containing your garden variety cocaine. Apparently, nothing about me screamed out law enforcement. Mission accomplished.

"Not this early in the evening." I laughed.

She shrugged and dug her manicured fingernail into the vile and snorted. "Suit yourself." She wiped her nose and checked her appearance. "Lolita?"

"Lola," I corrected.

"Right," she nodded slightly, "I guess it doesn't matter. You won't be around much. No offense, hun, but you're not what they want. Hell, I'm not what they want either. You either have to be blonde and blue eyed or something foreign and exotic. We're neither." She was jaded, not that I blamed her.

"Do you have an outside agent?"

She scoffed at my suggestion. "Tried things out with Rick the Dick, but that was a total bust. He offers to get my name out there, wants to show the world who I am, and instead, I'm still working these fucking cocktail parties, trying to find advertisers who want to market my face or body for their products." Someone was angry.

"Rick Sanderson?"

"Yeah, what other Rick the Dicks are there?" Her tone was scornful.

"Well, maybe Mrs. Tate can find better opportunities for us." Hopefully, lumping myself into the same category would solidify our bond and get her to open up. Obviously, she had a lot to say.

"Don't fool yourself." There was nothing but disdain in her voice. "The only one of us she gave a shit about was her beloved Caterina, and now that she's gone, the rest of this place is going to end up just as lifeless."

I pulled some mascara from my purse and reapplied to buy some time. Yves was making this job too easy. She had been jealous of Caterina, displeased with Tate, and angry at Sanderson. The anger was understandable given the internet video, and I considered broaching the subject but was afraid to push too hard this soon. I put the makeup away and raised an eyebrow, hoping she'd continue, but instead, she shoved the bathroom door open and walked out.

After she left, I exited the ladies room and discovered my previous pal abandoned me. Oh well, being solo made it easier to snoop. Plus, I had gotten more in the last hour than I ever imagined. I headed toward the bar to see how things were going for the undercover cops. On my way, I spotted Bruiser standing near a potted plant, sipping something that looked like vodka but was probably water. I 'accidentally' bumped into him.

"I'm so sorry," I said loudly, brushing the water off his jacket. "Make sure he never leaves your sight, got it?" I whispered.

"That's fine. You have a lovely evening, miss." He failed to conceal the amused smile. If Jones was here, Martin had to be close by.

Determined not to let Martin's unseen presence derail me, I continued to the bar when a voice stopped me. "Ms. Peters, so lovely to see you again," Sanderson greeted as I turned, and he casually embraced me. "I put in a good word for you. I'm glad to see Yolanda listened."

"Thank you so much, Mr. Sanderson. I'm only here on a temporary basis, but it's still a fantastic opportunity."

"How's everyone treating you?" His eyes were continually traveling the length of my body, and I fought the urge to slap him and vomit.

"Very well. I've been speaking to Monique Webber. She has the sweetest things to say about you."

"She's such a dear." His eyes moved upward, analyzing my hairstyle.

"And Valerie Yves." I threw out her name to gauge his reaction.

"She's a spitfire." He looked a little uncomfortable. It was about damn time someone made him feel uncomfortable. "Look at you, at a party and without a drink. We need to rectify this situation immediately." Or maybe he wanted to change topics immediately. "Barkeep," he bellowed. O'Connell turned around, and I raised my eyebrows at him as if to say look who I found.

"Yes, sir?" O'Connell asked. Surreptitiously, his eyes darted to the corner of the bar where Martin was sitting with his back to me.

"A gin martini," Sanderson ordered, before turning and looking expectantly at me. I looked at the bottles behind the bar. Drinking would be frowned upon while on the job, but not drinking would hurt my cover story. Well, I just had to take a sip, it wasn't like I had to drink whatever concoction O'Connell made.

"An IRA." I smirked ever so slightly, and Nick narrowed his eyes. "Bailey's and Irish Whiskey," I clarified.

"Girl knows how to drink," Sanderson said in an admiring tone. O'Connell mixed the drink and threw a warning glance my way, so I wouldn't do anything outrageous. "Oh." Sanderson spotted Martin, who turned at the sound of my voice. I hoped it wasn't that obvious to anyone else. "Let me introduce you to the man responsible for our initial introduction."

"Rick," Martin stood, "it's nice of you to come out in honor of Caterina. Everything that happened two weeks ago was devastating."

"I heard you got caught up in the investigation." Sanderson seemed to have forgotten I was in the room, which suited me just fine. "Did the cops ever discover who attacked you?"

"I haven't heard anything." Martin looked at me and smiled. "James Martin." He extended his hand.

"Where are my manners?" Sanderson chided. "This is Lola Peters. The girl you vouched for." I took Martin's offered hand, and he kissed my knuckles. My god, he was good at the playboy act.

"Thank you, Mr. Martin," I cooed. "I had no idea my uncle worked for such a well-connected man." Martin was wearing a black suit with a black dress shirt, opened at the collar, without a tie or pocket square. He wore all black for the memorial.

"I'll let you two get better acquainted," Sanderson said, disappearing into the throng of partygoers.

"Please." Martin indicated the barstool in the far corner. I sat down, glancing up to see if O'Connell had a minute, but there were ten guests in line, waiting for drinks. "You're stunning, and certainly, the most beautiful woman here."

"Bullshit," I whispered. "I'm just waiting to talk to the bartender."

Analyzing his appearance, he was dressed elegantly but somehow more dressed down than usual. His hair was still perfectly in place, but I didn't see his expensive watch. I was making mental notes of how he differed tonight from the night two weeks ago as I took a sip of my drink for lack of anything better to do. Putting it down, I knew there would be no more of that since I was on the job.

"So, Ms. Peters," he was still playing his little game, "interesting drink choice."

"What are you drinking? I've heard the cosmos are awful," I quipped, having issues staying in character when dealing with him.

"It's beer." He slid the glass forward for my approval. I picked it up and sniffed. "The bartender's afraid I'm a lush."

"Well, he's a professional. He's probably just looking out for your best interest, Mr. Martin." I tried to stay in character. Why did everyone decide to order a drink now when I wanted to talk to O'Connell? "Thank you for inadvertently providing me with this wonderful job opportunity." I managed to choke the words out with a minimal amount of sarcasm, and he looked intrigued.

"My pleasure." There was an evil glint in his eye, and he knew I wouldn't break cover. "I'm just wondering, Lola, what my chances are of picking up a girl like you in a place like this."

"I hate to disappoint you." Considering the very real possibility the killer could be watching us at this exact moment, I scooted my barstool closer and put my hand on his bicep, leaning in so we wouldn't be overheard. "But I'm working."

"That dress is working for me." His words were smooth, seductive, and the classic lecherous commentary I had grown accustomed to. I laughed for show and gave him a challenging look.

"In that case, feel free to bring your A-game," I smiled coyly, "or whatever it is you do to meet models because the more casual you look, the better off we'll all be."

TWENTY-NINE

Martin stayed perched at the corner of the bar the entire evening. A few people would go over and speak to him every once in a while, but there were more important things to worry about. Since O'Connell and Bruiser were keeping an eye on Martin, I had the opportunity to gather more information. Unfortunately, everything helpful I discovered occurred within the first hour and a half. I encountered Yves and Webber a few times in the ladies room, but they had nothing useful to add to their previous comments. The other models avoided me like the plague. Apparently, short was a serious condition someone could catch.

While I strategized on a new way to extract important information, I went back to the bar and took a seat next to Martin. "Back so soon, Lola," he asked. I smiled and returned some of the flirtation, justifying it based solely upon the premise it's what Lola would do. At least, it was what five models had done in the past, so who was I to break with tradition. The party was dying down, and people began to leave or disband into smaller groups situated on some couches or tables. "You know, I run my own company," he began, and I snorted at the absolute absurdity. "Maybe I shouldn't be talking to you. You see, there's this amazing woman I know with gorgeous blue eyes, great smile, intelligent, witty, and fearless." I blushed and hated it.

"Bartender," I yelled, looking for an escape, "I need a drink and don't be stingy with the liquor this time."

A break from the flirtation was turning into a necessity. Plus, yelling at the bartender was a plausible cover, even though I wasn't really drinking since I was working, but it was important for my level of intoxication to appear to be advancing. Honestly, I barely had half a drink the entire night.

"Am I making you uncomfortable?" Martin purred in my ear.

Turning, I caught sight of someone watching us, so I got off my barstool and made a spectacle of myself before sitting on his lap. "Just go with it," I whispered, hoping he'd play along with my charade. He tensed but wrapped his arms around me. "We have an audience." O'Connell leaned across the bar toward me. "Nine o'clock."

He shifted his gaze and grabbed a glass, pouring whatever he was holding into it. "Isn't that Yves?" he asked.

"I think so," I remarked. "Is she still staring?"

"Yep." O'Connell put the drink in front of me.

"All right," I picked up the glass, trying my best to sell the drunk thing, "I'll see what she wants." I glanced at Martin, who was still holding me on his lap. "I gotta make this look good. Just don't take it personally," I warned, kissing him full on the mouth and getting clumsily off his lap. "I'll be right back," I said loudly. "Don't go anywhere." I stumbled on my way to Yves.

She was pretty far gone. A few bumps of blow and tequila shots tend to have that effect. "Is that Sanderson?" she asked, pointing at Martin. "I swear Rick the Dick needs to have it cut off. Why'd you let him get all up in your business?"

"That's not Sanderson." I dropped the intoxicated act slightly, caught by her confusion. "That's James Martin."

"Huh." She assessed the back of him. "From here, he looks just like Sanderson."

I spun around. Maybe the fine clothes and expensive haircut were similar, but they weren't built the same. Martin was all toned, lean muscle, and Sanderson probably failed high school P.E. and hadn't visited a gym since. I squinted. They were close to the same height and had similar hair color. Maybe when everything was clouded due to alcohol and drugs, they looked even more alike.

"No shit." I suddenly made the connection. "Do you want to meet him and see for yourself?" Reverting back to my slurred speech pattern, I grabbed Yves's hand and dragged her to the bar. "See?" I giggled.

"Damn," she ogled Martin, "sorry, girl. I'll let you get back to that fine piece of man."

I leaned over the bar in front of O'Connell. "We need to talk. Now," I hissed.

"Taking a break," he told the line. "Hey, you," he pointed to Jacobs who was passing by with a tray, "fill in behind the bar for a minute. I gotta take a leak."

"What's going on?" Martin asked. He wrapped his arm around me, and I couldn't tell if it was part of the act or if he was just being himself.

"I have to talk to the bartender first," I said, still not breaking cover. "Do me a favor, and stay out of trouble for a few minutes." Walking off in the general direction of the restrooms and kitchen, I waited for O'Connell to follow.

Two minutes later, we were in the kitchen, standing off to the side. The room was empty, but that could easily change at any second. "What the hell's going on? You have that ah-ha look you get," he whispered.

"Martin and Sanderson were wearing the same suit that night. Just now, Yves thought I was with Sanderson. Caterina was obviously the target, but maybe Sanderson was the motive."

"I've seen the video. You really think someone would be jealous of Sanderson?" He raised a questioning eyebrow, but I didn't waver. "I don't see it, but that's just me. Maybe you're right, and it might lead to something. I'll radio it in, and maybe we'll find a new connection." He looked genuinely interested. "You're damn good at playing this whole thing up. If this were a movie, you'd get best actress," a brief look of curiosity flashed across his face, "unless maybe it's not entirely an act."

"Don't start." I went back to the bar.

It was easier to talk to Martin when I could whisper in his ear and not be concerned about being overheard, so I sat on his lap and wrapped my arms around his shoulders. "You smell nice."

"Shut up." I was getting annoyed. "I think you were mistaken for Sanderson that night. I don't know if it's why you weren't attacked or if that's the reason Caterina was. You said it yourself; the two of you were wearing the same designer suits. Do you remember when you woke up which way you were facing?"

"What?" He was confused.

"Were you facedown, turned to the side, on your back?" This was a very strange way to ask questions, when I couldn't assess his facial expressions, but his posture stiffened as he thought about it. Then again, maybe all interrogations should be conducted this way. It made it easier to read body language.

"I was facedown. Facing the bench seats," he clarified.

"Do you think the assailant would have seen your face?"

"How would I know? I don't know. Probably not."

I was completely still, processing through the few fleeting thoughts. If this were a case of mistaken identities, then Sanderson couldn't be the murderer, and we were down to three possibilities. Yves seemed angry at the world. She had a drug habit and possibly a drinking problem since addiction didn't tend to fall into one nice, neat category, and at least a brief stint in the amateur adult entertainment industry. Yolanda Tate's finances needed further sorting before we could determine if her monetary gains would have made killing her star model worthwhile, and I still didn't have much to go on concerning Monique Webber. She struck me as a ditz, but obviously, she had an affinity for Ricky.

"Hey," he shook me from my reverie, "unless you're planning to pretend to pass out, you probably should stop imitating a statue."

I stood up and sat on my own barstool. I was working the pieces backward in my mind. Drugs were given to Spencer to give to Alvarez to use on Caterina. How did Sanderson fit into any of that?

"What time is it?" I asked, but without his watch, he didn't know. "I'm going to run with something. If you leave before I get back," I got off the stool and leaned against him, "make sure Marcal takes a circuitous route for the drive home. I'm probably just paranoid as always, but it couldn't hurt."

I found each individual model from earlier and asked them about Jake Spencer. Monique's words rang true since every girl had some scandalous tale to share, but I wanted to know more than just Spencer's sexual prowess. Tread lightly, Parker, I reminded myself. Subtlety wasn't typically my strong suit, but I was after something that required finesse. Did Spencer have any kinky habits? I hoped it would be a lead-in to questions about intoxication.

A group of drunk, depressed models was easily pliable. By the time I questioned Seline, I had heard similar stories three other times. Spencer was no gentleman; he would gladly kiss and tell. Yves liked sex when she was stoned out of her mind, and bubbly Monique insisted on some threesomes. As far as rape fantasies were concerned, that had been Caterina's personal preference. It was all an elaborate game Spencer and she would engage in at random parties. He'd seek her out, taking her to some remote location, and wham-bam-thank-you-ma'am.

While I personally found the rape fantasy concept deplorable on every imaginable level, it was a far too common preference. Once again, I was amazed at how people who had never been placed in actual, horrifying situations could think this was exciting and pleasurable. There was no rape in the game they played. It was two consenting adults engaging in amorous activities, the opposite of the definition of rape, but I pushed my resentment at people's stupidity away for the moment.

There were two new angles to consider. First, maybe the drugs were a new dimension to Caterina's game. Hell, maybe even Martin was a new addition to the game in a very sick and twisted way. Second, did someone else interrupt the game before Spencer had a chance to find and bang Caterina? Jealousy was the ultimate motive for passion killings. So who was the assailant jealous of? Caterina, Jake, or possibly even

Rick? My head was starting to spin with all the new questions, and I wanted to interrogate Spencer for answers. If he'd admit to his own stupidity and name his drug connection, then we'd have a solid suspect with both motive and opportunity.

It was late, and I was useless at this point. The information from the models had run dry, and I was out of theories and questions. The only thing left was to work out the finer points of what I ascertained and hope it would lead somewhere definitive.

Back at the bar, Bettina was sitting beside Martin, getting a little too flirty. I sat in the empty seat on his other side and glanced at O'Connell for help. He poured vodka into a martini glass and knocked it over, spilling it all over her dress.

"You fucking asshole," she squealed, jumping up from her seat. "How dare you?"

"I'm sorry, ma'am," he replied, handing her a dish towel. "I don't know how that happened."

"Ma'am," she shrieked. "Ma'am!" She ran, practically in tears, to the ladies room. The few other people at the bar turned to watch the drama. And I thought I took issue with being called ma'am. Sheesh.

"I'm such a clutz," O'Connell offered as way of explanation, toweling off the bar, as the others went back to minding their own business.

"Afraid I might take my attacker home?" Martin quipped.

"Hey, I'm not the one spilling drinks," I reasoned. "But I did tell you to stay out of trouble, and she looks like trouble."

"Total accident. It just slipped right out of my hands," Nick deadpanned. Smirking, he caught the look on my face. "You look like the cat that swallowed the canary."

"I'm done here. I've gotten all I can. When can we

leave? I need to chat with Spencer. The crybaby might just have all the answers." Our end of the bar was completely empty, and I was tired of pretending to be Lola. Alex Parker was ready to get back to work on the investigation.

"We're stuck through clean-up, but you can head out and give Moretti a call." He glanced around the mostly empty banquet hall. "A lot of people already left. I'm sure the brass won't have a problem if you do too." He focused on Martin. "The two of you should leave together. It might reinforce your story if it looks like Lola's going home with someone." Martin stood and offered me his hand.

"What, you're not going to tip the bartender?" I asked. Obediently, he took a fifty from his wallet and put it in the tip glass. Fifties seemed to be the smallest denomination he was aware of.

I winked at O'Connell as Martin put his arm around me, and we strolled to the exit. Bruiser appeared from the shadows and met us at the car. Martin held the door, ever the consummate gentleman, and I climbed into the backseat.

"Have Marcal drive away but stay close. With any luck, I'll be rendezvousing with the surveillance van." I dialed Moretti. When he answered, I filled him in on the possible Sanderson mix-up, Caterina's sexual fantasies, and every relevant piece of information I had gotten on each of our suspects.

"Good job, Parker," he sounded impressed. "We received confirmation on the IP address, and Heathcliff's gone to pick up the warrant. A team is on the way to the marina to search Sanderson's boat. It was his wireless network which supported the video upload. With the addition of exigent circumstances due to the vehicular nature of the crime scene, we're impounding the boat and securing the area. Right now, we're just waiting to move in."

"Do you guys need some help?" I wanted to get in on the search.

"Were you drinking at the party?" He soured to my request.

"Not nearly enough for it to register on any discernible scale." I wasn't saying no since O'Connell served actual liquor.

"I'm not risking you fucking this up. If you want to be helpful, get a full statement from James Martin since you're sitting in his town car and then write up your report. I want all the I's dotted and the T's crossed. Bring it in first thing tomorrow morning, and if Lola's job is done, you can assist on Spencer's interrogation."

"But–" I was prepared to argue.

"Go home. Do the paperwork. I'll see you tomorrow." He disconnected, and I angrily snapped my phone closed, grumbling to myself.

"Good news?" Martin asked sarcastically.

"I'm stuck filling out paperwork while Heathcliff goes on a treasure hunt." An amused look crossed his face, further annoying me. "In the meantime, you can give me your official statement, and I have to write my report." I made a face. "Do you mind dropping me at the precinct first?"

"Sure."

THIRTY

Per Moretti's orders, I stayed away from the search and seizure of Sanderson's boat. I also avoided going inside the precinct since Moretti specifically said to go home and do the paperwork. It was irritating being sidelined after all the information I discovered, so I was going out of my way to follow his orders to the letter, hoping it would annoy him just as much. More than likely, he couldn't care less when he got my report as long as he got it, but it made me feel better to think I had the upper hand.

Martin kindly offered to provide his statement, if I felt like meeting him at his place. After the way Lola acted this evening, I wasn't looking forward to dealing with the aftermath, but I went anyway. When I arrived, Marcal buzzed me into the garage, and I retrieved my duffel from the trunk, hoping to change back into me before we started on the reports.

"I'm in for the night," Martin said to Bruiser and Marcal. "You guys can take off." Bruiser looked to me for approval, and I nodded. Once they cleared the room and the garage door opened and closed, Martin asked, "Why is my bodyguard looking to you for verification of his orders?"

"We've reached an arrangement over the last two weeks." I smiled at his perplexed look but returned to work mode after noting the time. "I'm going to change back into Alex Parker before we begin."

"Pity," he smirked, his eyes dancing, "I was under the impression Lola was actually interested in me."

I turned my back to him and pulled my hair to the side. "Can you unzip me?" He didn't say a word, but his fingers lingered for a moment before starting the zipper so I would be able to reach it. "Thanks." I headed for the guestroom. "By the way, Lola's completely out of your league."

With my face scrubbed, wearing jeans and a sweatshirt, I reemerged to find Martin sitting on the sofa in his living room. He smiled. "Still beautiful."

"Let's not," I said softly. "I'm sorry about tonight. I was practically molesting you in order to sell my cover. Anyway," I picked up the notepad and pen, "we should get started on this. I'm sure you have an early morning."

"Eh. Not that early."

Almost an hour later, after some cajoling, questioning, and memory jogging, he had written out a full statement, covering everything that occurred this evening. We rehashed the night of his attack, and I made sure he went into detail about his interactions with the other models, Jake Spencer, and Rick Sanderson. The biggest piece of relevant information was the similarity in his attire compared to Sanderson's.

"I think that covers it." I reread the statement and double-checked his signature and date.

"There should be a way to make police reports more fun," he quipped.

"Tell me about it. Do you mind if I write my report

here so I can drop it by the precinct on my way home?" My annoyance with Moretti faded. After all, the lieutenant had a point, and I didn't need to act like a diva. That was Lola's job.

"Help yourself to my office and computer." He indicated the room down the hallway. "Feel free to stay as long as you like, but I'm going to bed. Can you let yourself out and reset the alarm?"

"Same code?"

"Yes," he affirmed. "Watching you work tonight was pretty spectacular." I gave him a look, assuming he meant the way I pawed at him. "I'm serious. I've never seen you do any undercover work, except downplaying being my bodyguard. It makes sense why Mark wants you back."

"Good night." I wasn't sure what else to say. It felt like some dynamic between us was about to change, but I couldn't figure out why.

"Night, Alex." He climbed the stairs. "If Lola reappears and wants to join me, send her up."

"You wish," I remarked good-naturedly.

I retreated into his home office and began typing my report. My thoughts were jumbled, so I wrote it as a narrative, giving the information in the order in which I received it. I stared at the screen, rereading my own words and trying to make sense of everything. If I could find the end to this trail of breadcrumbs, I'd be able to follow it back to the beginning. After rearranging my report into a more logical order, I decided it would suffice.

Hitting print, I rubbed my eyes. Maybe if I dropped the reports off tonight, I wouldn't have to show up quite so early in the morning. Although, that would only be beneficial if I managed to halt the nonstop picking and evaluating of every single piece of information as it crossed my mind, and I actually fell asleep. Fat chance that was going to happen.

I was signing the last page when I heard a noise in the kitchen. My heart leapt into my chest, and I forced the memories of attackers past out of my mind. Cautiously, I went into the kitchen to assess the situation.

Martin was sitting at the table, staring into the steaming mug in front of him. "Did I wake you?" I asked. It had been a couple of hours since he went to bed, but it didn't look like he slept.

"No." He looked confused. "I didn't even know you were still here."

"I was just on my way out." Leaning against the doorjamb, I crossed my arms and watched him curiously. "What's going on?"

"I couldn't sleep." He played with the paper at the end of the teabag. "I just keep thinking about things."

"Things?" Was I the cause of his current distress?

"Waking up and finding Caterina's body, getting arrested," he focused on the mug, "those things." He looked up, searching my eyes for answers. "Tonight hit a little too close to home, being at a party with the same group of people." He snorted. "Why am I explaining this? You of all people know what it's like to revisit traumatic events."

I chuckled. It was a cynical, incredulous sound, and he stared uncomprehendingly at my reaction. "Seriously, you think that's traumatic? You live in this house and go up those stairs every single day, and some stupid party bothers you?" I shook my head, amazed. "I'm barely holding it together standing here right now with everything that happened *that* day, but none of that has any effect on you." I was referencing events long since passed. "And yet the thing you walked away from mostly unscathed is what keeps you up at night. Unbelievable."

"It's been almost a year. I've moved past getting shot. There's no reason to hold on to what happened here. It wasn't that bad."

Laughing bitterly, I wrapped my arms tighter around my sides, recalling the stabbing pain of fractured ribs. "I forget sometimes that you had the easy job that day." My tone was clinical, cold, and darkly scathing. "You just had to lie on the floor and bleed." I shut my eyes and bit my lip, trying to push the memories away.

"Alexis, we've never talked about any of this." I opened my eyes and found him gazing at me. "Talk to me. Tell me what it was like. Help me to understand. Everything that's filling up the space between us starts there."

"What do you want to know?" The entire nightmare began to play out in front of my eyes. "If you remember, two mercenaries entered through that door. I sent you up the stairs, hoping you would find someplace safe on the fourth floor. Then the two men started searching each level of your house. Their only objective was to kill you, but somehow, I managed to subdue one of them. His partner spotted me, and I fled. I hid inside the closet on the third floor, waiting, not knowing what would happen." Swallowing uncomfortably, I remembered the ensuing firefight. "I had taken his buddy's automatic rifle and—" My posture stiffened.

"I heard," he interjected. "It was nonstop. Deafening. I had no idea who was firing or what was going on."

"The rifle was out of bullets, so I switched to my nine millimeter. Even after all those shots, his body armor didn't even dent. It's like it was impenetrable. I got lucky, and one shot pierced his neck." Distinctly, I remembered seeing the blood slowly pool around his motionless form. Taking a life was difficult, even under justifiable circumstances, and I forced the lump down my throat.

"Alex?"

"That's when I heard something upstairs, and I found you in the office. I still don't know how the third gunman got there or when. Maybe he went up when I was dealing with the second mercenary, or he breached on a different level. I don't know." My voice shook, and I steeled myself against the impending barrage of images that I had tried so hard to forget over the last ten months.

"That's why you were looking around the room." He was recollecting his own version of the events. "You were facing away from the door, and I spotted him in the hallway. I don't know how I even noticed him, but," his jaw muscles clenched, "his gun was raised, and I had to get you out of the way."

Shutting my eyes, I bit the inside of my cheek, trying to get my emotions under control. "That was the stupidest thing you could have done," I scolded. "I didn't even know what happened. You shoved me into the wall, and when I turned around, that lunatic was firing wildly into your office, and," I gritted my teeth, "you were unconscious on the floor." I inhaled sharply. "The blood was pumping out of your body, and I was completely helpless to stop it."

"Alex." He pushed his chair back, but I put my hand up, stopping him from coming toward me. "Maybe you think I pushed you out of the way in order to save you, but did you ever consider it was because my chance of survival was greatly improved if you weren't dead." I stared at him, not believing for a second he had run those calculations in his mind before pushing me out of the way mere nanoseconds before my brain would have splattered against the wall like a Pollock painting.

"No," I said angrily. "Instead, you left me alone to take down the last gunman and stop you from bleeding out. I still don't see how either of us survived since he was intent on turning both of us into Swiss cheese." Forcing myself to breathe, I continued. "Somehow, I made it to the doorway before taking three shots to the vest. The gunfire should have shredded the Kevlar, especially at that range, but it didn't." I stopped, meeting his eyes and holding his gaze. "It knocked me onto my back, and I remember staring at the ceiling, trying to determine if my vest had been pierced. And then, he was standing over me, gloating. If he hadn't been so goddamn impressed by his own skills," my face contorted into a sneer, "I wouldn't have had time to put a bullet between his eyes."

Martin paled, aghast at my retelling. "Alexis, I'm sorry."

"Oh, it gets better," I hissed. "Then came the really fun part of forcing my lungs to work and my body to obey just so I could crawl back into that room. Crawl back to you. I spent an eternity trying to stop the bleeding, but you wouldn't wake up. You weren't responding. I was covered in your blood." I trembled, and my chin quivered. "There was nothing left I could do to save you. I heard more gunfire in the distance, and I was sure that was it. That day broke me," I admitted. "It was over. I felt it." There was a level of conviction in my words that sent more tremors through me. Death had come to claim both of us, and somehow, here we were. "I still don't know how or why, but Nick just appeared. And he picked me up and carried me down the stairs while the paramedics worked on you."

In a split second, Martin crossed the room and

enveloped me in his strong arms. He kissed my hair and my forehead. "Alexis, I'm sorry." The resentment I didn't realize I was harboring dissipated. Talking had released the pain of that day, and I no longer had to hide it in the darkest corners of my being. His apology acted like a salve on my raw nerves, and he kept repeating it as if it were his mantra.

"I killed two men that day." I was numb to my own statement, knowing I would gladly do it again given the circumstances. "And somehow saved you in the process." I looked up at him, feeling our entire foundation shift. His eyes held an understanding they never had before. It was the same understanding I had seen on his face earlier in the evening when he complimented my undercover work.

"I never knew. Why didn't you tell me?"

I shook my head, talking about that day hurt too much, and now it was out. I uncrossed my arms and placed my palms flat against his chest, unsure if I wanted to push him away or pull him closer. Tilting my chin up, we kissed. The force of nature which existed between us could no longer be denied or ignored. We stood in his kitchen, filling the void of hurt and destruction with gentle and tender affection. When we broke for air, I ran my fingers along his jaw.

"Martin, take me to bed." He searched my eyes, making sure I was positive in my decision, before scooping me into his arms and carrying me down the hallway.

THIRTY-ONE

We were lying in bed, completely sated. My cheek was against his chest, and I traced the ridges around his sculpted abdominal and pectoral muscles with my fingertips, making the conscious effort not to trace the scar on his shoulder.

"It's nice to know we're good at more than just arguing," he teased, running his hand through my hair.

Smiling at his assessment, I felt like time was frozen as we enjoyed the tranquility. Finally, I moved from my comfortable position against his chest and kissed him. "I should go." I rolled onto my back and glanced at our discarded clothing, littering the floor.

"Stay." He turned onto his side and wrapped his arms around me. "Please, Alex."

"You know this house is the source of my nightmares," I began, but he nuzzled my neck.

"I'll keep the demons at bay, and if it doesn't work, I'll wake you up if you start to have a nightmare." I looked again at my abandoned clothes and considered the unappealing prospect of getting out of the nice warm bed.

"Will you wake me when you get up?" I asked, insinuating myself closer to him, and he nodded.

"Good night, sweetheart," he whispered, kissing my neck before we both drifted off to sleep.

*   *   *

Rolling over, I caught a glimpse of Martin getting out of bed in nothing but his boxers. There were slight traces of light filtering in from behind the curtains. "What time is it?" I asked, my voice still thick with sleep.

"Go back to sleep," he insisted. "It's still early. I'll be right back." I shut my eyes, but before I could drift off, the mattress sunk in as he returned. "I didn't mean to wake you. What time do you have to be at the precinct?" I turned toward him and rested my head against his chest, finding the sound of his heartbeat comforting for some inexplicable reason.

"Whenever. It doesn't make a difference." I fell silent, shutting my eyes. "What are you doing?" I finally murmured as his cell phone continued to emit random beeps.

"Something for work." He sounded too awake for it to be this early. He leaned over and put his phone on the nightstand before wrapping his arms around me. "Sorry." I didn't bother to respond. I wasn't sure what time it was, but if he was up and thinking about work, every few remaining minutes of sleep were precious.

Time lost all meaning to my unconscious mind. A few seconds could feel like a few hours, but the feeling of my hair being brushed away from my face and soft kisses against my shoulder brought me out of the abyss. I opened my eyes and looked at Martin, who was propped up on his elbow, watching me.

"How long have you been staring?"

"Not long." He smirked, getting out of bed. "There are clean towels hanging in the bathroom." I grunted my thanks as he left the guestroom and presumably headed upstairs to get ready for work.

Shutting my eyes, I waited for regret or embarrassment to flood over me, but neither did. Eventually, I got out of bed, picked up my duffel bag and scattered clothing, and went into the guest bathroom to shower and get ready for the day. Everything about last night was unexpected, and I tried not to dwell on what it might mean.

By the time I emerged, Martin was in front of the stove. He was only partially dressed, wearing suit pants and an unbuttoned dress shirt. It was Friday, but he was clearly taking the definition of casual to extremes. He looked up from cooking and smiled wolfishly, his green eyes sparkling.

"Don't look at me like that," I remarked, leaning over the pan to see what he was making. It was an egg white omelet with tomatoes, spinach, and mushrooms.

"Like what?" he asked innocently, dropping the spatula and pinning me against the counter.

"Like you've seen me naked." He put his hands on my hips and lifted me onto the countertop, so we were almost at eye level.

He cocked his eyebrow up and kissed me. "But I have seen you naked."

"True, but you don't have to look at me like you did."

"We'll see." He grinned. "Can I interest you in some breakfast?"

I glanced at the clock on the stove. "Is that the right time? Shouldn't you be at work?" It was almost eleven.

"I took the morning off on account of a meeting," he responded, acting as if he had all the time in the world. I sighed and pushed him backward, so I could slide off the counter.

"A quick bite, and then I have to get out of here. If I don't show up soon, Moretti will have my ass."

I took my duffel bag to the car and retrieved the MT security guard applications from the trunk. My cell phone was dead, so there was no way to check for missed calls or messages to report to work. At least I had a car charger I could use on my way to the station.

"Coffee?" he asked as I came back into the kitchen with the stack of applications.

"Of course." I was starting to feel awkward. Fortunately, we didn't have time to discuss last night since I was already three hours behind. "I won't be able to stop by your office this afternoon to drop these off." I slid the applications across the table. "It's down to top six. If you want top five, I'll randomly pull someone out. Things have been getting away from me lately, but I worked on these a couple of nights ago."

"Six works." He picked up the papers and put them on one of the empty chairs. Then he put a plate and mug in front of me before retrieving a matching set for himself. "Are you working late tonight?"

"Probably. I don't know what turned up last night." I chewed thoughtfully, ignoring his roguish grin. "Or how long they've been at it today. I guess I should have gotten up earlier."

"I have some foreign business to deal with, so I have my own late night planned," he volunteered.

"The police might need you to verify details or something, but if you get a call, you can make them work around you."

I finished eating and put my plate in the

dishwasher, hurrying to drink the rest of my coffee. Even though I slept an extra three hours, our passionate activities lasted through the early morning, so I didn't even get a full six hours of rest. Coffee was a necessity today.

"Not a problem." He was being appeasing.

He finished his breakfast and added his plate and mug to the dishwasher. I tossed my mug in and did a quick mental check to make sure I grabbed my report, Martin's statement, and all of my belongings. His staff probably suspected there was something going on, but I didn't need to reinforce their suspicions by leaving anything behind.

"All right," I hedged, unsure of how to proceed, "I'm gonna go. Thanks for," I adopted my own mischievous glint, "everything." He drew me to him, and we kissed. Where was this going, and did I want to get off the train before it was too late? I shelved that thought for the moment, instead focusing on the present.

"Have a good day." He winked, disappearing up the stairs to finish getting dressed.

*   *   *

"Nice of you to finally show up," Thompson remarked, busting my chops as I sat at the empty desk I claimed as my own.

"Where is everyone?" I asked, looking around at all the vacant chairs in the squad room.

"O'Connell hasn't come in yet, and Heathcliff is down in evidence, sorting through what was found at the original scene. Apparently, he had some kind of epiphany."

"Well, it was bound to happen at some point."

I went into Moretti's office and handed him my

report and Martin's statement. He took the paperwork, barely glancing at it. "Some uniforms are bringing in Yves and Sanderson for questioning," he supplied. "Are you ready to retire Lola? Or do you think she might come in handy?"

"Lola's done all she can." He nodded, picking up the report to read, and I went out to the bullpen just as O'Connell walked in.

"What'd I miss?" he asked me since Thompson had disappeared from sight.

"I just got here, but from what I gather, Heathcliff's on to something. And Sanderson and Yves are getting picked up now."

"I tried calling you last night." He clicked a few keys, logging into his computer. "I thought you'd like to get a head start reviewing the information you obtained while we waited for the search to be conducted."

"Sorry, dead battery." I held up my phone. "I didn't realize until this morning, but it's working now."

He squinted, perhaps suspicions of where I had been. "I hate it when that happens."

Heathcliff returned with an evidence bag containing the pillow used to kill Skolnick. He paid no attention to us, comparing the item in his hand to an enhanced printout from Sanderson's video debut. "One and the same?" he asked, holding both of them up.

"I'm no expert, but you could make that argument," I said as he located the manifest which enumerated the items seized from Sanderson's boat.

"How many pillows do you put on a queen size bed?" he polled.

"Two," O'Connell and I responded in unison.

"Yeah. Apparently, Sanderson misplaced one of them. Maybe it grew legs and walked onto Martin's yacht." He was in a good mood today, playful, focused, and ready to make heads roll.

"I forget, is that one of the selling points for white, rectangular pillows?" I queried.

"I'll ask Sanderson when he arrives. Thompson and I are working this angle, and since both of you showed up late this morning, you can deal with Spencer. You might want to bring a box of tissues into interrogation with you."

"Oh, I'm sure I can give him something to cry about." I cocked my eyebrow menacingly.

When Thompson returned, I gave the three detectives my rendition of all the dirty, scandalous secrets the models divulged. They looked stunned, despite the fact they were all hardened cops and should have expected as much. Apparently, looks could be deceiving.

"If you find a solid connection between Spencer and the porno, let me know immediately. Every bit of leverage may come in handy," Heathcliff added.

An officer came through the double doors and informed us Spencer was waiting in interrogation room one. I got up, checking to make sure O'Connell was ready to go. We were hitting the ground running today, and it was about time.

"Do you want to take point?" Nick asked. "It seems you might have more information than I do. Plus, you're not a cop, so you can ask the crazy questions, and his lawyer can't take any official action against the department."

"Sounds like fun."

He opened the door, and we entered the room. "Mr. Spencer," O'Connell greeted, "I'm Detective Nick O'Connell, and this is our police consultant, Ms. Alex Parker." Spencer looked at me uncertainly. His lawyer whispered something to him, and his gaze shifted unsteadily around the room. "Shall we begin?"

"I've informed my client not to answer any questions without my approval," the lawyer told us. O'Connell nodded, taking a seat at the table across from Spencer's counsel.

"Mr. Spencer," with any luck, my interrogational skills weren't that rusty, "you have one hell of a reputation when it comes to the ladies. Are there any models you've photographed that you haven't slept with?" His lawyer looked uneasy, but Spencer kept his mouth shut. "Monique and her threesomes, Seline and her bondage fetish, Valerie and her drug use," I paused, letting my words sink in, "and let's not forget Caterina Skolnick and her adventurous fantasies."

"I never raped her," he sputtered, and his lawyer glared angrily at him, advising him to be quiet.

"No, you didn't. Having a twisted desire to fantasize about nonconsensual sex and having nonconsensual sex are two very different things. So how far were you willing to go to please Caterina?" I asked, pulling out a chair and taking a seat.

"Look," it was O'Connell's turn to play, "we have proof you gave the Rohypnol to the bartender, Raymond Alvarez, with instructions to slip it to Ms. Skolnick." His lawyer looked uncomfortable. It was understandable since his client might be guilty of conspiracy to commit murder or an accomplice to murder.

"But," I interjected, "given Caterina's sexual proclivities, maybe it's not as bad as it seems."

"If you tell us exactly what the two of you planned for the evening, who else knew of your sexual escapades, and where you got the drugs, we'll have the more serious charges dropped," O'Connell promised.

"Let me consult with my client in private," the lawyer said.

O'Connell and I left the interrogation room. We had him on the ropes. It was only a matter of time before everything would fall into place.

THIRTY-TWO

Spencer had given us everything we could have possibly hoped to gain. The only problem was we couldn't exactly verify any of the details with Caterina, unless we bought an Ouija board and found a medium. Spencer insisted Caterina wanted to up the ante and devised the entire plan for their foreplay. She allegedly wanted to make her experience as real as possible and had him procure the Rohypnol from one of Valerie Yves's drug connections.

The plan was simple. Caterina would wait at the bar, hoping to find a man who would take an interest in her. Once things escalated to the point of no return, she would ask the unsuspecting third party to order a cosmo. This would signal Alvarez to dose both drinks, and then Spencer would follow Caterina and her companion as they left the event, thereby adding to the illusion by taking her in front of another man. Their plan was deplorable, dangerous, and stupid beyond belief.

My stomach roiled at the absolute depravity, and a

part of me wished O'Connell could lock him up just because he was a pervert. James Martin had become the unknowing and unwilling participant in this sick, twisted game, but some things still didn't make much sense as I paced the interrogation room, just to get a few feet farther away from this sicko.

"Why did you have sex with Caterina in the bathroom beforehand?" I asked harshly.

"The anticipation was driving her crazy," Spencer said, saddened. I wanted to slap him. "There was no reason we couldn't take advantage of things ahead of time. If I knew what was about to happen," he sniffled, "I never would have gone through with any of it. I would have called the whole thing off." His voice caught in his throat, and he began to sob uncontrollably.

"Goddamn," I cursed, deciding to continue questioning him anyway. What was the worst he'd do, blubber some more? "Why the hell didn't you follow her when they left the party?"

"Parker." O'Connell looked at me sharply, suggesting I back off. I stood in the corner near the two-way mirror and leaned against the wall, throwing my head back and staring at the ceiling while I regained my composure. "Mr. Spencer," O'Connell pushed the tissue box toward the crying man, "we need your cooperation if you want us to find who did this to her."

Spencer nodded through his tears and blew his nose loudly. "After our tryst, I got distracted. Tate asked me to take some photos of the event for her website. I figured," he sniffled again, choking back the tears, "I had plenty of time to search for Caterina since it would take some time before the drugs wore off."

"Disgusting pig," I muttered under my breath, but

luckily, no one heard me.

"Did you ever look for Caterina?" O'Connell asked. I thought back to the surveillance footage, but I didn't remember seeing him leave the party.

"No. I told Monique to find her and make sure she was okay."

O'Connell turned to me. Webber was on our list of suspects but had little connection to anything else until now. When I encountered her last night, she didn't strike me as killer material.

"What was she supposed to do?" I asked. "Why would you tell one of your conquests to find another of your conquests, whom you've drugged and left with some strange man?"

Silent tears fell from Spencer's eyes, but he kept his crying to a minimum. "I thought she'd wait until the Rohypnol wore off and take Caterina home, or the three of them would have some fun."

"You fucking piece of shit." I lunged forward, losing my patience with this worthless asshole and his entire story, but O'Connell grabbed me and shoved me out of the room.

"Calm down," he warned. "Stay out here. I'll deal with the rest."

I stalked the hallway like a caged tiger. Spencer was a revolting piece of work. Assuming everything he said was true, and that was a big fucking if, then did Monique kill Caterina?

I was outraged by everything Spencer had said and done. The situation was disgusting anyway I looked at it. How could a person let someone they care about do something that dangerous? Out of nowhere, I felt the familiar twinge, deducing something I didn't want to know or even consider, and filed it away for a later time and place.

"You okay?" O'Connell asked, exiting the

interrogation room.

I rubbed my eyes and pushed a strand of hair behind my ear. "I guess. Sorry about in there."

"I'm glad it was you and not me. If it were me, you would have let me hit him, and that would have been the end of my career."

"You could always be a bartender," I teased as we returned to the bullpen. "What's the verdict with Spencer's story?"

"We'll bring Monique Webber in for questioning. Perhaps she'll corroborate his story. In the meantime, maybe Thompson and Heathcliff got something substantial from Sanderson."

*   *   *

O'Connell and I stood in front of the theory board, trying to connect the dots while we waited for Webber to be brought in and Sanderson's interview to be concluded. "What part of Jake Spencer's story enraged you the most?" O'Connell asked as I scribbled some notes, depicting the most reasonable scenario.

"All of it," I responded automatically. Pulling out the evidence manifest from Sanderson's boat, I looked to see if the video camera used for the adult film had been recovered. "He is morally abhorrent. It speaks against every fiber of my being."

Nick chuckled. He knew me well, and normally, I didn't judge this harshly. "I thought it was his comment about Martin and two models having a drug-induced threesome that you found particularly offensive."

"Right, because it has nothing to do with the fact Spencer was encouraging dangerous behavior from someone he claims to have a deep emotional attachment for and then abandons her, directly resulting in her murder."

"Well, when you put it that way." He fell silent, focusing back on the case.

I searched for the report the Bureau sent over regarding the questionable film, hoping for new leads. If we could cross-reference Skolnick's TOD with the time of the filming, we might be able to knock a few more suspects off the list.

"How'd it go?" Heathcliff asked, joining us. O'Connell informed him of our interview, kindly leaving out my untimely outburst. Heathcliff nodded and jotted a few notes before sharing what he learned. "Sanderson had no choice but to admit to the filming; however, he insists he has no idea how the pillow from his boat turned out to be the murder weapon."

"Did you find out who the filmmaker is?" I asked.

"You're not going to believe this," Thompson interjected. "Yolanda Tate."

"This would be so much easier if everyone wasn't so damn interconnected," I complained.

Everyone would have to be brought back in and questioned in light of all the new evidence. Moretti suggested I keep my head down, just in case Lola had to go back to Tate's agency, so I was in the evidence room, reviewing the items recovered from last night's search and seizure. From what was uncovered during Sanderson's interrogations, the surveillance feed, the crime scene, and our Bureau provided internet report, I managed to piece a lot of things together concerning the adult film. Obviously, the solitude of the evidence room was good for something.

Tate's agency was going under. She was hemorrhaging money by having a slew of models that couldn't land a gig to make ends meet. The downward spiral in the economy hit everyone hard, and advertisers wanted established names instead of wannabes. Caterina Skolnick was supposed to take Tate's agency out of the red, but her ad campaign wasn't scheduled to shoot for another few months.

While they waited for their cash cow to produce milk, Tate and Sanderson devised a plan to gain publicity, albeit initially negative publicity, by having some of the willing and lesser known models flood the internet with sex tapes. It would cause a media buzz and get their names, faces, and other assets out to the world. With a bit of luck, the popularity gained through these despicable means would get the girls hired for some kind of work, even if it was just lingerie ads.

Valerie Yves was selected to be the guinea pig. Like she said at the memorial, only blondes and exotic, foreign beauties were getting hired. By breaking into the amateur internet porn industry with a barely known, practically never-was model, Tate and Sanderson would be able to determine how advantageous this new marketing technique could be. If it made Yves a household name, just think what it could do for the others. This was the best way Sanderson thought to test their new business ploy or a great excuse for him to bone a model, and since Valerie was desperate, she was a willing participant. It also explained her absolute aversion to Sanderson, whom she affectionately dubbed Rick the Dick.

While all of this made for a fascinating tale into the dark side of the modeling world, it did little to explain how Caterina ended up dead on Martin's yacht. I skimmed through the financial records and insurance policy, thinking that Tate might have murdered Caterina in the hopes of finding an immediate, untapped revenue source with the life insurance policy. However, the policy was chump change compared to what she stood to gain from the nationwide ad campaign. Tate didn't have a strong enough motive to kill her only moneymaker, and the same was true for Sanderson.

"We've finished up with Tate, and we made another go at Sanderson," O'Connell proclaimed, entering the room and filling me in. "Neither of them is good for it. They've both alibied out."

"No motive either," I added glumly. "What'd you get from your stint with the catering company? Any idea who swiped a knife? Let's not forget, Skolnick was stabbed, probably for emphasis, after being suffocated."

"No idea. It could have been anyone." He helped put all the evidence bags back in their boxes.

"It's either Yves or Webber. They're the only two left on our list who had opportunity. Plus, Skolnick was their rival, so they both have motive." Was there any way to figure out who did it? Webber had been sent to look after the drugged Caterina, but Yves provided the drug connection to Spencer. They both looked equally likely, unless Yves was still screwing Sanderson at the time of the murder. Too bad we didn't have TOD and the time of filming down to the minute. "Is the DA filing charges against Tate and Sanderson for making the video?"

"Probably not. Yves might be able to bring them up on civil charges or claim coercion, but it's beyond our jurisdiction if two consenting adults want to film themselves."

"How much longer do you think it'll be before they finish with the models?" It would be nice to escape the dank and dusty evidence room.

"We've booked both of them. Valerie Yves was in possession of narcotics when we brought her in, so if nothing else, we have her on some coke charges. And until we get things sorted out, Monique Webber is being held on suspicion of murder. Neither of them is going anywhere. Not anytime soon, anyway. Sanderson and Tate have cleared out, so Moretti said you can come upstairs and rejoin the world of the living."

"Fun," I muttered, following him up the steps. We were talking through our theories on motive, so I was distracted and didn't notice the uniformed officer and his charge exiting the interrogation room to our right.

"You fucking bitch," a woman screeched and slammed me against the wall, her nails slashing across my face. "What did you tell them?" She continued to rant and rave as my instincts kicked in, but before I could fend her off, O'Connell and Heathcliff simultaneously grabbed Yves and threw her into the opposite wall. O'Connell cuffed her and berated the officer for allowing this to happen.

"You okay?" Heathcliff asked.

"Yeah." Although temporarily stunned, I was fine. Unless a model was holding a pillow or a knife, she couldn't inflict too much damage. "But feel free to add assault charges to her rap sheet."

Seated back at my desk, Heathcliff was annoying me with antiseptic and butterfly bandages. "Stop moving. I'm trying to clean that nasty scratch. Do you want to contract rabies?" I laughed and let him treat the two scratches on my cheek that actually drew blood.

"I won't get rabies. She didn't bite me. She scratched me." I was joking around. Getting assaulted in the middle of a police station was bad business for the cops and tended to make me believe that my attacker was guilty of a serious crime, hopefully murder.

"If this were a vet's office, they'd put her down," Thompson commented.

"Maybe we need to start calling the two of you Doc," I said to Heathcliff and O'Connell, "since you both got there at the same time to put her down, hard."

"You know I have your back." O'Connell winked. Eventually, Heathcliff grew tired of playing doctor and put his first-aid kit away, and the four of us got back to work.

THIRTY-THREE

"I don't want to hear this isn't admissible because it's entrapment," I complained as a tech taped a wire to my bare torso. "Cold, cold, cold." I slinked away from his hands.

Monique Webber waived her right to counsel, but she was taking her right to remain silent very seriously. She hadn't spoken a word to any of the officers after she was booked, so they put her uncooperative ass downstairs in the empty drunk tank, secluded from Yves, hoping some time alone might loosen her lips. Since Valerie assaulted me, my cohorts thought it'd be a great idea to give Monique the same opportunity.

"Don't worry about it. Anything she says freely in a police station after being informed of her rights should be fair game," Heathcliff said from the doorway. I put my shirt back on, and the tech performed a sound check. "Plus, the scratches ought to help sell your story."

"Are you gonna knock me around a bit to add some

realistic bruises too?" I asked cynically.

"No, but here," he produced an almost empty bottle of bourbon, "swish and spit."

"Did this come from your bottom desk drawer?" I narrowed my eyes, assessing his reaction. "This is why you're so possessive of your desk, isn't it?" He caught the smartass look on my face and rewarded me with a slight smile.

"I thought you were over breaking my balls."

"Keep dreaming."

Inside the women's locker room, I transformed back into Lola. It was a good thing I didn't actually go home last night or else the dress and shoes wouldn't be in my car. I mussed my hair and reapplied my makeup, splashing water on my face to give it an old, runny appearance. Returning to the bullpen, I wondered which of the detectives would have the privilege of throwing me into a holding cell.

"Whenever you're ready." Heathcliff's cuffs were on top of the desk.

"Oh, come on." I could suck it up and deal, but only if I really had to.

He noticed my trepidation and clipped them back on his belt before escorting me downstairs, making a show to speak to the officer in charge before opening the door to the drunk tank and shoving me inside. "Behave yourself while we get this sorted out," he warned.

"I know my rights. Let me out of here," I yelled after him. I made the effort to stumble and act as if I were dealing with a horrible hangover. Keeping my head down, I sat on the bench away from Monique, pretending not to notice her.

"Lola?" she asked, glancing out at the officer who was working on a crossword puzzle.

I looked up, conveying utter misery. "Why are you

here?" I sounded confused, scrunching up my face and rubbing my temples. "Don't tell Mrs. Tate or I'll never get the job." This would be a priority for Lola.

"Don't worry, I won't say a word." She sat next to me, looking at the scratches. "Are you okay?"

"I guess. The asshole from the party last night took me home, and this morning, his wife threw me out. How the hell was I supposed to know he was married?" I bellowed to the officer, who ignored me. "That asshole used me like a tissue and threw me away." I wiped at nonexistent tears. "So I wandered into some pub after it happened, and the douchebag working called the cops for unorderly conduct or some shit like that because I accidentally knocked over a glass. Can you believe that? Two shitty guys in two days. Fuck." Unintelligent tended to work well with hungover, and Monique wrapped her arm around my shoulders supportively.

"Men will tear your heart out, sweetie," she said softly. "That's kinda the reason I'm here, too." I looked at her uncertainly, waiting for an explanation. "Can I tell you a secret?" I nodded emphatically, probably too emphatically for someone with a hangover, but she didn't notice. She was dying to talk to someone. "Ricky's always been so sweet to me, but lately, he's been distant."

"Are you dating?"

"No, but we will. I'm sure of it. The way he looks at me, checking me out, and he calls all the time. We're in the pre-dating phase." She smiled to herself. "But that stupid bitch just kept throwing herself at him. At everyone, really. We all had some fun with Jake, but Ricky was mine. Everyone knew it. You could see it, right?"

"Definitely. He was completely yours." I tried to sound sincere, even though Monique actually fell into the crazy bitch category, as in foaming at the mouth, clinically crazy. "Who didn't see it?" Luckily, she hadn't attacked me, or I'd be begging to get vaccinated for rabies right away.

"Caterina," she sneered. "That little bimbo got everything. The most attention from Yolanda and the best modeling jobs. Jake even went out of his way to make her happy and do everything she wanted. Can you believe he paid off the bartender not to serve martinis to anyone else because it was some special codeword or something the two of them were using for their game?" Her sigh sounded like a growl. "I just couldn't take it anymore. It wasn't fair. She controlled everything, even what I was allowed to drink."

"Wow, what a bitch."

"Don't I know it." She rolled her eyes. "We all knew Cat got Jake to agree to roofie her because Val has a big mouth and was bragging about how she hooked him up with the stuff. But something happened at the party. I don't know what it was, but Jake asked me to go find Cat. She apparently just disappeared." She shook her head. "After all that shit with the drinks and the drugs, and then she just leaves. Who the hell does she think she is?"

"I don't know. I don't see why anyone would do that," I commented, trying to seem sympathetic to her plight and not uneasy about being seated this close to a psychopath.

"It's just how Cat is," she scoffed, "but Ricky was gone too. I couldn't believe he'd play that disgusting game with them, but there he was, passed out on a random yacht with that whore."

"Oh my gosh." I sounded a little too valley girl, and I tried to tone it down. "What did you do? I hope you set him straight." Confess, my internal voice screamed.

"I was going to, but he looked so helpless, lying there," her tone shifted to something soft and motherly. Her psychosis was making me edgy, if not downright frightened. "I went back to Ricky's boat to get him some things since apparently Cat thought it'd be more exciting to fuck on a stranger's boat," she snarled. "Why else would Ricky be blacked out on the floor of some shitty yacht?"

I stared in awe, pretending to be deeply interested in the drama. "What happened then?"

"I was going to bring him his own pillow. Something comforting and familiar, y'know. The poor thing was on the deck while that selfish bitch was sprawled out on the cushioned seats like she was royalty." Apparently, Skolnick's body wasn't positioned. She must have collapsed on the seats above Martin. "And then I just couldn't stand it anymore. The walk down the pier made me angrier and angrier. How could she treat my guy like he was garbage? I couldn't let her do it. Not to me. Not to him. Not to anyone." Monique's tone changed from caring to venomous as she shifted from talking about Sanderson to Caterina.

"Of course not," I piped up. Solidarity sister. "What did you do?" My tone was excited, maybe slightly manic, hoping to feed into her insanity.

"There was a knife near the trashcans that must have gotten thrown away by accident, and I figured I'd scare her with it."

"Did you?" My stomach twisted in knots because I knew what happened next, but apparently she forgot last night's party was a memorial.

"I tried, but she just lay there with her eyes open, staring at me. I hit her with the pillow, but she just kept staring. That bitch couldn't even be bothered to offer an explanation. She did nothing. Said nothing.

So I–" She stopped abruptly, remembering herself and her surroundings.

"What?" I pushed.

"Caterina's dead." She remembered this as an afterthought. Even if she didn't say another word, she said quite a bit already. Suddenly, she looked wary. "Were you with Ricky last night? Val said you were sitting with him at the bar?" Before I could respond, Heathcliff opened the door to the drunk tank.

"We have more questions for you upstairs, Ms. Peters," his tone was professional as he dragged me away, locking the cell behind him.

"She was about to crack," I insisted once we cleared the double doors. "Why'd you pull me out?"

"Because she was about to crack your skull over her beloved Ricky."

"So you're not sending me back in?"

"No. We have an explanation for how the pillow ended up on Martin's yacht and where the knife came from. It ought to be enough," he insisted, but I had issues being optimistic. I feared when Monique was confronted, she would spin the story into a different tale of woe, but it was still nice to untape the wire from my torso since it was starting to chafe.

After changing back into my normal garb, I located the group of detectives standing around the theory board. Thompson was playing an elaborate game of connect the dots. He organized our suspects, motives, and evidence into a flow chart. Spencer had given the drugs to Alvarez, but when he couldn't attend to Skolnick himself, he sent Webber to find her.

"Wait," O'Connell was processing the information, "after Webber found Skolnick and Martin, she detoured back to Sanderson's boat. Weren't Sanderson, Yves, and Tate on board filming?" Our timeline was going to shit.

"No. Sanderson and Tate alibied out because they left the filming fiasco together and met with a third party business backer. We had uniforms question the backer and verify their story." Thompson put the additional pieces together.

"How long did the filming process take?" I wondered aloud. O'Connell tossed the Bureau's report on top of my desk, and I skimmed through it. "Twelve minutes from start to stop. Add in some time for setting up and posting online, so maybe thirty minutes?" I got a round of head nods. "Did the ME ever narrow down Skolnick's time of death?"

"Not down to minute increments," Thompson responded. "But according to the surveillance feed, Webber was the last person to leave the party within our window of opportunity, and that was twenty minutes after Yves. If things happened in the order she claims, she probably missed their tryst by a few minutes."

"Maybe Webber ran into Yves on Sanderson's boat," O'Connell speculated. "Yves probably knew Webber wasn't stable, and instead of risking her wrath, she might have told Webber she'd seen Skolnick go off with Ricky in order to cover her own ass."

"But if Webber is head-over-heels for Sanderson, why would she try to make him into a scapegoat?" I asked.

"I don't think that was her intention," Heathcliff muttered. "She probably killed Skolnick, freaked, and did her best to hide the evidence. She's probably delusional enough to assume no one would think the unconscious guy was the killer, even though he was the only one on the goddamn yacht."

Moretti came out of his office and stood in the center of our discussion, silently observing for a few minutes. "Some good solid police work," he said mainly to himself as his gaze settled on me. "Get cleaned up and go home."

"Sir?" I hated my OIO brainwashing.

"You've been incredibly helpful in this investigation, but I don't want you to make this department appear incompetent. Despite popular belief, we can find our asses with both of our hands." Reading between the lines, Moretti was afraid of the appearance of impropriety if I worked out the few remaining details resulting in the positive identification of Caterina Skolnick's killer. "We'll call you when the paperwork needs to be finalized or in the event the ADA's need anything from you."

"I'll keep my phone charged." I tossed a slight grin to O'Connell. "I brought you boys this far, so don't screw it up."

THIRTY-FOUR

The next morning, there was loud knocking at my front door. I looked at my nine millimeter, but shooting whoever it was could be considered an overreaction. Instead, I put on my robe and answered the door. After signing the delivery form, I was handed a large white box. I put it down and eyed it suspiciously. Nondescript packaging always made me leery. Slowly, I lifted the lid to reveal a bottle of French wine and a dozen, long-stemmed, white roses. The card was scrawled in familiar handwriting: *For everything you've done, and everything still to do. Thank you. - J.M.* Could Martin be any more cliché?

I picked up the bouquet, filled a large water glass, and shoved the stems inside. I wasn't the floral type, but it was a sweet gesture, I suppose. It would have been sweeter if he thought to send pizza to accompany the wine, but maybe that's where he and I differed. Deciding to ignore the gesture for the time being, I got ready and went to my office.

Staring at my notepad, I was unable to resist

working on the final solution to Skolnick's murder. Moretti had a point. It didn't look kosher to have the initial suspect's security consultant identify the actual perpetrator. Then again, Martin had friends in high places, and it seemed unlikely anyone would bat an eye. Better safe than sorry, though.

The only remaining question was whether Valerie Yves was an accomplice in Caterina's murder. Yves knew the unconscious man wasn't Sanderson, but she had an axe to grind with Skolnick. Being desperate for money and fame would make a great reason for killing the star model at Tate's agency, and since Webber was willing to kill over nothing more than conjecture, Yves might have convinced her Martin was actually Sanderson.

Considering Webber was insanely possessive of her beloved Ricky, what would she have done if she saw the sex tape? The light bulb blinked on, and I knew it was the threat Heathcliff would make to get cooperation or at least substantiation from Yves. Valerie wouldn't risk her own safety to cover for Skolnick's killer. After all, accessory charges didn't carry the decades that homicide did.

If Webber saw the porno, there'd be no way to predict how she'd react, and Yves wouldn't risk being locked up with a deranged killer. Then again, besides the drug contacts and insider information on Sanderson and Tate, if Yves wasn't involved in the murder, she wouldn't have anything useful to give the police. But why did she attack me? There had to be more to the story. I leaned back in my chair, trying to clear my mind and leave the investigating to the men with badges since I was benched for the rest of the game.

The phone rang, providing a great distraction. "Parker Investigative Services," I answered. I had no idea what to call my business, so I was trying out new things.

"Don't we sound professional?" Jack Fletcher mocked. "I just wanted to make sure you received our invoice."

"Mail's a bit slow," I replied since I didn't bother to check it today. "Don't worry, you'll get paid. You know where I work, after all."

"I was kidding about the invoice. I was just calling to tell you that other issue concerning our mutual adolescent acquaintance has been resolved. No record and no court appearances. He didn't do anything wrong, so it's all been swept under the rug."

"Any word on the dealers?" I had no idea why Fletcher was calling to fill me in. Maybe he missed one too many professional ethics classes, but I wasn't complaining.

"They're small potatoes, but I heard through the grapevine the DA's compiling a major case against some bigwig supplier. I don't know if they work for the same guy, but if they do, the DA's office is prepared to make a deal with them. Once again, there won't be any blowback on anyone we might concern ourselves with."

"Thanks." I was genuinely appreciative. "Are you harboring any ill will toward me for declining your generous work offer?"

"We're good here," he reassured. "In the future, if we need an investigator for a random third party, should we file your name in the Rolodex?"

"Only if I have the option to decline again."

"Thanks for the referral, and thanks for straightening out the other situation." He disconnected, and I wondered if the police made any more progress on the Skolnick case in the last twelve hours or if Fletcher's gratitude was a general statement and not focused on anything specific.

Since he reminded me that I failed to check the mail, I went outside to the box. There was a bubble mailer with the Smidel's return address. It must be Christmas with all the packages I was getting today. Inside was a thank you card from Roger and a brand new mancala game board. I smiled, placing it on top of my desk. At least the kid didn't take after his mother. Although, with the way she was, this probably wasn't the last time I'd hear from either of them.

After dispensing with the rest of the mail, I used my office time to catch up on some phone calls. First, I dialed Mark's work number and waited. When the call was redirected to his voicemail, I left my thanks for smoothing the waters with Director Kendall and an apology for my less than positive attitude when it came to consulting at my former agency. I knew when I asked for a favor it would lead to at least one more gig at the OIO, and I didn't want there to be any hard feelings for when I returned. The police department put me through enough hazing hell for one lifetime, and I didn't want the OIO to get the same idea. I was running damage control for the future. Maybe I was completely pessimistic or just afraid what another stint would do to my private life.

Speaking of private life, I tried Martin's cell phone. It was Saturday, and there was a fair chance he'd be at home. "Hey, beautiful," he greeted. "I was afraid to leave you alone to your own devices for too long."

"Thanks for the flowers and wine. It wasn't necessary."

"It's the least I could do. God, Alex, I wish I realized what I put you through. At least I understand why you were so adamant about protecting me before and why you pushed me away. I'm sorry."

"You've said that already. Let's leave all of that in

the past. You've moved beyond it, so it's time I do the same." I let out a breath. "On a more current matter, nothing's been set in stone, but I feel confident the police have Caterina's killer in custody. I can give you a brief synopsis the next time I see you." I promised to fill him in, and everyone at the police department probably expected as much.

"Well, I'm free all day." The swagger was in his voice. My god, he was one confident son of a bitch.

"Okay," I relented, "I'm leaving my office now. Do you want to meet at my place?"

"Sure. I'll see you soon."

On the way home, I picked up takeout from the Chinese restaurant. I wasn't sure how well Chinese food would go with French wine, but it was the easiest option for reheating. Apparently, we were international tonight.

I just put the food into the fridge and placed Roger's gift on my coffee table when there was a knock at the door. Someone was impatient. Opening the door, I nodded to Bruiser, who immediately retreated down the hallway.

"Hey." How Martin made a single word sound sexy was some talent. He was giving me the same look he did yesterday in his kitchen. My face flushed, and I turned away, hoping he didn't notice. This was ridiculous. "Maybe I should have sent a vase instead of wine." He cocked an eyebrow at the flower setup on my kitchen counter. "I've missed you."

"You need new material, especially since we haven't even hit the thirty-six hour mark yet."

"I didn't realize there was a moratorium before such sentiments could be uttered." He cracked a bemused smile. "Is there a rulebook or something that I can refer to?"

"Jackass." I snorted. "I picked up some Chinese

food for dinner in case you were planning to hang around for a few hours, unless Bruiser's waiting in the lobby again?"

"You don't have a lobby, so I sent him home," Martin remembered, picking up the mancala box. "What's this?"

"A gift from yet another of my adoring fans." I pulled two wine glasses from the cupboard. "Wine?"

"Open it now, so it'll have time to breathe," he instructed, taking the box and setting the game on my kitchen table. "I haven't seen this in years. We had to make our own for some social studies class in high school or junior high," he mused, appearing nostalgic. "Want to play while you tell me about the police investigation?"

"Sure." I uncorked the wine and found my decanter, which I never used, and emptied the bottle into it. Over the next forty-five minutes, we played nonstop mancala and drank some wine while I told him everything regarding Sanderson and Webber. "I still don't see the resemblance," I concluded, "but I've been removed from the investigation for now. Moretti wants his guys to finish things up, unhindered and unassisted."

"Smart move," he responded. I glanced up, noticing he was struggling with something, and I had my suspicions on what it could be.

"One thing," I poured more wine into our two glasses, perhaps needing the liquid courage, "a guy goes to a party with a wad of cash, his Rolex, overly popular designer suit, his Harvard business school ring, and a condom in his wallet, and proceeds to drink himself stupid. It seems to me he's looking to get laid."

"Don't do that." But his face read guilt in bold letters. "You have some great deductive skills, but don't use them on me."

Too bad, I was never one to follow directions very well. "Thing is, I wouldn't have thought anything of it because that's just how you are," I took a long sip, "except Thursday night, you were dressed nicely but simply. No Rolex, no ring, and I didn't check your wallet since protection was in the nightstand, but I had to tell you to tip the bartender."

"But it was O'Connell," he protested. When I didn't waver, he sighed and cleared his throat, knowing damn well I was right. "It had been a month since we spoke, and I had given up on you. On us. What do you want me to do? Nothing happened with Caterina or anyone else. I wish I could take back that night, but I can't."

"How many serious relationships have you actually had?" I asked, surprising him with the question. This wasn't about flings with models. This was about his ability to focus and commit.

"Two." He was confused by my line of questioning.

I nodded thoughtfully. I didn't have a better answer than his. From my determination, we were both fairly dysfunctional and destined for a mayday spiral before crashing and burning yet again.

"I don't want you to think I'm easy." The words came out, but I had no idea where I was going with this.

"You're anything but easy," he agreed. "I've known you for almost a year. Just think about all the time and effort and friendly dinners that went into things. I've never worked this hard for anything else. Anyone else."

"Manipulative bastard," I teased, smiling at him. On a more serious note, I added, "We have a history. Not a good history. Nothing's changed really. I still do this, and I never want to be put in a position to relive what happened. So I will isolate myself and avoid you like the plague when things get rough."

"But I get it now." He reached for my hand. "You should have given me more credit on the first go 'round. After all, I'm brilliant. I would have understood, but you didn't tell me. Maybe if you had, we could have avoided some heartache." His eyes were sincere. "Can I assume you've decided we should try this again?"

"I guess so since the decision was made in your kitchen the other night, but we need some ground rules or something. I don't know. We're both workaholics. I say our careers take priority. If you have to work late, travel, and be gone for weeks at a time, it's okay, but I expect the same level of understanding. Part of the problem last time was your clinginess."

"Sorry, but how was I supposed to react after you told me you were almost killed?" His thumb absently traced the scars on my wrist.

"Hazard of the job." I pressed my lips together, wondering if that would be a deal-breaker. He nodded, thinking about the week I had exiled him during our first, fleeting attempt at a relationship. "It's not going to get any easier," I warned, "and if you wake up on a boat with a model again, I will leave you in jail to rot."

"What if it's Lola?" he asked playfully. "Is she the exception?"

"She's still way out of your league."

We ate dinner and spent the rest of the evening drinking the remainder of the French wine and a bottle I had stocked for a rainy day. We played mancala off and on to occupy the time between conversation and seductive glances. We turned it into a game of twenty questions.

"Are you sure you're straight?" I asked. "Because I am still positively baffled by your endless knowledge of fashion, clothing, and accessories." His face drew into a bittersweet smile, and I wasn't sure I wanted to know the answer anymore.

"My mom was a fashion designer. She was sick for a long time, but she didn't want her work to suffer. When I was in high school, I used to help out after class. Then when I was in undergrad, my summers were spent working at her business. It counted as an internship on my business school application since, by that point, she spent most of her time in the hospital, and I had to learn how to run her business."

"I'm sorry." I tended to blunder into these situations far too often.

"It was a long time ago. It's fine," he insisted.

"Is this when you started dating models?" I teased, lightening the mood.

"If only I had been that smart." He snickered. "Then again, from what I hear, they are a scary, deranged lot." We fell into a comfortable silence, pouring the last of the wine and automatically resetting the game board. "Why are we still playing?" he asked, draining his glass. "Maybe I'm jumping to conclusions, but I'm pretty sure I know where this evening is headed." He looked confident.

"Fine, last game for high stakes," I smiled coyly, "the winner gets to be on top."

"Or we could forget the game and just take turns," he whispered seductively, standing up from the table and offering me his hand.

THIRTY-FIVE

"You have to stop watching me sleep. It's too stalker-esque," I murmured, opening my eyes to find Martin lying next to me. He was absently playing with a strand of my hair.

"I can't help it if we disagree on what is considered morning," he replied. "I tend to wake up early, and there isn't much to do except watch you."

I rolled my eyes and turned away from him, snuggling deeper under the covers. He put his arm around my waist, and we stayed in the quiet for a while. Unfortunately, I was awake now. Damn morning person.

Even though there was no chance of falling back to sleep, I had no desire to emerge from bed. Things were simpler here, isolated from reality and the harsh dangers the world had to offer. The problem was, even here, my mind was back to work on the Skolnick case.

My thoughts wandered to Jake Spencer. He was clearly a player, but the girls knew it and didn't care. They probably had other partners on the side too. But why did Webber latch on to Sanderson when nothing else in their world indicated monogamy was even possible? Her alleged love for the guy was what drove her to murder, but I wasn't even sure they had ever been intimate. And if they had, she wasn't faithful either, especially with her threesomes.

Perhaps Webber had reached this frenzied, possessive state after she thought Skolnick was eyeing Sanderson. Maybe all the little things, like the modeling jobs, Jake's attention, and no martinis made her snap. Obviously, someone didn't like to share. After all, Sanderson was Webber's agent, and his questionable ogling translated into flirtation in her mind. Did she assume that Sanderson would be Skolnick's newest sex slave, like Jake, and it would be detrimental to her career?

Caterina Skolnick was the only star at Tate's agency, and all the models loathed her because of it. Hell, it was a miracle they hadn't strung her up like a piñata and beat her to death. It was a crazy, sexed-up version of Cinderella and the evil stepsisters all over again, but this story lacked a prince and a happy ending.

"What's the kinkiest thing you've ever done?" I shifted around to face Martin.

"Why?" The intrigue was obvious on his face. "Was there something you wanted to try?"

"No," I responded quickly. "I'm of the mindset if something is already amazing, there's no need to change things up. I was just thinking about the photographer and the models. They all have some kind of kinky hang-up."

"I'm fairly conventional, but I remember when the bondage thing became so in vogue, this woman wanted to tie me up. It lasted for maybe thirty seconds." I hid my laughter, and he corrected himself.

"The knot. It came undone. Have you ever?"

"No," I interjected sharply. "When you've actually been bound," I rubbed the slight scars on my wrists, "it makes no sense how anyone can find the torture or pain a turn on."

"It's just," he swallowed, "sometimes, I don't see how you're okay. All the things you've seen and done. Everything that's happened to you." He held me tightly. "You're incredible." This was our entire problem. He wanted to protect me from my life, and I wanted him to stay away from it.

"I give us three weeks," I stated neutrally, derailing the serious topic.

"Three weeks?"

"Maybe I'm overestimating. We've been together twice, have you gotten me out of your system already?"

"Not even close, Alex."

"Then I say three weeks until our fiery end. Unless you think we'll go the way of a Robert Frost poem, then maybe it'll be an icy end."

"Don't bet against us," he purred in my ear. "I'm in this for the long haul."

"It's not the 1950s. We're not going steady, but," I wasn't going to fight anymore since I wanted things to be good for as long as they could be, "monogamy does have its perks. Casual's about all I can handle, but no more models on the side." He kissed me, silently agreeing to my terms, and we spent the rest of the day together.

*   *   *

The next day, Heathcliff phoned. They were wrapping things up, and I was recalled from my brief exile. Valerie Yves cut a deal for herself. The possession charge was being pled down, and the police department was willing to overlook the assault in exchange for testimony against Monique Webber. I went to the precinct and listened to the story unfold.

Valerie Yves was still on Sanderson's boat when Monique Webber entered to retrieve a pillow from the freshly made bed. According to Yves, Webber didn't notice she wasn't alone, picked up the pillow, and sauntered down the pier. Being curious, Yves followed and watched Webber search the ground near the dumpsters, but she didn't see what happened after that because she was too busy self-medicating away the horrors that just occurred. Fortunately, despite the haze, she still remembered Webber throwing something onto a neighboring boat after untying Martin's docked yacht.

"We asked for permission to check the neighboring vessels, and we found Caterina Skolnick's cell phone and the knife used to stab her," Heathcliff informed me, sliding some photos over for my perusal. "We presented this evidence to Ms. Webber, and she sang like a canary." He was pleased and maybe a little bit relieved to have the albatross removed from around his neck. "She even admitted to turning on the engines, which is what led the yacht to drift so far from the docks. We fingerprinted her and checked the controls. The prints were smudged, but there's a three point match. It isn't sound forensic evidence, but it corroborates her guilty admission. The real kicker is the knife. It's covered in Skolnick's blood, and Webber's prints are all over the handle."

"Unbelievable." I frowned. Even though we identified the killer, no one was clean. "I'm glad you caught the psychopath responsible, but Spencer's going to walk away with a misdemeanor, maybe. Meanwhile, Tate and Sanderson are busy breaching the realm of adult entertainment by bribing out of work models with the hope of a turnaround in their careers, and Alvarez, for all his faults, ends up getting an accessory charge for trying to make a quick buck to support his family."

"The whole thing's been fucked up from the start," he admitted. "We do what we can. One less raging psychopath on the street is still a win in my book. Let's be honest, Parker, no one is getting a bum rap here. Maybe some got off easier than they should have, but we aren't in the business of booking innocent parties."

"Well," I gave him a pointed look, "not when the innocent party gets his high powered attorneys involved."

"Don't forget his personal security either," O'Connell chimed in.

"I still maintain any of us would have done the same thing given how it looked. One guy in the middle of the water with a dead model, nine times out of ten, he's going to be good for the murder." I couldn't argue with Heathcliff's logic. If it looked like a duck and quacked like a duck, it normally wasn't a mongoose.

Since things were settled with major crimes, I took a trip upstairs to the narcotics unit to see if I could discover anything useful relating to Roger Smidel and the two brutes from the park. Heathcliff escorted me to the detective in charge and made the proper introductions. I was given a very brief synopsis of everything that transpired.

Roger, Karen, and Oliver had simply been in the wrong place at the wrong time when they witnessed the two drug-dealing thugs meet with their supplier. No charges were ever filed against the three teenagers, courtesy of the ABC law offices and junior partner, Jack Fletcher. The two thugs agreed to roll on their connection for reduced sentences and were sent to the U.S. Marshal Service for protection until their testimonies. The state wanted to stop all drug running since the war on drugs would never be over, thanks in large part to the Reagan administration and the continued efforts of the DEA. Of course, the expansion of RICO laws to apply to drug cases and the government's ability to confiscate any and all property in drug busts was added incentive. This allowed the two thugs the chance to avoid hard time and salvage their lives if they cooperated.

Roger Smidel's name would never be linked to any of the proceedings or used in concert with any of the information. He was in no danger of being threatened by the supplier, and he and his friends could go back to resuming their lives as normal, obscenely wealthy teenagers. I would call Mrs. Smidel sometime soon to reassure her and see if she finally stopped her incessant nagging and shrieking. The narcotics team thanked me for the heads up. At least I managed to make a few more friends at the precinct.

Back at the major crimes division, I filled out whatever remaining paperwork the police department needed and relinquished the use of my commandeered desk. I gave Thompson and O'Connell a friendly smile. They knew this wouldn't be the last time our paths crossed.

"It was nice working with you, Detective." I extended my hand to Heathcliff.

"Are you always so formal, Parker?" he asked, ignoring the gesture and getting up from his desk. "I'll walk you out." He held the door as we exited the precinct and headed toward my car. It was dark. The day had flown by, but everything was copacetic. "Hey, do you maybe want to go out sometime, get dinner or a drink?" I tilted my head to the side, trying to determine if he was just being friendly.

"Are you asking me out?" I was in utter disbelief this no-nonsense cop had any interest in anything that wasn't strictly job related.

"Yeah, something like that." He grinned.

"I'm flattered, but I don't date guys I barely know. Hell, I don't even know your first name, and until five seconds ago, I thought it might be detective." Not to mention, I'm seeing someone.

He laughed good-naturedly. "It's Derek, but at least you had the first two letters right. I take it you aren't much for dating cops either. Probably goes back to the whole cops versus feds thing, right?"

I chuckled. "It's not that. It's the shit hours, work never sleeps, on-call all the time, horrible odds of coming home with a few holes, or not coming home at all."

"You only date outside your own species then," he replied knowingly.

"Are you saying you're a dog and I'm a bitch?" I playfully teased, opening my car door.

"Your words, Parker, not mine." He held the door as I got into my car. "Have a good night. Stay safe out there." He shut the door and tapped the side of my car before going back inside. Maybe dressing like Lola had been beneficial to my ego, I thought ironically.

THIRTY-SIX

The next morning, I went to my office, determined to show up at least twice a week since I was mostly unemployed again. I called Mrs. Smidel who seemed civil and accommodating on the phone. Apparently, she had been abducted, and the imposter wasn't aware of what a shrew the real Lynette Smidel was. Graciously, she thanked me for recommending Mr. Fletcher to deal with Roger's legal issues. She was relieved her son's future had not been irrevocably damaged, and he was no longer in any danger.

"I'm sending you a check to cover the extra time you put in to help Roger," she promised.

"That's not necessary, ma'am." Her money came with too much screaming and nagging for my liking.

"It's in the mail." As an afterthought, she added, "I've forbidden Roger from going to that park anymore. No good can come from him sitting around alone. Maybe you were right, Ms. Parker, and I need to be more present in his life."

"Glad to hear it." I doubted her conviction, but I wasn't a parent. Maybe she really did all she could.

After cleaning my office and paying a few bills, I had no more business to conduct. To waste time, I was online shopping for office furniture and cute shoes. Apparently, no good could come from sitting alone with a credit card and countless shopping opportunities either. The bell above my door chimed, saving my bank account, and I caught a glimpse of Roger entering my office.

"I hope it's okay I stopped by," he sounded sheepish.

"Take a seat." I gestured to my client chair. He sat down and stared unnervingly at me. "What's up?"

"I wanted to say thank you in person. Mr. Fletcher truly helped me out. Karen and Oliver, too."

"Yeah, I know. That's what he does. How are your friends? Are they okay with everything that's happened? Are you doing okay with everything?"

"They broke up." There was a happy glint in his eye. "And I'm good. Oliver isn't supposed to hang out with us anymore, but Karen's been around the last few days. The only bad thing is Mom won't let me go to the park anymore."

"Well, your mom worries about you, and in case you haven't figured this out yet, that's actually a good thing."

"Yeah, if it lasts." He didn't think her resolve was going to stick either. "In the meantime, my cash cow has dried up."

"Who are you kidding? Twenty dollars a day is far from making bank," I remarked, looking out the door at his Lexus. "What the hell do you need extra money for anyway, besides buying drugs?" I gave him a stern look.

"It's just nice to have cash sometimes. It impresses the ladies." Sometimes, I wondered if all rich boys read the same damn guidebook to life and love.

"All right." I was considering something which I had a feeling I might regret. "If your mom gets too busy and you're home alone, contemplating getting into trouble, give me a call. There might be an opening for a part-time gig. The money will be shit, but it would give you something to do for a couple hours a day, maybe two or three times a week. Nothing difficult, but it's bound to be better than getting assaulted in a park." Worst case, I could hire Roger to throw out my junk mail and save me a drive to the office. It'd probably be cheaper than my habit of killing time by online shopping.

"I'll keep it in mind, but I gotta go. Mom wants me home for dinner."

After he left, I ordered a pair of black pumps I didn't need and called it a night. I locked my office and drove home. The Skolnick case was solved. The Smidel case was settled, and I was already bored.

*   *   *

Thursday afternoon, I was sitting behind my desk, achieving my goal of checking in twice for the week. All this time in my office reminded me why I didn't check in more often; there was nothing to do. Why was work an all or nothing thing? I was either busy doing three things at once or nothing at all. There must be some kind of compromise in order to reach a happy medium. I just needed to figure out what the trick was.

As I was dusting and considering upgrading my furniture, my office phone rang. "Parker Security Firm," I answered. I still didn't know what to call my business.

"Ms. Parker, please hold for Mr. Guillot," a woman's voice replied. I didn't know why Luc would be calling. It must be in reference to a personal matter, or else Martin would have called himself. Luckily, before I could consider something horrible having happened to him, which at this point seemed extremely likely, Luc's voice sounded over the line.

"Mademoiselle Parker," Guillot was cordial as always, "Martin Technologies is aware that your security contract is up for renewal in less than two months, and we would like to have a meeting before time has lapsed." Maybe Guillot was scheduling a conference to officially fire me. It was okay. I shouldn't be sleeping with the boss, too many ethical qualms. "Are you free next Thursday at two?"

"Let me check my schedule." I couldn't resist. I had nothing on the books for the foreseeable future, but it was fun to pretend I was a sought after commodity. "Sounds good."

"Okay, I will have an assistant e-mail you the details. Have a nice day."

"You too."

Apparently not only did I tend to work more than one job at a time, but I also concluded more than one job at a time. Maybe I shouldn't be considering buying new furniture or giving Roger a job as my assistant since I might be working out of a cardboard box by next month. Let's just take one day at a time, I thought as I drove home.

*   *   *

I was in workout gear, pounding out the miles on the treadmill and trying to clear my head from the last few weeks. I wanted the Skolnick case out of my mind. It was completed, and any remaining issues could be dealt with by the courts and Skolnick's estate attorneys. Maybe her parents would file civil suits against Spencer, Tate, and the rest of the guilty lot. It was no longer my problem. My problem was finding a new job. I slowed the speed on the treadmill until it stopped, and then I stepped off.

Just as I got out of the shower, the phone rang. Wrapping the towel around me, I went to the kitchen and managed to grab the receiver seconds before the answering machine kicked on. "Hello?" I waited to see if the caller hung up.

"Alex?" Mark asked.

"The one and only." I took the cordless into the bathroom, so I could dry off and conquer the feat of dressing with one hand. "What's going on?"

"I got your message. It was incredibly pleasant and congenial, so obviously, I was afraid you were being held for ransom or aliens abducted you."

"Unfortunately, no." I zipped my jeans and switched hands as I put on my shirt. "Is that the only reason you called?"

"No. I wanted to congratulate you on a job well done. I heard some chatter confirming the model's murder was resolved."

"Thanks. The police department has some good detectives. They could have handled it on their own. Well, mostly on their own."

"Uh-huh." He didn't sound convinced. "Remember, the OIO helped run down the internet information and IP address, and I believe you made reference to the promise of returning the favor."

"And you won't let me forget it." I went back to the kitchen to get a bottle of water. "If you plan to cash in, I'd prefer it be at a later date. It hasn't even been a week since the Skolnick case concluded. I have an upcoming meeting at MT, and," I sighed, "it's only been a few weeks since I finished that last consulting gig for Kendall. Can you give me a few more days before I start on another one?"

Without seeing him, I could still picture the knowing look on Mark's face. "I knew you'd come back to work here. At the bar, you went on and on about how you were done, and now look at you. Do you want to make it permanent this time? Or are you still too busy entertaining fanciful ideas that you're a cop or completely private sector now?"

"I am private sector, and with my stellar record, my consulting rate has just gone up." He chuckled. "By the way, I'm not willing to travel for work. If it's something here, I'll consider it." I was taking Martin into account when making my work decisions, even though this violated my rule about the job coming first, but he didn't have to know about it.

"Okay. Just a heads up, you'll probably get a call sometime next week. We have an open case that hasn't gone anywhere. If it doesn't move in the next few days, Kendall is demanding we do something different."

"I'm something different?"

"You're definitely something different. Talk to you soon."

My job hunt wasn't lasting as long as I thought. Even though being back at the OIO was familiar, like returning home, it took a painful toll every time I walked into the building and remembered the agents that had been lost. If I had to consult again, maybe I could do it remotely. Jeez, I needed to be more careful making wishes.

*   *   *

As Mark predicted, Wednesday afternoon Kendall asked if I would take a meeting. Everyone wanted a meeting with the great and powerful Alexis Parker.

Maybe the title on my business card should be changed to reflect my newly gained popularity. Thankfully, Kendall agreed to wait until Friday since I had the mysterious appointment at Martin Technologies scheduled for Thursday.

Even though I spent last weekend with Martin, he didn't mention anything about the meeting with Guillot, but he was preoccupied with his impending business trip. He was going out of town for the next two weeks, first stopping in Istanbul and then Prague. He was leaving Saturday morning. Maybe this was why he was so oblivious. I accused his trip of being a delay tactic to disprove my three week theory, but he vehemently denied my accusations. By Sunday evening, I told him about my upcoming meeting at the OIO, even though it wasn't a certainty at that point. Now it was, and it'd be interesting to see how we fared in the face of both of our careers. He insisted we'd be fine, and for once, I was inclined to believe him.

THIRTY-SEVEN

Thursday afternoon, I dressed in a tailored skirt and jacket, prepared to be fired. Fired probably wasn't the proper terminology. My contract would be allowed to expire, or my contract would not be renewed. I was ready for it. I would be gracious and thank the Board for the opportunity the MT corporation had provided over the last year, and I would complete my remaining seven weeks with dignity. I even went so far as to check for an appropriate replacement they could hire.

I was ushered into a conference room on the fifteenth floor and asked to take a seat at the end of the table. Four of the board members, whom I met previously, flanked me at the conference table. They gave slight nods and polite smiles while we waited awkwardly for Mr. Guillot to arrive.

"Ms. Parker," he sounded less French today, probably trying to seem more professional, "thank you for coming. I'm not sure if you are aware of our current proposal." He looked questioningly at me. "Perhaps Mr. Martin has discussed this with you." I shook my head, puzzled, so he continued. "As you are aware, there are branches of Martin Technologies all over the world. There are five in this country alone. The Board has voted to improve our staff efficiency by consolidating our security personnel."

"Basically, we want to overhaul the entire system," Charles Roman, one of the board members, offered. "All of MT's security personnel need to have similar training and backgrounds. The emergency protocols must be updated and made uniform throughout the corporation, and this way, there will be a pool of candidates available in case we need to temporarily relocate someone whenever there is an extended absence." I thought about Jeffrey Myers and the search for his replacement.

"We were hoping you would consider heading the committee on the consolidation. We're still months away from enacting this plan, but the Board has approved it. There are still some business documents and contracts from legal to be drawn up, but we're all confident it'll pass," Guillot concluded the pitch.

"Mr. Guillot," I interrupted, "I'm not familiar with corporate practices. I have no idea how any of this even works. I'm honored, but I'm not the right person for the job."

"Don't be so humble," Roman teased. "You kick ass and take names. What more could we possibly want?"

"I believe what Mr. Roman is trying to say," Guillot interjected, probably not understanding Roman's sense of humor, "is you have the know-how to be incredibly beneficial in coordinating the overhaul. The Board and I will deal with the corporate implications. We just need someone capable of finding and training individuals and devising emergency protocols and procedures. Your expertise has streamlined the security in the Paris office and here." I was still completely out of my league and was going to decline the position, but Guillot must have predicted my response because he added, "You have time to decide. Let us know before your contract expires so we can draw up the proper paperwork."

How could a total restructuring of MT's global security wait almost two months for my decision? But I didn't question it. Instead, I thanked everyone for their generous offer and headed out the door.

As I climbed into my car, Martin called. "Come over tonight," he requested. "I'm leaving Saturday morning, and I don't know what I'm doing tomorrow. But it'd be nice to see you before I leave."

"Yeah, okay." I blew out a breath. Apparently, my complaint about his previous clinginess had fallen on deaf ears, but we needed to have a chat. "I just came from a meeting at your company, and we have a few things to discuss."

"Shall I pick up champagne on the way home?" The bastard knew the entire time and didn't say a word. Unbelievable.

"There's no reason for champagne since you've lost your damn mind."

"We'll see." I heard the smirk. "See you at seven?" Sighing, I agreed and drove home.

Would it seem forward to bring my interview clothes to Martin's since I didn't expect to make it home tonight? Then again, I could leave early in the morning and stop at home before going to the OIO if tonight turned into tomorrow morning. But either way, I still wasn't a morning person. It was better to be safe than sorry, so I packed a professional looking outfit and laid it flat in my trunk. It never hurt to be prepared. The boy scouts always were.

Arriving at Martin's, I ignored the uncomfortable twinge that always accompanied me whenever I stepped foot inside his place. He picked up French food to go with the last remaining bottle of French wine he had brought home from his trip to Paris. Trying to appear more refined and patient than I was, I waited until after dinner before broaching the subject of work.

"First, I shouldn't be working for your company anymore. Second, I don't know who came up with the cockamamie idea to put me in charge of some kind of security firm creation merger thing, but they need to have their head examined. The fact that I don't even know what the proper terminology to use here is indicative of my lack of knowledge in this particular area."

He laughed. "Just so you know, I've deferred all things security related to Guillot since I know how much you loathe mixing personal with professional." He winked. "Heaven forbid if someone found out we were dating. What would they think?" His voice dropped an octave. "Hell, I'd probably get a few dozen death threats from jealous employees, and half of the Board would conspire to have me killed." I glared, but he chuckled. It was still way too soon for that to be funny. Honestly, I didn't think it'd ever be funny. "And to address your second point, the Board doesn't actually expect you to do any, what was it, security creation mergers?" He laughed again at my absurdity.

"So what the hell was the entire presentation about?" I didn't take being made fun of very well.

"It was mostly a fancy way of asking if you wouldn't mind doing more security guard applicant reviews, finding qualified people to train the security personnel, and establishing proper protocols for all of MT's branches." At least his explanation made more sense than Guillot's.

"And the slideshow was for?"

"Entertainment purposes only." He snorted. "It's business. We like our charts, graphs, tables, and bullet points. We really love our bullet points."

"I do too, but mine involve actual bullets."

"From my understanding, we're still months away from beginning the first phase, but Guillot thought you needed some time to think about it. For some reason, he's under the impression you don't particularly care for corporate work."

"What do you think?" I asked, helping him clear the table.

"I don't think you like corporate work either." He shrugged. "But I'm not giving you an opinion. We're keeping business separate, remember?"

I set the plates in the sink and put my palms against his chest, balancing on my tiptoes and brushing my lips against his. "Wow, something I said actually sunk in," I teased, "but there are things I can do to force you to answer the question."

"Remember, my safe word is grenadine." His eyes crinkled playfully. "Plus, you said you didn't have any kinky habits."

"I didn't realize you considered FBI interrogation techniques kinky."

*   *   *

The next morning, I was glad my business attire was in the trunk of my car. Martin let me oversleep again, and I was in a mad rush to get ready. He watched, amused, as I grabbed my phone and car keys and ran down the steps.

I arrived at the OIO barely on time and went straight to Director Kendall's office. Why was I so concerned about being on time and making a good impression? The last time I was here, I hated every second and made it painfully obvious to everyone. Maybe I changed in the last few weeks, or I was desperate for a paying gig. More than likely, the sick, twisted part of my psyche needed another morbid puzzle to unravel.

"Ms. Parker," Kendall greeted, "I thought you were standing me up."

"No, sir," I responded automatically, hating how easily the auto-pilot kicked in. "Thanks for the use of Bureau resources to assist the police department in their homicide investigation."

"Glad to be of service, particularly since you owe us a favor." I nodded slightly. "Great." He produced a stack of consulting paperwork that I read and signed. "C'mon, Parker, it's been a year. Aren't you ready to come home?" He opened his top drawer and pulled out my old credentials. "The badge looked good on you."

"I can't. The woman on that ID isn't me. Not anymore."

"If you ever change your mind," he shoved the gold emblem back inside his desk, "I'm sure we can find a place for you." I shook my head, considering running for the exit and never looking back. That's what I tried to do many times, and each time, I failed. "Agent Becker will give you a formal briefing in the conference room."

The briefing took a few hours, and despite my reluctance to be back at the OIO, I was looking forward to having something new to occupy my time. They even guaranteed my consulting work would all be local, and most of it could be done remotely. There was a lot of information already compiled, so I'd be evaluating collected evidence, watching interviews, and sifting through the investigator's notes. It sounded simple enough, even though the actual dynamics of the case were not. It would conclude on its own time, but for once, my work at the OIO wouldn't interfere with my ability to work other cases or maintain a personal life.

Stopping by Mark's office on my way out, I was relieved we were back to normal, or at least, the way we had been before my stubbornness interfered with our friendship. We discussed the current case, the Skolnick case, and my new job offer at MT.

I was about to leave when my phone rang. "You left your house keys at my place," Martin said enthusiastically.

"Shit. Are you serious?" Mark looked confused by my cursing, but I wasn't ready to tell him about my relationship. It was still too new. "Hang on a second." I covered the mouthpiece. "I'll see you tomorrow," I promised Mark. "It's your turn to buy the coffee, and remember the extra foam in my cappuccino." He pantomimed writing himself a note as I walked out of his office and headed for the parking garage.

"Are you still there?" Martin asked as I waited for the elevator to open again. The reception inside was too challenging to talk through.

"Yes, sorry about that."

"I'll bring them to your place and save you a trip. What time are you leaving?" He was up to something.

"Now. I just got in my car."

"See you soon."

During the drive home, I tried to recall when I took my house keys out of my purse. There was definitely something weird going on, and Martin was probably to blame. I grabbed my belongings out of my car and went inside the building. It felt strange entering unannounced, but it would have been even odder to knock. Opening the door cautiously, I found Bruiser watching television.

"Parker," he nodded and made a beeline for the door, "nice seeing you again."

"Jones," I replied as he let himself out. Either he had a hot date, or he thought his boss did.

I dropped my car keys and purse on the coffee table and put my gun and holster down before going into the kitchen. Martin was in front of the stove, stirring something.

"I thought I'd make you dinner," he remarked.

"I didn't expect to see you today." I insinuated myself between the countertop and him. "I'm sorry about the keys." He looked pleasantly guilty. "Did I actually forget my keys, or did you borrow them?" Being a pickpocket was not a skill in his repertoire that I had any knowledge of until now.

"Taste this." He held the spoon to my lips, deflecting my question.

"Needs pepper."

He gave me a 'yeah right' look and kissed me. Leaning back, he smacked his lips together. "I agree."

"The keys," I tried again, but he wouldn't give me a straight answer. "You know, this could be construed as breaking and entering." I slid out from between him and the counter and set the table. After all the wine I'd been drinking lately, it was no wonder I hadn't turned into a lush, so I poured a couple glasses of water and handed him one.

Over dinner, I offered a vague rundown of my plans for the next few weeks since I was officially consulting for the OIO again, but he didn't seem concerned. He would be away on business, and I was working a case. Maybe the universe was done conspiring against us, at least for the moment.

* * *

The next morning, familiar soft kisses pressed against my shoulder, and then Martin climbed out of bed. I rolled over and muttered something about the shower and where to find clean towels before shutting my eyes and listening for the water to turn on. Once the shower was off, I considered getting out of bed, but I wasn't completely committed to the idea and decided to wait before making any rash decisions. Martin came back into the bedroom completely dressed and collected his discarded clothing from the night before, stowing it inside his overnight bag.

"What are you doing?" I asked. He was on all fours, looking under my bed.

"Trying to find my shirt." He looked up and smiled. "Never mind. It looks a hell of a lot better on you, anyway." Sometime during the course of the night, I had gotten cold and slipped into the first thing I could find. "Keep it."

"I'll get up and make you coffee or see you out or whatever." It felt like I should be doing something besides lying half asleep in bed.

"Stay there." He sat down, leaning against the headboard. "Marcal and Jones are picking me up and taking me to the airport. There's no reason why you have to get up."

"Is Jones going with you? Foreign countries can have a lot of issues, especially when it comes to rich Americans."

"Yes, he's coming with me."

"Good." My eyes closed, and my head slumped against his shoulder. "Make sure he stays with you everywhere you go. Don't start with *it's a party, I'll be fine*. We both know how well that works out."

"Yes, ma'am." He said it just to irk me. "I'll be fine. Can you manage to stay in one piece while I'm gone?"

"Of course, Mark has my back." My doorbell rang, and I moved over to my pillow. "Stay away from models."

"I'll see you in two weeks." He kissed me good-bye, and I heard the door open. He spoke briefly to Jones and locked it behind him. After a few minutes, I got up, slid the deadbolts into place, and went back to bed. I lay against his pillow, breathing in the scent of his cologne and shampoo before falling back to sleep. A few hours later, I was dressed and rushing to meet Mark at my office to start work on my next case.

Mimicry of Banshees

DON'T MISS ALEXIS PARKER'S NEXT
ADVENTURE.

SUSPICION OF MURDER IS NOW
AVAILABLE FOR PURCHASE IN
PAPERBACK AND E-BOOK.

ABOUT THE AUTHOR

G.K. Parks is the author of the Alexis Parker series. The first novel, *Likely Suspects,* tells the story of Alexis' first foray into the private sector.

G.K. Parks received a Bachelor of Arts in Political Science and History. After spending some time in law school, G.K. changed paths and earned a Master of Arts in Criminology/Criminal Justice. Now all that education is being put to use creating a fictional world based upon years of study and research.

You can find additional information on G.K. Parks and the Alexis Parker series by visiting our website at
www.alexisparkerseries.com

35459233R00199

Made in the USA
Lexington, KY
03 April 2019